RIDE OR DIE

BETH BOLDEN

Beth Bolden Books

www.bethbolden.com

beth@bethbolden.com

Ordering Information:

Quantity sales. Special discounts are available on quantity purchases by corporations, associations, and others. For details, contact Beth Bolden at the address above.

Ride or Die/ Beth Bolden. -- 1st ed.

PROLOGUE

"YOU ARE LITERALLY THAT heart-eyes emoji right now and it's too goddamn early for that." Ren—he avoided his overly flowery name of Lorenzo Domenico as often as he could—Moretti shot his cousin a look that would've cut anyone else down a peg, but he barely blinked.

Annoyingly.

Gabriel had a spring in his step and a gooey look in his eyes that meant his mood was impenetrable.

Ren knew, because Ren had tried.

"It's almost noon," Gabe said. "That's not early."

"Too early for the heart-eyes bullshit," Ren said, not mincing words, because Gabe already knew how he felt about it, and there was no point in pretending that he wasn't annoyed. And not just because instead of working, Gabe was staring sappily out of the front window of the food truck they owned together. No, he was annoyed because he'd barely seen his best friend over the last few weeks, ever since he'd officially gotten together with his boyfriend, Sean.

It was one of many reasons why Ren thought love was stupid.

It changed you. It irrevocably altered your life.

Ren was not interested in that kind of change.

He was interested in getting naked and sweaty with a cute guy, and then both of them going their separate ways. Nobody had ever made him feel that he needed to do it a second time, or to stay after, and confess all his secrets or share all his dreams.

"*And* I've barely seen you for a week," Ren added, not bothering to hide the bitter edge in his voice.

He wasn't surprised to see the sudden guilt swamping Gabe's features. He was the King of Feelings, after all.

"You've seen me at work," Gabe said.

"Yeah, but half the time you're staring off into space, like you're the main character in some Shakespearean tragedy. Sorry, dude, but you're no Romeo."

"Well, Sean isn't Juliet, so I'm good with that." Gabe hesitated. "I intend to stay alive for long enough we actually get past the honeymoon phase."

Shit like that—*dying* for the person you loved—was why Ren had no intention of ever getting caught up in feelings that he couldn't help, and couldn't hope to control.

"Hey, look, there's that Lennox guy," Ren said, glancing out the window and changing the subject.

He realized only after Lennox stopped and stared, shock written across his features, that he hadn't been to their food truck since they'd changed the name a week ago.

He came stomping over, and Ren couldn't help himself. He smiled.

People's reaction to their truck being called *Buns and Balls* was always amusing. Lennox's was just going to be more amusing than most.

He could be awkward and cold, and well, he'd turned Ren down for a hot night in between the sheets hadn't he?

"What are you doing?" Lennox demanded.

Ren leaned over, bracing his forearms on the front counter, so he was almost eye level with Lennox, and that was when he realized the enormity of that casual choice.

Because Lennox wasn't alone.

There was another guy, trailing behind him.

He was tall, even taller than Lennox, who wasn't exactly short. He was built similarly, too, filling out his loose navy-blue t-shirt and jeans in a way that made Ren's fingers itch to take them off, so he could see the body underneath. His face wasn't the most handsome Ren had ever seen. In fact, his nose was crooked, just a hair to the left, and Ren found he couldn't look away. His hair and scruff were close-cropped, but the reddish gold glowed under the LA sunshine. And his eyes?

Ren felt the earth shift when they met his.

They were a cool gray green, but they weren't cold at all. Nothing like Lennox.

He laughed, and the warm amusement in his gaze stole Ren's breath.

He was *never* like this.

He flirted. He propositioned. He indulged in plenty of hot hookups. He was the one who always left guys wanting more.

He hadn't even had this guy yet—but he *would*, he knew that much—but he was already worried that the one who would want more after would be him.

If he was smarter, he'd leave this one alone.

He didn't need to get burned.

He definitely did not need to be converted to love and affection and *forever*, like his cousin.

But he couldn't help himself.

Self-control had never been his strong suit.

"We're serving food," Ren said, answering Lennox—but not taking his eyes off the other guy.

"Food? Or terrible puns?" Lennox demanded to know.

"Why can't it be both?" Ren thought most things were better that way. Like humor and sex—they naturally went hand in hand. He liked having a good flirt, a fun date full of laughs, and then a hot night after.

"I suppose you think you're very funny," Lennox said.

"Funnier than you," Gabe said, joining Ren at the front counter.

Ren could hear the undercurrent in his cousin's voice. He felt guilty, still, and he'd come over to defend him—to defend *their* choices.

"Leave the guys alone," the guy said, speaking for the first time. "I think it's pretty damn funny myself."

He had a deep voice, melodious and slightly tinged with a Southern accent.

Ren could imagine it telling him to *come*, and his insides tightened.

Lennox shot his friend an annoyed look. "Nobody asked you."

He couldn't help it; Ren inserted himself. "I did," Ren said, leaning over further. He was having a good hair day, and well, a good face *life*, and he could tell the guy appreciated both. The appraising look in his eyes made that clear enough.

"Well," he said, "then you might as well put down, *Seth thinks it's hilarious*."

"Seth, huh? I'm Ren. Lorenzo, but nobody calls me that." He filed away Seth's name for later.

Later, when he was screaming it.

Because there was no way they weren't going to have sex.

Ren had woken up this morning and showered and gotten dressed so he could be here right now, to meet this guy, and make sure they had sex.

"It's nice to meet you, *Lorenzo*," Seth said with a glimmer of a knowing grin that should have pissed Ren off, but it didn't. At all. "I work with Lennox here. I've been on a long assignment, but I'm back in LA now, and this place was the first one Lennox said we needed to visit." He frowned, clearly confused. Or maybe, Ren thought, *jealous*? Was he worried that Lennox was interested in *him*?

Yes, Lennox had turned him down, when he'd offered, but he'd only done it as a matter of routine, and frankly, with this magnificent creature in front of him now, Ren could barely remember the exchange.

"Something about salad?" Seth added.

Gabe laughed, getting it before Ren's sluggish brain understood.

Right, Lennox was interested in *Ash*.

Poor Ash.

"We'll let you discover for yourself why salad's so attractive," Gabriel said.

Lennox frowned. "It's not . . ."

But it was.

Everyone could see it—even if Lennox wasn't ready to admit it yet.

But Ren, well, Ren was plenty ready to admit his own inclination.

"Like that?" Ren raised an eyebrow. He knew how this particular expression made him look. It had brought better men to their knees.

Seth just continued to look amused—and intrigued.

"I'm sure a big strong man like you thrives on salad," he added.

"Uh, not exactly," Seth said with a dry chuckle. Their eyes met again, and it was just as cataclysmic as the first time.

Ren wanted to know exactly what, in explicit detail, a man like Seth thrived on.

Of course, Sean chose that moment to show up and to break Seth's focus from what was really important: *him*.

"What's going on?" he asked.

Ren had zero compunction about groaning loudly, and saying, "You again?"

"Me again," Sean said, not looking even the tiniest bit upset.

"What's going on?" Gabe asked, his gaze softening so much that Ren wanted to apologize for his completely lovestruck cousin.

"I needed some more glaze, Ren said he'd run some over, but he must've forgotten."

Gotten distracted more like.

"Sorry," Ren said, not feeling sorry at all. "We were busy. Well, scratch that. *I* was busy, doing work for both of us, and your boyfriend was just staring sappily out the window."

"That was not me," Gabriel defended himself staunchly, but Sean laughed, grabbing the container of Thai meatball glaze from the fridge underneath the counter. Probably because he knew just what Gabe was capable of.

"Yes, it probably was," Sean said.

It would've been so much harder to like Sean if he didn't just love Gabriel, he *saw* him.

"Yeah, it probably was," Gabe admitted.

"I'm not bummed about it," Sean said.

Ren glanced away from the annoying pair, back at Seth, who was still examining every word on their menu.

"You gonna order?" Ren asked. Hoping that he understood exactly what he meant. And he wasn't talking about sandwiches.

"Oh yeah, I definitely am," Seth said, and Ren's stomach fluttered.

There was something so decisive and *grown up* about this guy.

Like he'd throw Ren over his shoulder and cart him back to his bedroom.

"What can I get you?" Ren asked.

Me. I can get you me. And you'd enjoy every second of it. Trust me. I'm delicious.

"That's a real good question," Seth said.

"I'm going to get lunch," Lennox announced, and nobody was surprised to see him head off towards Ash's food truck.

"Well, if you want a recommendation," Gabe said, and Ren wished that his cousin would go do *anything else* right now, "you can't go wrong with the Thai meatball crunch wrap."

"Does everything have balls or buns?" Seth wanted to know.

Oh, Ren wanted to show him.

So badly that he deployed the smile that he usually saved for closing the deal. But then, he was closing the deal right now, wasn't he? He could feel it in his bones.

Specifically one bone in particular.

"Yes," Ren said.

"Straightforward," Seth said, taking a step nearer, and now Ren could really get a good look at him. He was even sexier in higher definition and he'd made Ren's mouth water even without the close-up look. "I like it."

"See anything else you like?" Ren decided there was no point in delaying. They were both clearly interested. "Lucky for you, I just happen to be free tonight."

Somehow, impossibly, Seth's own closing smile was even more devastating than Ren's own.

Ren was unmoored. Blown away. Blown apart.

What would it be like to be under him, when he smiled like that?

What would it feel like to kiss that smile off him?

He was going to get to find out. Ren could feel it. Could nearly taste it.

"*Really* straightforward," Seth said, not sounding like he hated that at all.

"Why bother pretending that you don't just want a sandwich?" Ren shrugged. "We're both interested. I'm free tonight, and I know we'd both enjoy ourselves."

"What about tomorrow, then?"

Ren had learned the hard way that it was better to *always* be honest about his intentions. But this guy, even if he didn't do one-night stands, was so hooked that Ren knew there was no way he'd ever turn him down.

Ren could feel the other side of the hook, buried in him, tugging him even closer, and he dared anyone to try to resist that completely irresistible pull.

"What *about* tomorrow?" Ren asked archly. "Why do we have to worry about tomorrow?"

"I'm all about the tomorrows," he admitted with a shrug. "I'm not here for just the tonights. I want to know there's going to be a tomorrow, too."

Ren frowned. "I don't *do* tomorrows. Not when tonights are so freaking great."

"Then I guess I'll have to make do with just a sandwich." Seth sounded genuinely regretful, which was why Ren didn't even register the rejection right away. He'd been so goddamned *nice* about it. Like he hadn't wanted to say no.

Like he'd wanted to say *yes*.

"Just a sandwich?" Ren knew he was quick and intelligent, but this guy just took it right out of him.

"Just a sandwich. I'll go with Gabe's—I think Lennox mentioned his name was Gabe—suggestion of the Thai meatball crunch wrap?"

Ren couldn't believe it. Seth wanted to talk about food right now? Could *think* about food right now? After he'd just turned him down?

He had a healthy ego; Ren knew it. But he was worried it wasn't just his ego that was smarting right now.

"Is it another guy? Is it Lennox?" Ren knew he was being stupid. Stupid *and* obvious, two things he tried never to be. But there was something about this guy . . . he didn't want to just let it go.

It wasn't that he rarely got rejected.

He'd *never* been turned down by someone he really wanted before.

Not once.

"Lennox?" Seth laughed. "No. We're just friends. I just . . . I don't do the one-night-stand thing. It's not my style. I don't suppose I can persuade you to go on a date with me?"

Ren stared at him. "A date without sex? A date . . . with just the expectation of another date?"

Seth nodded. "I'd like to take you out."

Guys didn't *take Ren out*. He never let them. He'd never even been tempted before.

It was easy enough turning them down.

It was not easy turning Seth down, because he wanted it so badly.

And because he wanted it so badly, he knew he had to.

He could get into this guy. He could . . . well, Ren wasn't sure he was capable of falling in love, not the way other people did, but if he could, maybe he would, with Seth.

But he wasn't going to.

He didn't *want* to.

And one guy, no matter how attractive, no matter how many butterflies he gave Ren in the base of his stomach, wasn't going to change him.

"I don't do that," Ren said frankly. "Ever."

He watched as Seth sighed. "I was afraid of that."

"So . . ." Ren swallowed hard. "Just the sandwich?"

"Just the sandwich."

Ren turned towards Gabe, who was still somehow, impossibly, saying goodbye to Sean. Like they hadn't spent all night together.

"He wants the Thai meatball crunch wrap," Ren said shortly.

Gabriel raised his eyebrow. "Don't you want to make it for him? With your own two hands?"

It was an unsurprising question. After all, if his proposition had gone well, he'd have wanted to do exactly that, so he could deliver it to Seth and make some thinly veiled innuendo about how he'd touched it all over.

"No." Ren wasn't going to give Seth the satisfaction.

He'd had a chance, and he'd turned it down.

Turned *him* down.

Flat.

Gabriel said goodbye to Sean *again*, and then finally turned back to the stove, setting a pan on it.

"You asked him and he said no? Really? Maybe he's dating someone."

It would've been easier—barely—if that was the case.

There might've been some kind of hope for the future.

But no.

Seth just didn't want to fuck him. He wanted to *romance* him. Ew.

"He's not. I asked."

"Well, maybe he's like Lennox and just . . . well . . . *cold*," Gabriel suggested. Trying to be nice. Because Gabriel *always* tried to be nice.

It was exhausting sometimes.

And *cold*? Seth? There was no fucking way that was true.

He'd been plenty hot. Just not for Ren.

"Lennox isn't cold, he's just interested in Ash," Ren said, because it was easier to diagnose Lennox's problem than discuss his own.

"Maybe there's a good explanation for him turning you down." Gabe still was attempting optimism, like he could excuse away the sting Ren was feeling.

"Maybe." Ren knew the reason why he'd gotten turned down, but the last thing he wanted to do was explain it to Gabe, because then he'd have to hear again how he was wrong, and love was wonderful, and didn't he want to open himself up to new possibilities?

No, that was not what he wanted to open himself up to. He knew that for sure.

Three months later

It had been hard enough to turn down Ren Moretti the first time.

It was hard in a completely different, and so much *harder*, way, to be confronted with the guy he'd rejected over and over and *over* again.

When he'd done it, Seth hadn't realized that Lennox spent so much time at Food Truck Warriors—or that he would fall in love with Ash, who owned one of the trucks. Or that Tony, the owner of the lot, would fold him and Lennox into their friend circle without even blinking.

Or, that, most difficult of all, Seth would find himself face-to-face, again and again, for the last three months, with the irresistible guy he needed to resist.

It was easier only because Ren clearly carried a grudge and never bothered with any small talk or friendly greetings or even the barest acknowledgement that Seth even existed.

That helped.

But he did talk to everyone else, and he was his snarky, charming, absolutely sinfully hot self. Truthfully, he was tough enough to resist even without turning all that charisma on Seth.

Tonight, he was standing over by the firepit, laughing with his cousin and Sean, throwing his head back, endlessly amused by whatever it was that Gabe and Sean were teasing each other about.

His profile was devastating enough, but with the flickering firelight playing across it, he could have been a Renaissance painting, hanging on the wall at the Louvre or the Met. Seth couldn't get enough of looking at him.

If he'd known how difficult this was going to end up being, maybe he should've just slept with the guy.

But he'd known, after talking to the guy for less than ten minutes, that one night wouldn't ever be enough. He was going to want more, and more, every single goddamn night. He was going to want to unpack his secrets, and twist Lorenzo around his finger, until he never wanted to leave.

He'd never have left it at one night, and since Ren didn't do tomorrows, only tonights, it would've been impossible.

In fact, it probably would've been a catastrophe.

But then, it felt like a fucking catastrophe now, that he'd never gotten to touch him.

"You're glowering. Again."

Seth looked up, and Ross Stanton was standing in front of him. Awkwardly, because Ross Stanton did most things out of the kitchen awkwardly, but over the last few months, they'd become friends.

Especially after Ross had ended up getting together with Shaw, who co-owned this bar with his brother. He'd drifted from the fringes of the friend group to the center, and Seth, who spent a lot of the time on the fringes himself, understood how baffling it could be to have your center of gravity change so drastically.

"Am I?" he asked casually. He knew he had been, but it was one thing to feel it, and it was another entirely to admit it.

Even to Ross, who was a friend.

Though, it would still be easier to admit to Ross, than to someone like Lennox. Someone who knew him a little too well.

Who knew all his demons.

"You are," Ross said succinctly, sitting down.

One of the reasons he'd always liked Ross was that both of them liked to speak the truth bluntly.

"Your guy inside working?" Seth asked, referring to Shaw.

Ross nodded. "With this crowd, he won't be off early. So I thought I'd come down. See who else was here."

"Just about everybody," Seth said, glancing around. Considering it was a Friday, and a gorgeous clear night—cold but not overly chilly with the space heaters scattered around the edges of the patio, and the firepits that all gathered a crowd—that wasn't all that surprising. He'd known Ren would likely be here. But he'd told himself at the very beginning that he wasn't going to change his life or his routine or alter his friendships because of what had happened between them.

And, he'd been so sure that over time the feeling that he'd let something precious slip away would fade.

Except three months later, it was still going strong, and he'd considered starting to beg off some of these social evenings, but if he did, then Lennox would want to know why, and he couldn't talk about it.

Not with Lennox.

Not when Lennox was so happy, and wanted everyone else to be happy too.

"Tony and Lucas, and Gabriel and Sean, and even Ren, came," Ross said.

"Must not have had a hookup planned tonight," Seth grumbled under his breath.

But he hadn't been nearly quiet enough, because Ross tilted his head. "You're worried about Ren with other guys?"

"No, of course not. Ren can go out and fuck anyone he wants. That's . . . it has nothing to do with me." But Seth heard the lie in his own voice.

Ross gazed at him, the expression on his face making it crystal clear that he'd heard it too. That much was obvious, but for once, he must have decided to let it slide.

"Then why are you avoiding each other, still?"

Seth tilted his head. "You weren't even around back then. Can you say *still* in that scenario?"

"Yes," Ross said seriously. "I can."

"Okay, well, fine, I guess we *are* avoiding each other, but I don't know why."

Ross's gaze was sharp. "You don't know?"

"Okay, probably because he's pissed off that I turned him down."

"I turned him down," Ross said frankly, "and so did Lennox. And he's not avoiding us."

To illustrate his point just about perfectly, there he was, standing now with Lennox *and* Ash, talking and laughing like nothing was wrong.

He'd not done that once with Seth, not since the first day they'd met and everything had gone to hell almost as soon as it had begun.

"He's . . . well, maybe *I'm* avoiding *him*," Seth said. Partially true.

"Because you're . . ." Ross shrugged. "I'm not good at this under the best of circumstances, but you two are beyond me. I can't even guess, but I'd assume it's not because you're mad at *him* for you deciding not to sleep with him."

"Of course not. That would be ridiculous," Seth said. But there was something in that thought that resonated deep inside of him.

Was he in fact annoyed and frustrated and a little bit bitter that Ren had chosen the path he had and refused to budge from it? Even for Seth?

Oh, absolutely.

It was completely unfair for Seth to be pissed off for his lack of flexibility, when Seth hadn't exactly bent to Ren's demands either.

But that didn't mean he wasn't, still.

Still.

Okay, it *was* ridiculous that three months had passed, and they were still circling around each other. Seth couldn't deny Ross' point—not when Ross was staring at him like he'd just said everything that needed to be said.

He stood. "Okay, you're right."

Ross smiled. "See, that wasn't too difficult."

They joined the group surrounding the firepit.

Ash and Lennox were there, as well as Ren and Gabe. Seth didn't know where Sean had gone, but he wouldn't be far, not with Gabe here.

Ren glanced over and Seth *swore* his gaze slid right over him, like he wasn't even there, like he didn't even exist. He had a temper; he'd learned the hard way to control it, but it still spiked inside of him. Hot enough and high enough that he wasn't going to take this. Lorenzo couldn't just pretend that he wasn't here, the same way he'd been pretending he wasn't here for the last three months.

"Hey, Ross," he said to Ross, specifically, even reaching over and patting him on the shoulder. "Good to see you again."

That was another thing, Seth thought, trying not to inwardly seethe, Ren touched everyone. Friendly, happy, sweet touches. His cousin, Sean, Tony, even Ross. But he'd never touched Seth.

How could he, when he was in the middle of pretending he didn't exist?

"Lorenzo," Seth replied back, cutting Ross off, not letting Ren get away with any of his usual bullshit. Usually he went along with it. But tonight, he was through pretending.

Ren looked surprised. Then his gaze swept from the top of Seth's head down to his toes, in a leisurely, possessive, and ultimately dismissive, way that had his temper spiking again.

"Seth Abramson," he finally drawled. "Nice to see you around." Implying, with only his tone of voice, that actually the opposite was true.

Seth knew he had banged up Ren's pride. But hadn't Lennox and Ross done the same thing to him? Why was only *he* singled out for Ren's dislike?

He still wants you.

The thought surfaced, unbidden, in Seth's mind, but it couldn't possibly be true.

But nothing else explained why Ren would still be so mad months later.

He wants you, and you want him. It would be so easy . . .

It would be so easy.

And it would get him nothing in return, except probably a spectacular night and a bruised heart in the morning.

Then why did he feel so compelled to call him on all his bullshit?

"I thought you'd forgotten my name," Seth said casually.

Ren raised an eyebrow. "Oh?"

"You've spent the last few months pretending I'm not around. Makes sense you'd have forgotten all about me. But I guess not. Guess I'm still on your mind, even if you won't acknowledge I exist."

It was the verbal equivalent of a mortar shell, knocked right into Ren's walls. Because he had them. Seth had spent enough time watching him, listening to him, that he knew they existed. He wanted to see the guy behind them, the *real* Lorenzo, but Ren didn't lower them, at least never in Seth's vicinity.

Maybe not in anyone's vicinity. But Seth saw enough, just little tantalizing glimpses, that he knew there was a whole other person back there. It was stupid and pointless for him to want to know that other man, but he did, all the same.

"Maybe you're just beneath my notice," Ren said, and *yeah*, that was more than a little mean.

But maybe not unwarranted. Seth had hurt his pride, maybe Ren had the right to hurt his in return.

"Oh, we both know that's not true," Seth said gently.

Ren looked caught.

Ross put a hand on Seth's shoulder, surprising him. "Neither of you are going away, because I like both of you. So figure it out."

Trust Ross to cut right through to the heart of the matter.

"What is there to figure out?" Ren said, a little recklessly, his dark eyes wild.

"Maybe we should start over," Seth said. He wasn't idiotic enough to extend his hand for Ren to shake. He hadn't touched the man yet, and he knew it was better that he didn't. His self-control was only so good. "Hi, I'm Seth Abramson."

Ren eyed him uncertainly. He rarely looked anything other than completely and utterly confident, so Seth knew how much this exchange had cost him.

The cost was a knife that cut both ways, and his own composure was more than a little rocked.

"Ren Moretti," he finally said shortly.

He didn't say it was nice to meet him.

Seth understood; the idea behind this was to break the standoff, to make them both more comfortable existing in the same friendship space. He wasn't dumb enough to believe that it would fix everything.

They were both going to still want the exact same thing—and also two different things, at the exact same time.

"I think I'll call you Lorenzo," Seth said, just to see Ren's eyes flash again.

That right there was why they'd never be friends.

He couldn't resist his own worst impulses when it came to this man.

"See?" Gabe inserted himself into the awkward silence. "You two can actually be civil to each other. There's hope for world peace, yet."

Except that Seth knew, as he watched Ren take a drink from Sean's hand, that nothing had really changed.

And nothing would, not until this attraction finally burned itself out.

CHAPTER ONE

REN HAD BEEN ON many dates during his twenty-six years, but none of them had ever been this bad.

It wasn't that the guy was ugly.

He wasn't boring, either.

He was also making a decent effort at being charming and funny, and Ren knew that a few months ago, he'd have enjoyed the evening, gone back to this guy's apartment or his house or his loft downtown—it was at this moment that Ren realized he didn't even remember this particular dude's name—and had some perfectly satisfactory sex.

The guys sitting across from Ren hadn't changed.

Ren didn't even think *he* had changed.

What had changed was sitting across the bar, in the corner, having a quiet drink with Lennox and Ash, conveniently right in Ren's line of sight.

Every single fucking time Ren tried to actually get into the conversation, or dig deep to find some shred of interest, Seth was *right there.*

To Seth's credit, he wasn't normally right there.

No, normally his interference was only in Ren's head.

But tonight, fate had apparently decided to be an extra bad bitch, and make sure Seth was in the one spot at the entire bar where there was no way that Ren could ignore him or shove the thought of him to the side.

". . . and that's why he told me he was the best at hackey sack." The guy stopped with an anticipatory gleam in his eyes, and Ren assumed this was the end of the story, and he was supposed to laugh at . . . well, at *something*. But since he hadn't been paying attention, he had no idea if it had actually been funny.

He dredged up a half-hearted chuckle.

It wasn't this guy's fault that he'd drawn the unluckiest hand, and this date was fated to be a bust.

The guy laughed heartily at his own joke. "Wasn't that hilarious?" he asked, like he needed to remind Ren that he was making an effort.

"Hilarious," Ren echoed.

He had a feeling that even if it *had* been hilarious, he wouldn't have found the story particularly funny.

Ren sighed, and leaned back, shoving a hand through his carefully styled hair.

Something he'd never do if this was a date that he actually wanted to succeed.

Not that he needed flawless hair. He knew he was really attractive, and was lucky enough to be really attractive even when he didn't make any effort whatsoever.

Which was why he tried never to rest on pretty.

"Have you ever played?"

"Hacky sack?" Ren questioned.

There was no way he was going to end up going home with this guy. He couldn't even remember his name, not with Seth sitting right over there.

Taunting Ren with his rejection.

The guy opposite him, nodded. Way more engaged than Ren could hope to be.

"Listen, I need to be honest," Ren said. There was no point in letting this guy work this hard. He was asking about *hacky sack*. Ren wasn't a freaking emotionless monster.

He felt . . . *things*. Not love. At least not ever in a romantic way—because he definitely loved his cousin Gabe and his mom and his whole extended family—but he'd gotten used to not feeling it for any of his hookups. He'd barely ever been tempted to hook up with the same guy twice. But that didn't mean he was callous or a monster.

The guy's smile gleamed in the muted light of the Funky Cup. "Honesty," he said, "is always the best policy. Your place or mine?"

Ren ran another hand through his hair. It was probably standing straight up now. It took work and effort to tame the dark curls he'd gotten from his Italian parents. But this guy didn't seem deterred in the least.

"I mean," Ren said, leaning closer and lowering his voice, because he was also not into humiliation kink, "I should be honest that this isn't going to work out."

He tried to school his expression into something like resigned regret as the guy stared at him incredulously.

"What?"

"It's not you, it's me?"

The guy rolled his eyes.

"Do you actually buy any of this bullshit you're spouting?"

"I said I wanted to be honest." Ren met the guy's narrowing gaze without flinching. "This is me being honest. I told you I would be, when we met."

"You also told me we'd go on a date, and there wouldn't be any strings." He had. He usually did. It was always better to be up front about his complete lack of interest in a boyfriend or a relationship or *love*.

"Me telling you that this isn't going to work out is a string?" Ren questioned.

"No," the guy said, "the whole point wasn't any strings, but I at least expected to fuck you at the end of all this effort." He waved, like meeting Ren at a bar and then buying him a drink was a "lot of effort."

Ren didn't roll his eyes but *that* took effort. He already knew the guy wouldn't appreciate just how much it took —especially if he thought buying a drink was a significant enough effort to get Ren into bed.

"Well, I'm sorry," Ren said. "I'd suggest a do-over, but I have a feeling this ship has sailed."

"No fucking kidding," the guy grumbled as he stood and dramatically stalked over to the door.

This would've, Ren thought as he nursed the rest of his drink and heard the door slam behind him, been a hell of a lot easier if he'd actually remembered the guy's name.

It was embarrassing that he hadn't. That he still didn't.

He wasn't one of those guys who slept with everything that moved, and didn't give a shit.

He enjoyed the dates and the slow burn of anticipation, always. Even stayed friends with a lot of his hookups. He just didn't feel the need to revisit any of them. To deepen the connection.

Gabe had told him that he'd gotten stuck in a rut . . . and well, maybe that was why Seth's rejection had stung so badly.

By turning him down, Seth, Ren decided with annoyance, had ruined everything.

Even him.

He did not appreciate it.

And on cue, because he apparently *knew* how difficult he'd made everything, Seth met Ren's eyes and tipped his glass in his direction.

That did it.

He was fucking done with this bullshit.

Ren stood and he did *not* stalk dramatically over to where Seth was sitting with his business partner, Lennox, and his boyfriend, Ash, but he walked with a purpose. Because he most definitely had a purpose.

It wasn't his fault that most of the eyes in the place followed him.

He was used to it; he could hardly complain about being attractive, but sometimes it got old to always be the center of attention, even when he didn't want to be.

He stopped in front of Seth.

"I need to talk to you," he said, between clenched teeth.

Also not something he'd *ever* do when faced with a guy he wanted to sleep with. But they'd clearly established that Seth was an exception to just about every rule of Ren's.

Except one.

He wasn't going to have a relationship with the guy, just to get underneath him.

"Well, hello, Lorenzo," Seth said, all innocence. Like he had no idea that he'd just ruined Ren's date.

He doesn't know he just ruined your date, he's just being nice, his brain informed him, but he pushed the logical truth away. He didn't want to hear it right now.

He also ignored the fact that Seth was the only one who ever called him Lorenzo, and somehow he made it about ten syllables long, each one sexier than the last.

"Hi," he said shortly. "I need to talk to you."

Seth smiled.

He wasn't the hottest guy Ren had ever seen.

Or the most charming.

Or the funniest.

But somehow his grayish-green eyes, his close-cropped auburn hair, and rather ordinary features had taken up residence in every single one of Ren's dreams.

It was unfair, but it was finally time to get this guy out of his head, for good.

"You said, so *talk*," Seth said. He was straightforward. It would've been refreshing, except for the straightforward rejection he'd given Ren last time they'd had this conversation.

Despite the fact that Ren had told himself, very explicitly, that he would *never* be making a second offer, here he was again.

"I think we should have sex."

See, Ren congratulated himself, *you didn't ask, so it wasn't an offer. Instead, you made sure it was a strongly worded suggestion.*

Lennox had been taking a sip of his beer and he choked on it, starting to cough. He might be dating Ash, who had loosened him up, but he still had that closed-off vibe to him.

No doubt he wasn't used to people making such obvious propositions in front of him.

But Seth didn't say anything, just smiled, slowly. "Oh, we should?"

"We should."

Ren had marched over here with almost no plan, messed-up hair, that single sentence, and a burning need to *make* Seth accept his offer.

Except Seth did not look particularly receptive. He looked kind. He looked *sympathetic.*

Ren wanted to fall to the floor and crawl out the door. One rejection had been humiliating enough. He hadn't even gotten the second one yet, and already it was worse.

Why had he thought this was a good idea?

Oh, that's right. *Desperation.* Because that always led to reasoned decision-making.

"Are you saying you want to go on a date with me?" Seth asked.

Ren nearly nodded, but then remembered the trap.

He and Seth considered a "date" very different things.

Ren saw a date as a fun way to pass an evening before he enjoyed a satisfactory sexual encounter. Seth saw a date as a stepping-stone on the way to a *relationship.*

"You know what I'm saying," Ren said. Nobody could blame him for not being crystal clear. He'd never try to fool Seth into bed with him. Because that was a heinous thing to do, yes, but also because he wasn't desperate enough to miss the hints of steel hiding behind those kind gray eyes. You did not fuck with this guy and live to tell about it.

He *and* his best friend and business partner, Lennox, were both ex-military and probably knew a couple hundred ways to kill a man.

"What you're saying is clear, but what I don't understand is why you're saying it." The words were trademark Seth—brutally honest with a veneer of kindness that would fool you if you weren't paying attention. He finished his drink and set it down on the table with a click.

Ren knew that Ash and Lennox were staring at them like they were an episode of their favorite Netflix show, but he couldn't tear his eyes away from Seth's.

Why couldn't he see through him? Why couldn't he see what made him tick? Why couldn't he unlock his mysteries . . . in bed? Because that was where he wanted him, right?

Right?

"You know why I'm saying it. I want you. You want me." It was arrogant, maybe, but what else could Ren do when faced with this implacable calm?

It was annoying. It made him want to ruffle it.

The same way Seth had ruffled him.

Ren braced himself for the second rejection, but instead, Seth stood.

"Come on," he said, "we should talk about this privately."

"That . . ." *That's what I was trying to do when I said I needed to talk to you.*

But then he hadn't waited, he'd just blurted it out, all desperation and a hell of a lot of misplaced hope.

"Did you really want to discuss this in front of Lennox and Ash?" Seth asked as he walked towards the little hallway that Ren knew contained both the bathrooms and Jackson's—who owned the Funky Cup with his brother, Shaw—office.

"I . . ." Ren hated how indecisive he sounded.

The hallway was empty.

Seth leaned back against one of the walls.

It was really a very narrow hallway. All Ren would have to do was lean forward and they'd touch.

They'd never actually touched before. Even when Seth had done his whole "starting over" routine. He had very specifically not extended his hand for Ren to shake.

And honestly, Ren couldn't blame him, because if they did, he wasn't sure he would trust himself either.

"I guess you didn't care." Seth's voice didn't sound damning, it sounded contemplative.

"Sex isn't something anyone should be ashamed of," Ren said. On the other hand, *he* sounded annoyingly defensive.

"No, but I consider it my private business."

Ren hated how this man made him feel out of control. Out of control and *petty*. "That's because you're not having any."

"But I could be." The insult just glanced off of Seth, and he looked speculative. Like he was actually considering it.

Even though Ren knew he wasn't.

"I asked, didn't I?" Ren took a step closer, even though he hadn't meant to.

In the dim light of the hallway, Seth's eyes looked almost mossy green. He had several days' worth of reddish-gold scruff on his face, and he was so much everything that Ren wanted over him and under him and around him that it didn't even matter that he wasn't close to the hottest guy he'd ever been with.

He wanted to know what it would be like to have all that straightforwardness, all that *honesty*, focused on him.

"You did." Seth sighed. "And I wish you hadn't."

It shouldn't have hurt.

But the sting of it made Ren reckless. Even more reckless than usual.

He was so close now, if he tipped his head back, he could pick out the hundred different shades of green in Seth's eyes. The nearness of him lit something inside of him, in a place that felt like it hadn't been touched by anyone else.

"I know you want me."

Ren could feel it. Like a separate entity with them in the hallway. His lust had form and shape and weight. Just the same as Ren's own.

Why was he fighting this?

"That's why I wish you hadn't asked." Seth's voice was low, rough. "I'm only a man."

"Having trouble resisting?" Ren teased. It would be so easy to just lean in, another few inches, and press his lips against Seth's.

It would be so good.

Ren had never been more certain of anything in his whole life.

The sex would be so hot, it would burn Seth out of his system for good. Ren was sure of it.

If he could just persuade him to give in . . .

He leaned in another inch.

Not quite far enough, but close enough that he could see Seth's jaw clench.

Men always wanted Ren; that was definitely not new. But he'd never felt so accomplished than he did right at this moment.

"This isn't a good idea." Seth's voice was quiet, but it carried. Hit Ren like a series of bombs.

"But . . ." Ren felt numb. Like defeat had just been snatched from the jaws of victory. "But you *want* me."

Seth reached out and pressed a single finger against Ren's mouth. It was rough, calloused. Glorious. Ren wanted to bite it. "I do want you. Doesn't mean it's a good idea."

And then he was gone, and Ren didn't know what to think about it.

Lie.

He knew exactly what he thought about it.

That it was total and complete bullshit.

Seth Abramson took one deep, shaky breath, and then another.

He'd walked out of the bar five minutes ago, away from Lorenzo and the clear plea in his bedroom eyes, but his breathing still hadn't returned to normal.

When Seth had turned him down six months ago, he'd never expected that Ren would ever ask again. After all, it wasn't like Ren was lacking in admirers. Just tonight he'd been out on a date. And though Ash and Ren weren't particularly close, Seth heard enough gossip that he knew after he'd turned Ren down, Ren had gone about his regular routine.

It had been what had convinced Seth that he'd made the right call.

Not that he blamed Ren for his lifestyle; he was happy with it, and he'd chosen it, clear-eyed, without a hint of shame. And there was something admirable about that.

It wasn't what Seth would've done. Not with his history. But the lack of shame had been refreshing. He'd almost *enjoyed* watching Ren enjoy himself.

But still . . . having him ask again, that had not been something Seth had ever anticipated would happen. He definitely had not expected that the question would come phrased as a strongly worded suggestion either. Or that Ren would deliver it with that desperate look in his eyes, like if he didn't have Seth—and that was *him*, which was kind of blowing his mind—he wouldn't be able to live with it.

Seth had always assumed that it was because he didn't get turned down often, and Ren's pride was smarting. But tonight's offer put a whole different spin on things.

Ren had been thinking about him for six months.

"Hey."

Seth looked up and saw Lennox standing in front of him.

Just Lennox.

Which meant that he'd come out here without Ash, specifically because he was concerned about Seth.

"Hey," Seth said. Fighting his own instincts to stay calm. The good news was that he'd had lots of experience doing it, and it came easier today than it had four years ago.

"You okay?" Lennox took a step closer. He looked concerned. Seth wondered how upset he'd looked when he'd practically run out of the bar.

Probably pretty upset, if Lennox had come out here to check on him.

Especially since Lennox *knew* he didn't do distressed.

He'd walked out of God knew how many firefights and five tours in Iraq and Afghanistan with a calm smile and normal blood pressure.

But Ren reaching for him made him breathe a little too fast.

Both because Ren was *Ren*, and Seth would have to be dead not to want exactly what he was offering, and a whole lot more, but also because he didn't know what to do about it.

He was conflicted, even though he didn't want to be.

"I'm fine, just . . . surprised." That was the truth. He had been shocked as hell when Ren had stalked up, and with barely any preamble had suggested that they have sex.

He'd been so surprised that he'd almost said yes.

And what would be so wrong if you said yes? that annoying voice in the back of his head wondered. *You want him. He wants you. You aren't a freaking monk.*

He wasn't.

But he also knew himself, and it was impossible to deny that the pull he felt towards Ren was strong. He was going to want more. And wanting more, when Ren was around all the time?

A recipe for disaster.

It had been fine enough when it was just Seth feeling that way. Easy enough to deal with.

It was not so easy to deal with if Ren felt it too.

"You're telling me," Lennox said, leaning against the outside brick wall of the bar, and his voice was easy. The easiness in it helped Seth relax a little more. "I'm still not used to guys walking up to other guys and being so . . . well, so open about it."

"Welcome to the real world," Seth said, fighting a smile. "And Los Angeles, where nobody gives a shit who you are or who you're fucking. Nice change from the base, right?"

"Why were you surprised?" Lennox punctuated his question with a sigh, like he was secretly disappointed that Seth had tried to change the subject.

"I just didn't think he'd ask again." Still the truth. He'd thought he was alone in his weird Ren-and-Seth-sleeping-together-*and*-more obsession.

Apparently he wasn't, and he didn't have a clue what to do about it.

Especially since the *more* was still not on the table.

It was pointless to ask Ren for a date, because all Ren would do was laugh in his face and go for his dick.

In that super sweet, charming, funny way of his that made it seem like it was all good at the time, until later when Seth had to see him with another guy, and then another guy, and then another, and he realized that he was just another in a line.

He could do a lot of things but not that.

"You didn't think he'd ask again?" Lennox looked surprised now. Which was a new expression for Lennox.

Seth reminded himself to congratulate Ash when they went back inside, for turning Lennox into something resembling a real boy, not the closed-off, buttoned-up version that had existed for so many years.

"Of course I didn't."

Lennox chuckled. "Then you haven't been paying attention. You guys gravitate towards each other."

Not *helpful*.

"That's because we ended up in the same friend circle," Seth said, valiantly trying to circumvent the truth. Which was that *yes*, he did gravitate towards Ren, because he was the human version of a black hole: both irresistible and impossible. "That's how friends work, Lennox."

Lennox tilted his head, still smiling. "You like him. He likes you. I fail to see the issue. Apparently he *also* fails to see the issue."

"He wants to take me back to his room and fuck me, or let me fuck him, or something. He doesn't want . . ." *Everything I want.* "It's a bad idea. Bad all around."

"You know bad ideas," Lennox said, "they like to draw you in. And then keep you there."

Lennox would know. He'd had his own version of a bad idea, but he'd broken the pattern. He'd left Brandon and their fucked-up secret relationship that was never going to be anything other than buried in the deepest, darkest closet.

"You're not wrong," Seth said wryly.

"You should do something about it."

Seth opened his mouth to say that yeah, he was trying. And he'd been doing a halfway decent job of it, too, before Ren had sauntered over and blown his carefully constructed mirage of half-truths to bits. But Lennox kept going.

"No, you're not trying. What did you tell me once? I need to get out? See some things? Meet some people?"

Seth waved a hand. "I am pretty sure I gave you about a hundred different versions of that speech. Maybe a thousand. I'm glad you finally listened to me. And I know Ash is glad too."

"We both are. But it's time you take your own advice."

"What am I supposed to do? Ask out the cute barista at the coffee place down the street? Spend a Saturday night at Temple? Join that new app everyone's talking about?"

"All of those and any of those," Lennox said with finality, like it was easy.

Maybe for him it was.

It had never been easy for Seth. Turning away from something he wanted was never simple for him. Even when he'd been burned by all that wanting too many times.

But maybe Lennox . . . maybe Lennox was right. Maybe he needed to try something different. Try to break out of this rut. And maybe doing it would convince Ren that it was a bad idea once and for all.

Not that Seth believed that he *wasn't* convinced after this last rejection.

Not many men got to reject Lorenzo Moretti once.

He'd gotten to do it twice.

He knew he wouldn't get to do it a third time.

"Come on, let's go back inside, buy your man another drink," Seth said, wrapping an arm around Lennox.

"You good?" Lennox asked, looking up at him, like he wasn't quite sure.

"Well, I will be," Seth said. Hoping that saying it meant that it would eventually be true.

CHAPTER TWO

"YOU LOOK GRUMPY THIS morning." Gabe shot an appraising look over the huge pot of red sauce he was babysitting on the stove.

Ren stared at the onion he was chopping. Normally he whipped through the prep on the truck quickly and efficiently, because he hated doing it, so he might as well get it done as fast as possible so he could move on to something he *did* like.

Like making the thousands of meatballs they sold a day.

But instead he was sulking in the middle of the onions.

He knew it and it was annoying, but predictable, that Gabe had called him out on it.

"Regular grumpy or extra grumpy?" Ren asked, even though he already knew the answer.

"Regular grumpy I can handle. When your knife is flashing over there, trying to emulate an Iron Chef, I know better than to interfere, but you're definitely pissed off about something because you've been on that one onion for the last five minutes." Gabe eyed him again over the huge pot of sauce.

Ren loved his cousin. There was nobody else he'd ever tolerate running a business with. He was funny, he was lighthearted, he was a hell of a great cook, and he ran a tight ship. And, more importantly than anything else, he was loyal. To the Moretti family, and also to anyone he called a friend. And he called just about everyone a friend. But he was also so fucking *emotional*. He always wanted to talk about his feelings.

On a normal day, that was bad enough.

But now he wanted to talk about *Ren's* feelings.

"Maybe, maybe not, but I don't have to talk about it." Yeah, he was sulking. It wasn't attractive, but if you couldn't be unattractive at eight in the morning while dicing onions, when could you be?

"Yes, you do." Gabe pointed a wooden spoon perpetually stained red at him. "You absolutely do."

"You're the King of Feelings, of course you think that." Ren finished with the onion, finally, and moved on to the next. Only about a million to go.

He loved working here. He *loved* it. Coming to the truck, a situation that happened six days a week, always made him feel better.

Except this morning.

He'd woken up, and the bitterness of Seth's rejection had tasted like ash on the back of his tongue.

It was bad enough he'd stooped low enough to ask again.

Doubly bad that it had gone just about as terrible as it could have gone.

It would only have been worse if Ren had done the unthinkable and actually, honest to God, *kissed* him, only for Seth to say, "Yeah, thanks, but no, thanks."

What was the world coming to, if the *second*-worst possibility had come to pass?

Ren did not want to know.

"I *am* the King of Feelings, and you should be impressed that I'm embracing that horrible nickname these days," Gabe said.

"It's not horrible, it's accurate."

It was the worst kind of day when even bantering with his cousin—but more importantly, his best friend—didn't make him feel any better.

"Then it's my duty to convince you to tell me at least a little of why you're so mad."

"How do you know I'm mad? I could be . . . well, *sad*. Or disappointed. Or hungover."

"You're not hungover, because I saw you leave the bar, from the back porch, and you didn't even look unsteady. Also, you only ordered a double instead of a triple espresso this morning, and you always get a triple if you had too much booze the night before. And you're not disappointed, because you'd tell me about that. The precise way you're cutting that onion tells me that you're mad." Gabe gestured again with the spoon.

Ren looked down, and *yeah*, Gabe wasn't wrong, because there was definitely a murderous intensity to the way he was currently slicing this onion.

He'd kind of been imagining that it was Seth's dick.

If he wasn't going to get to take a ride, then *nobody* should get to.

Fair was only fair.

Besides, they could always sew it back on, right? They did that these days. He'd just be the new gay Lorena Bobbitt.

And *that* got weird fast.

Ren set his knife down.

"Okay, fine, I'm mad," Ren said. Hating that Gabe had suckered him into this, but wondering if maybe . . . if maybe Gabe could actually help him.

After all, Gabe was now a man with some real relationship experience.

Ren didn't want to consider it, but what else could he do? Continuing on this way was fucking futile.

"Good, now tell me why," Gabe said, a glimmer of a smile on his face.

"Seth fucking Abramson," Ren said succinctly. "I asked him to have sex with me *again*, and he turned me down flat."

Gabe looked astonished. "You asked him to sleep with you *again*, and he said no, *again*?"

"That's exactly what I just said." Ren picked his knife back up and began cutting through another onion. It didn't feel too good to hear the shock in Gabriel's voice, or to hear the evening's events repeated back at him, incredulously.

At least Ren wasn't alone. Gabe couldn't fucking believe it either.

"You don't do that, though. Like . . . I thought you'd asked and he said no, and you moved on. And *wait*, you went on a date last night. Did you break up your date so you could proposition Seth again?"

"We agreed mutually that it wasn't going to work out," Ren said, close-lipped. "I didn't break it up to ask Seth or anything."

"Ah," Gabriel said. There was a multitude of opinions in that one single sound.

You, Ren reminded himself, *love your cousin. He's your best friend. Your roommate. Your business partner.*

"Just say it," Ren said.

"Well, again, I thought you'd moved past this?" Gabe leaned against the side of the counter that ran along one side of the truck. "It was . . . well it was some time ago, wasn't it?"

"Six months ago."

"Right, six months ago. I guess I didn't realize you were . . ." Gabe paused, clearly trying to search for the right term. "Crushing on him still?"

"It's not a crush," Ren said firmly. Except . . . what else could it be? The man was under his skin. He wanted him. Bad. What else was that except for a crush? An inconvenient affliction of lust?

If it was actually a crush, the first thing he wanted to do was get rid of it.

The second thing he wanted to do was totally smash it dead.

The third and most important thing was to completely annihilate it.

He didn't need this bullshit in his life.

No, thank you, he'd done perfectly fine without it for the first twenty-six years, and he wasn't intending to change now.

"I really think it might be a crush," Gabe said thoughtfully. "You're kinda hung up on him. Obviously. Unless you're . . . what? Afraid? Afraid you might like him? Afraid he might really like you? Afraid he might get to know what you're really like, unlike all these other guys who never stick around long enough to find out?"

"That is complete bullshit," Ren retorted. "Stop it."

"Fine, fine, fine," Gabe said, holding his hands up in faux surrender. "It's complete bullshit that you're afraid."

Ren glared at his cousin. Why was he like this?

Unfortunately there had never been a satisfactory answer to that question.

"I just hate this," Ren said, annoyed by the sulkiness in his own voice.

It had been amusing watching Gabe struggle with the same thing last year, when he'd had this ridiculous crush on Sean, his mortal enemy.

But then Sean had never *really* been a mortal enemy. Ren had known that much from the start. Gabe had just been a little slow on the uptake. But once they'd gotten their shit together and fallen in love . . .

Well, there was going to be no falling in love here. That's what happened when a crush got serious.

It was bad enough that he was crushing. He didn't need to complicate everything by doing the one thing he'd sworn he'd never do: fall in love.

He'd told Gabe he didn't think love existed, but *obviously* it did. It had been fun to see Gabe get all worked up about it, though. Of course love existed. He'd seen it blossom and bloom and grow settled and sweet between his mom and his stepfather. He'd seen it grow, despite all the odds stacked against it, between Gabe and Sean. Lennox had even *shot* a guy for Ash.

Admittedly, he'd just blown up Ash's food truck, and he'd definitely deserved it . . . but it was still a grand romantic gesture, born out of the deepest love.

But love? Not for him.

And *not* because of what Gabe claimed, because he was afraid or something. He wasn't afraid of anything. And letting a guy get to know him? *He let people get to know him.*

"So what are you going to do about it?" Gabe asked after a long silence.

The answer to that was obvious enough.

"Move on, move past, pretend it never happened," Ren said. "Take your pick."

"But you've already been trying to do that, right?"

Ren hated it when Gabe was right. Especially about things like this.

The good news was it didn't happen all that often.

"Yes, of course I have. I don't *enjoy* feeling like this," Ren said through clenched teeth.

"Then maybe you should try something else," Gabe said thoughtfully. "Like . . . try to find someone else."

"I did that, remember? Last night and quite a few times before that. Hasn't helped."

"Maybe you haven't met the right guy," Gabe said. Ren could tell he was working his most persuasive tone of voice. The one he used when he was trying to convince Sean that *yes, he actually did want to go to the Star Wars movie marathon with him.*

"And how am I supposed to do that? I meet plenty of guys."

"You could always try that new app, that one I've been hearing so much about."

"An app?" Ren could hear the derision in his voice. "I do not need an app, thank you very much."

"No, of course not, but it might . . . widen your search? If you're just gonna stick to the guys who you meet here, at the truck, or at the gym, or at the Funky Cup, it's a much smaller group. You want to find the guy that's gonna make you forget all about Seth? You gotta widen your sample size."

"I guess." Ren did not love the idea of the app, but he also could concede that *one*, he was fairly desperate, and *two*, Gabriel was making some kind of logical sense.

How long would he be stuck in this stupid crush if he just stood here and passively waited for the right guy to come along? A guy who would make him feel the same kind of electric spark that Seth did?

He might be waiting a long-ass time, and one thing Ren did not possess in abundance was patience.

"Just think about it." Gabe's gaze was shrewd. Like he knew that Ren wouldn't be able to stop, now that he'd put the idea in his head.

Ren turned back to his onions.

That was the downside of working with Gabe: he knew Ren better than he sometimes knew himself.

Seth didn't give in to the inevitable for two whole days.

He didn't want to ask out the cute bartender—who wasn't Shaw, because he was very taken—at the Funky Cup. He didn't want to invite the barista at his favorite coffee shop for a drink, because he'd learned the hard way that if things didn't work out with someone he saw all the time, it got awkward.

So that left the last possible choice.

The app.

Lennox had told him the name of it, and he'd mentally noted it, not really intending to try it. But it was quiet and lonely in his house.

Lennox and Ash had headed to the Funky Cup for a late drink, and they'd invited him to go, but he wasn't in the mood to socialize.

He definitely wasn't in the mood to watch Ash and Lennox and the happiness they'd found—and *yearn* for things he couldn't have.

It was easier than he'd anticipated to download the app, and then to create a login, but it was much harder to make a profile.

For job, he kept it simple, putting in, "Private security."

When he hit the interests section, he got really stuck. What *were* his interests? He had them, right? The military hadn't killed them all, right? Even if they had, he'd been out for over four years. He *had* to have interests, besides work. Finally he typed in, "Sparring and weightlifting. Art." He did enjoy museums and galleries. The more bizarre the art installation, the more interested he was. But when the Protectorate had taken off and he and Lennox had gotten busy, that was the first thing that had fallen off his radar.

Maybe he could find someone who'd like to go with him again.

"Now," he said out loud as he stared at his phone screen, "the tough part."

He had no idea what to do about the profile pic. For security reasons, he'd already decided that he didn't want to show his face, and the last thing he wanted was to post some kind of tacky headless, ab-heavy shot. Everyone would just think it was fake anyway.

He wasn't in this to just hook up—though it might be nice to work off some of all this sexual tension if he met some guy that he didn't see a future with—so the picture needed to indicate that.

He took a quick selfie, partially turning away from the camera, using the print of his favorite Picasso as the background, and then blurred what you could see of his face. Turned it black and white.

When he was done, Seth was mostly satisfied with how it had turned out.

He was just a dark-haired muddle—his memorable red hair dimmed—with the shapes of the Picasso print behind him.

Nobody would ever guess it was him.

It was, Seth realized as he finished his profile and saved it, kind of fun to not be himself. He could see right away what attracted people to this kind of anonymity.

There was no time to waste, and Seth started a search on the app, filtering out anyone who didn't live in LA, and everyone who was *really* young. He didn't mind dating someone younger, but he wasn't interested in some young kid, either.

"No," Seth said to himself as he started to scroll through the results. "No, no, no, *definitely* not. Too hot. Too full of himself. Too . . ." He made a face. "Too fake. Is anyone supposed to believe that jawline is real?"

It seemed that doctored pictures were the special of the day, because he had been through two pages of them so far.

He was beginning to be really glad that while he'd touched up his picture, he'd done the opposite. Nobody would ever bother messaging him. Not without him advertising just how hot he was as blatantly as everyone else.

He'd just congratulated himself on taking the first real step to get over this horrible fucking obsession when there it was.

Midway through the third page of results, Seth stopped scrolling abruptly.

"Seriously?" Seth exclaimed out loud.

Out loud.

Like just *thinking* it hadn't been good enough.

Ren's face stared out at him from the screen.

He hadn't taken a really thirsty pic, because he hadn't *had* to. Not with a face like that.

When Seth clicked onto the profile, it said things that he'd have expected. Like how he was a culinary mashup genius—*true*, Seth thought resentfully—and that he was into trivia nights, which Seth knew too, because he was a certified creeper who'd spent too many hours purposefully eavesdropping on a guy who wasn't interested in him.

But Ren's profile also said that he liked *finding the kind of secret spots that you can lose yourself in.*

And that right there, encapsulated in a single phrase, was why Seth hadn't been able to let this guy go.

It was right there, the depth of the man, only tantalizingly hidden, just out of view. Ren might pretend that he was shallow, but Seth knew better.

Seth also knew that this was one hundred percent, not-a-doubt-in-his-mind, Lorenzo Moretti.

And he'd joined the app, it said, only one day ago.

It shouldn't have bothered him that after he'd turned Ren down, he'd gone looking for guys to sleep with.

That should not have been even remotely surprising. Ren was Ren, and Seth had never really expected him to change. *Wanted* him to change, sure, but *expected*? No.

But it still stung.

"Well, fuck you too," Seth said out loud, throwing his phone down on the bed.

He didn't need any further evidence that Ren was trying to move on, just the same as he was. It shouldn't hurt. It was still a terrible idea to sleep together, especially when they wanted two such completely different things. But even with his limited experience, Seth had never had a guy work so goddamn hard *not* to sleep with him before.

Seth stood up and instead of letting himself pace, went to the kitchen. He'd just make a nice calming mug of tea, which was a practiced task that usually helped him calm down. If he was really lucky, it would put him right to sleep, and he wouldn't be tempted to do . . . whatever it was that he was suddenly tempted to do.

Not message Ren.

No way.

That would be both counterproductive and also idiotic.

The man doesn't want to talk to you. He just wants to fuck you. That's all.

Seth filled the teapot with water, and set it on the stove with a loud, satisfying bang.

But what if he didn't know it was you?

The idea was tantalizing.

Pointless. But tantalizing.

Of course, Seth would end up having to reveal who he was. It wasn't like they could meet in the dark. Seth couldn't insist that they wear masks. Though that could be kinda sexy.

And, Seth knew, it wouldn't matter.

In fact, there was no guarantee that Ren wouldn't figure it out immediately. He was smart. And Seth, while hiding his face in his profile picture, hadn't gone out of his way to lie about what he did or what he enjoyed.

Seth drummed his fingers on the counter.

Besides, Ren was just trolling for guys to sleep with.

What would messaging him accomplish? Even if he pretended to not be himself?

You could give him a chance to know you. You've never gotten to just talk *to the guy before.*

Seth took a deep, short breath, and then let it out.

He knew exactly what he'd be trying to do: win Ren over. Convince him that they might have something more than just sexual chemistry.

Before he could change his mind or decide that this was mad and crazy and absolutely the worst idea he'd ever had, Seth picked up the phone and selected the message option under Ren's profile.

With a face like that, he'd have no end of guys desperate to talk to him and fuck him. He needed to be . . . different.

Somehow.

Hey, he wrote, **I thought we were discouraged from using fake or touched-up profile pics.**

It was a gamble. Hardly the riskiest thing Seth had ever done in his life, but it got the blood pumping anyway. His chamomile tea was going to be completely fucking useless.

He knew that every single guy who messaged Ren would immediately slobber all over how gorgeous he was.

The only way to play it was to take the opposite tactic, and hope that Ren found that amusing enough that he wouldn't just ignore him.

Maybe he wouldn't even answer.

Though Seth thought he knew human nature well enough. And *Ren's* human nature?

Well, the guy was still hung up on his rejection from six months ago.

He wasn't going to take an insult lying down.

Ren was in a bad mood.

A mood he'd been trying to eradicate since Seth had turned him down forty-eight hours ago but that kept persisting despite all his attempts to improve it.

He'd gone out with Sean and Gabe for a drink after they'd closed up their trucks, hoping he might meet someone at the Funky Cup that might distract him, but no dice. The crowd had been quiet, and Ren hadn't seen anyone who had any shot at making him forget that Seth Abramson existed.

He'd come back alone, Gabriel going to stay at Sean's house, and had flopped down on the couch, sticking his bare feet on the edge of the coffee table. He leaned forward, picked up his phone, and because he'd exhausted every possibility *except* this one, he opened the Flaunt app and started to scroll through all the messages he'd gotten since creating his account yesterday.

He'd known he'd be getting a lot of private messages.

There was a gratifyingly long list of them, in fact. But most of them were the exact same. Some variation of, "You're superhot, let's hook up."

A few of the senders might have intrigued him, though he was sure most of them were using either a touched-up pic or a fake one, but the complete lack of imagination was a boner killer.

Ren skimmed through the list and then back up again, only to suddenly realize that someone had sent him a message accusing him—*to his face*—of using a picture that wasn't his.

"Okay," Ren said out loud, "I'll bite."

It might be insulting, but it was at least slightly more imaginative than all the ridiculous messages telling him how hot he was.

Of course, Ren knew whoever the guy was, he'd done it on purpose. Which meant he was smart.

There was a reason a lot of guys used the apps. Usually it was because they were shy or not great in person or worse, it was because they were dumb.

And dumb guys always thought they were great in bed —but never were.

Ren stared at the message, and then clicked over to the guy's profile pic. Unlike everyone else who'd slobbered all over him, he wasn't showing his face—or any other muscley features—in his profile picture, and his description was also vague. He was in security, and it seemed he liked art. That was all the profile gave away, though the fact that he liked Picasso, based on the picture visible behind him, was interesting.

Intriguing enough that Ren decided *what the hell*, he was bored and he was a little bit lonely and a lot horny, and nobody else was doing it for him. What did it say about him that the only time he'd even been remotely intrigued, he'd needed to be insulted first?

Gabe would probably tell him, in painful detail if he was here, but he wasn't.

Maybe I'm really just this hot, Ren typed back.

The guy, PICMAN1881, replied almost immediately.

You got photoshop to go with that ego?

Ren's mouth fell open. Okay, he was *hot*. Every single guy who'd messaged him on this app said so. Customers at the truck said it all the time, staring at him like they couldn't quite believe he was real, and serving them a meatball sandwich. Ren's *mirror* said it, frequently.

This guy was just an asshole. An intriguing asshole, but an asshole.

Just as Ren was about to click out of the screen and find somebody else—*anybody else*—PICMAN1881 sent him another message.

You must get really tired of people telling you that you're gorgeous all the time. I bet you that nobody ever says you've got a really good personality.

In fact, Ren *was* tired of only being seen as a pretty face.

It was annoying and frustrating, because he thought his personality wasn't half bad.

But who was ever going to pay attention to that when they could tell him how hot he was?

You're not wrong, he typed back. **I thought you were in security, not psychotherapy. How'd you guess?**

I like to think I know people pretty well. Long history of needing to analyze them before they hurt someone

I'm trying to protect.

Ren did not want to be intrigued.

He wanted to tell the guy, *hey, let's meet up and fuck*, but there was something about the bald honesty there that he found refreshing.

So your weakness is clearly anger management, Ren guessed. **Ex-military?**

I knew you'd be interesting.

Ren, who was used to compliments being flung his direction multiple times a day, actually *enjoyed* this one.

People never expected him to be interesting. Just beautiful.

Let me guess, PICMAN1881 (which Ren found ironic, considering that he had *no* real profile picture, no way to confirm that he was good looking at all) replied, **yours is vanity.**

And stubbornness, Ren said. **Bet you guessed that one too.**

Actually no, that one you surprised me with.

Ren decided that he didn't care if he was hot or not. He was *interesting*, and he found *Ren* interesting.

He was going to absolutely fucking sleep with him. Even if he was ugly.

If I was really vain, I'd put up a pic of Timothée Chalamet and hope nobody would notice. So, that's character development, right?

PICMAN didn't waste a moment. **Is that your type, then? Timmy?**

Who was his type?

He could be honest and say that *all* kinds were his type. That he'd never cared much before.

But in this moment, he discovered that he cared what kind of guy he slept with next.

It was going to have to be someone spectacular, someone who got all his blood flowing, and not because they were hotter than the sun.

It was going to have to be because he felt that same zing, the one he'd felt with Seth, except *stronger*. Because nothing else was going to help him forget that guy, except the fuck of a goddamned century.

Doesn't matter what they look like, Ren wrote. **But I want someone who doesn't bore me. Someone who's got a brain and knows how to use it. And not just in bed.**

Ren stared at the words, thumb hovering over the send button.

Not *just in bed*? Had he just typed that? Did he *believe* that?

Well, shit, he thought he might.

It wasn't that he wanted to *date*. It wasn't that he wanted a relationship. But he wanted more than a six-pack and a pair of great biceps, more than a guy who knew how to suck cock.

Maybe he might want to actually *talk* to the guy and not be bored to tears.

He hit the send button. And for a long second, proceeded to freak the fuck out.

So, PICMAN said, **you want to have fun in the sheets and outside of them, too. Just what everyone wants: the holy grail of someone you can actually give a shit about.**

Ren laughed. He'd never talked this much on any other foray onto any other app—and he'd tried them all. He'd looked at the profile pic, and decided, almost immediately, whether he was interested or not. But then he'd never had this much fun just *talking* before either.

Is that what you want?

Suddenly it occurred to Ren that all this talking might be because this guy had certain expectations. Expectations of things that Ren didn't do.

But when he clicked onto the guy's profile, he hadn't filled out any of the "Looking for" section.

I thought I wanted one thing, but I'm trying to shift my expectations, PICMAN finally wrote back, **so yeah, what you said sounds good. I think I could use some more fun in my life.**

It was the perfect opening for Ren to say, "Hey, let's meet up tomorrow night for a drink."

He almost did it.

The Ren of six months ago never would've hesitated.

But this time, he didn't.

It sounds like you could, Ren said instead. **You think you spend so much time protecting people, it feels like second nature to protect yourself?**

It was the polar opposite of what Ren would have normally said.

He'd normally have gone super flirty.

Well, *normally*, he'd have already asked to meet up with this guy.

But something about doing that, just for sex, felt wrong.

This guy was interesting. Maybe he deserved for Ren to work a little harder.

You're definitely way more perceptive than your profile pic suggests. And you might be right? Who knows. I have been single for a long time.

Ren leaned back on the couch, humming to himself thoughtfully. Single a long time, huh? Maybe this guy was *just* out of the military.

He was reminded, annoyingly, of Seth.

Was he just trying to recreate that situation, with a different ending? An ending that didn't frustrate the shit out of him?

Ren couldn't discount that, but then this already felt different. Like this time they'd gotten started on the right foot instead of the wrong one.

So what if they'd both been military? So what if they both worked in private security? Ren wasn't going to give up on the most intriguing guy he'd met in ages, just because he *happened* to have a few things in common with Seth.

In fact, he wasn't going to think about Seth. At all. Period.

You know, that's the kind of shit you're not supposed to confess on this app. But yeah, I'm single too. Out of choice. Not much for serious relationships. Or, uh, relationships at all, actually.

PICMAN replied almost immediately, wasting no time at all.

Ren found he liked the lack of game playing more than he thought he would, even though he'd once done it right along with the other guys he'd met.

I'm going to be shitty at this, PICMAN said, **so I guess we should get that out of the way now.**

Anger management and shitty at apps. Wow, it's no wonder you've been single so long, Ren teased back.

Looks like I've got pretty good taste, though.

Ren felt the zing all the way up his spine.

Oh, he liked this guy. Liked him enough that he hoped he might talk to him again.

Better at this than you think, Ren replied.

I'll take that as a compliment, PICMAN said, **as long as you promise not to ghost me.**

That was an easy enough request. Ren didn't want to stop talking to the guy; and he was clearly right there on the same damn page.

No ghosting around here.

Ren realized, unexpectedly, that it was much later than he'd realized. He needed to get to bed, no matter how much he wanted to stay up all night chatting with this guy.

And I've got to get to bed, actually, since I've got an early day tomorrow, Ren typed, **but I hope you remember the no-ghosting rule. Don't stay a stranger.**

CHAPTER THREE

SETH WAITED UNTIL LENNOX left to go to a client lunch meeting before he pulled his phone out.

He wasn't stupid enough to think he could keep this conversation with Ren a secret from Lennox forever, but it was so new, and so tenuous, he wasn't ready to share yet, even with his best friend.

But even though Seth wasn't entirely sure it was a good idea yet, he'd already learned things about Ren that he never could've guessed.

He'd always known Ren had hidden depths, and now he was finally getting to see them. And maybe show a few of his own, in return.

Seth unlocked his phone, and sure enough, there were a handful of messages from Ren. AKA ITALIANBOY5.

Ren, who didn't know the man he was talking to was the one who'd turned him down twice before. Seth felt a twinge of guilt. But it felt like he was finally getting closer to him, in a way he'd wanted for ages, and he couldn't stop now.

Good morning, the first message read, **I hope your early morning isn't too early. Mine was. My cousin**

always insists we start prep at a ridiculously early hour, but I'll confess, it wasn't the veggies I chopped I was thinking about. But I realized it was kinda weird to think of you in my head as PICMAN when you don't even *have* a picture, so maybe you'd be willing to share your name. You must be private, which I get, so I won't ask any other details.

Seth took a deep breath.

He'd been careful up to this point to not lie. He did not want to lie to Ren. There were some things you could do that you couldn't take back.

When—because Seth knew he would find out, it was inevitable, whether Ren guessed or whether Seth found the balls to tell him himself—not *if*, Ren found out, he had a feeling that the lying was going to make it so much worse.

He went on to read the next message.

I realize how much of a creeper that makes me sound. I'm not a creeper. Promise.

Seth laughed.

And finally, lastly, the fourth message: **I did promise not to ghost you. So this is me, not ghosting you.**

Seth took a deep breath.

When Ren had asked him last night what he wanted from the app, he hadn't known what to say.

I want to get you out of my system, but instead, you're burying yourself even deeper under my skin, and I don't know how to get you out.

It had been hard to be honest. It was the most honest he'd been in ages. He didn't know *what* he wanted. Only that Ren seemed to be the key to it, if he would just listen to Seth long enough to realize that there was so much more tantalizing possibility than just fucking and then going their separate ways.

His mother always said that honesty was the best policy, and he'd believed her then, and he still believed her now. He was going to have to toe the line. Probably not what she'd meant when she'd lectured him about their neighbor Mrs. Grossman's broken window and his baseball in her kitchen, but Seth *knew* that if he confessed his identity now, Ren would close right back up.

Good morning. Got my ass handed to me by my partner, probably because I was so fucking distracted, and then he wouldn't go away so I could text you back. But you're right. I am kinda private. Ten out of ten, you get a gold star for your observation skills AND for not ghosting me. I'm not sure I feel comfortable sharing my whole name yet, but you can call me Jake.

It was the least amount of lying that Seth could come up with. His middle name was Jacob.

Seth was just about to get up and heat up his sad frozen meal for lunch when his phone buzzed again and he picked it up.

Jake, it's very nice to meet you (officially). I'm Ren. Short for Lorenzo Domenico, but *nobody* calls me that, for good reason. Because it's ridiculous.

Seth let out an unsteady breath.

He was actually doing this.

He'd known, of course, that this was Ren. He'd *known.*

But it was another feeling entirely to have Ren tell him who he was.

He'd already promised himself that he wouldn't tell any other lies, but now that promise became ironclad. He couldn't betray Ren that way.

Not when he was so . . . so . . . *Lorenzo*.

Lorenzo, that's what you'll be in my head.

His response came in almost immediately.

I just told you . . . but you know what? I should have expected it.

Seth chuckled and typed back: **Gotta keep your ego cut down to size.**

Ha, I see what you did there. Trying to make my heart beat a little faster, huh?

He'd always known that Ren had a very dry sense of humor. But he'd never gotten to really experience it for himself. Only vicariously, through everyone else, because he'd been so rigid, so unrelenting, so sure that they could never be friends that he'd kept the man at an arm's length.

Always the goal. But I bet since I'm the only one who ever calls you that, you won't be able to forget me. Bet it's beating faster already.

Ren seemed surprisingly eager. Lennox had grumbled about him more than once, about all his supposed game playing, but there was a straightforwardness to Ren now that Seth found incredibly refreshing.

You'd be surprised. So what are your other plans for the day? Besides getting your ass kicked? Ren asked.

Seth: **I'm going to see a new client this afternoon. I'm not sure I mentioned this, but I'm in private security. Own a business with the guy who kicked my ass this morning.**

Ren: **Private security, huh? Does that mean that I've got to keep my creeper tendencies to myself?**

Seth: **That all depends on if you have any.**

Ren: **Would I know who this new client is? Are they famous?**

Seth: **It would make me automatically cooler if I told you, but unfortunately gotta keep this one under wraps.**

Ren: **What *can* you tell me?**

Seth: **That going to see a new client always makes me nervous.**

Ren: **Why?**

Seth: **This is going to make me seem very uncool, but it's about taking personal responsibility for someone's safety. I never want to be the one who lets them down, even though I know I'll do everything in my power to make sure that doesn't happen.**

Ren: **But shit happens.**

Seth: **Exactly.**

Ren: **That's not uncool, that's actually incredibly admirable. You don't take it for granted, giving your word like that.**

Seth: **Never. Thanks for understanding. My friend thinks I'm a little crazy, because they're paying a lot of money for our expertise, but it's never about the money. They come to us because they need help. I wouldn't wish being famous on anyone.**

Ren: **Oh God, you're not famous, are you? Is that why you're hiding your face and didn't want to tell me your real name? You're the opposite of those idiots on this app that upload some famous person as their profile pic and hope nobody notices.**

Ren: **You really don't have to tell me if you are, I'm cool, I promise. Except I just told you that I wasn't cool at all. If you needed any evidence of this, these three messages would do nicely.**

Seth: **I'm not famous, stop hyperventilating.**

Ren: **Thank God.**

Ren: **I know some guys who play for the Riptide who come to my place to eat. I don't think fame is ever an easy thing to deal with.**

There was a split second where Seth stared at the screen, heart beating a little bit faster. He'd hoped that he'd see the man behind the kind, affable smile, the one who told the truth, but was never cruel or dramatic about it.

But he'd never imagined that he'd learn so much, so quickly.

He's lonely. Gabe is with Sean now, and he's alone. Whether he wants to admit it or not.

Seth: **The Riptide, huh? You a football fan?**

Ren: **I like watching them in their tight pants, if that's what you're asking.**

Seth: **I bet your pants are even tighter than theirs.**

Seth knew Ren liked to wear skinny jeans. But he hadn't meant to give it away that *he* knew. That "Jake" knew.

Shit, he thought, *you're gonna have to be a lot more careful than that.*

Ren: **How did you guess?**

Seth: **You work in a restaurant. Your restaurant, I'd guess, by your insinuation earlier, but I'd bet you're one of those hipster types. Dark-rimmed glasses that you don't actually need, ironic t-shirts, skinny jeans that look like they're suffocating your balls.**

Ren: **The glasses would be a waste, because why would I want to hide my face. But the rest? Pretty spot on. Think you know me already, huh?**

Seth: **I'm trying to. Want to figure you out.**

Ren: **Do you do this with all the cute boys you talk to?**

Seth: **You *are* vain LOL. But no. And nice, assuming that I talk to *any* cute boys.**

Ren: **I find that difficult to believe.**

Seth: **I'm not against relationships. Would even like to try one sometime, but I did tell you last night that I haven't dated anyone in a very long time.**

Ren didn't reply right away, and Seth found himself sweating.

Had he figured it out? Had he not covered the skinny jeans mistake with a good enough explanation?

Seth: **You got real quiet there. I knew I'd scare you off, eventually . . .**

Ren: **You didn't scare me off. I was just surprised that a handsome, charming man like you isn't beating them off with a stick**

Seth: **You've never seen me, how do you know I'm handsome?**

Ren: **That's easy enough, you've got a confidence and a swagger to you. You wouldn't if you weren't hot as hell. Besides, I'm less interested in that than in how fucking charming you are.**

Seth took a deep breath, and then let it out again.

He was not ever going to be able to let this go. He wanted this man so goddamned bad.

Was this the moment he told Ren the truth? Or was it too soon?

Seth didn't know.

Seth: **There was someone . . . we wanted different things, though.**

You, Seth thought, *it was you, but I think you might be changing your mind. God knows, I'm just about ready to call it quits and tell you the truth.*

I'm not cut out to lie.

Not to you.

Ren: **What did he want?**

Seth: **At the risk of sounding even more uncool, he just wanted to fuck, and then forget about anything else.**

Ren: **Why would that be uncool?**

Seth: **Wanting more than just a quick fuck isn't always popular on these kinds of apps.**

Ren: **What if I told you that was why I was on here, originally?**

Seth: **Is that all you want, still?**

Ren: **No. Not anymore.**

Seth set his phone down on the desk and began to pace.

This was the moment.

Except, what if it wasn't?

What if Ren was pissed? What if Ren wasn't in deep enough yet?

Seth didn't know how he'd figure out when that was true—but he wasn't willing to stop winning Ren over until he was just as sure as Seth was. He walked back to the desk, picked up the phone and typed out something else.

Seth: **I was hoping you'd say that.**

Ren: **I didn't know what the truth was, until you asked me just now.**

Seth's phone dinged. Not with the notification he wanted. With a reminder that he had a meeting of his own to be getting to, and he had to eat first. Things had been going so good, but he needed to do this. Lennox would skin him, slowly, if he blew it.

Seth: **I've got to go get ready for my meeting, but I hope we can chat later.**

Ren: **I wouldn't miss it.**

Seth: **Good. Me either.**

"Hey, Ren."

He glanced up, and saw Ash standing there.

He'd been so absorbed in his conversation with Jake that he hadn't even noticed him approach.

Ren had taken a seat at the table he considered "his spot" twenty minutes ago because he could always tell if Gabe ended up with a line big enough that he couldn't handle it on his own—and after setting down the wrap he'd gotten from Sean's truck, pulled his phone out of his pocket. He'd spent most of the morning, despite how busy it had been, wondering if PICMAN would reply to the message he'd sent first thing this morning.

If he'd been glued to his phone during prep, Gabriel definitely would've noticed and demanded he explain, so even though he'd felt it vibrate a handful of times, he'd avoided looking at it for the last few hours.

But the lunch rush had finally ended, and Ren had told his cousin he was taking a break. Gabe had been flicking through their sales numbers on the truck's tablet, and had barely paid attention when he'd slipped out.

"Oh, hey, I didn't see you there," Ren said. "What's up?"

He normally really enjoyed talking to Ash, but honestly, all he wanted to do was keep talking to Jake. Even if he had a meeting to get to.

Ash sat down opposite Ren. He had his own lunch in his hands, and set it down in front of him.

"I just had the weirdest visitor," Ash said, digging into his salad.

Please don't say Seth, please don't say Seth.

It made no sense that it would be Seth, but Ren felt like he was *finally* making inroads on forgetting he even existed, and the last thing he needed was for Ash to bring him up again.

"Who was it?"

"He said his name was Jonas, Jonas Anderson," Ash said. "And that he's starting up a food truck lot a few blocks from here. Less than a mile, he said."

"What?" After only a bite, Ren set his wrap down again. "Is he really? Tony is gonna freak out."

"Tony is gonna freak out more when he finds out that this Jonas dude is trying to poach his food trucks."

"You're kidding," Ren said, this new problem *almost* pushing the thought of Seth out of his head.

"I wish I was kidding," Ash said solemnly. "I told him right away that I appreciated the attention, but that I wasn't interested. But he wouldn't take no for an answer, and kept upping the offer, trying to sweeten the deal, I guess."

"Wow."

"I know." Ash sighed. "I'm not even sure he really believed that I'd say no, even though he finally left."

"I wonder if he's going to ask anyone else."

"Oh," Ash said grimly, "I'd bet on it."

"You need to tell Tony," Ren said.

"I will, eventually." Ash speared a piece of chicken in his salad. "Here's the weirdest thing though. This guy he's . . . well, you'll have to meet him, and frankly, I think there's no way you won't, because why would he go after me, when he could have you guys? You're notorious. But if you do meet him, you'll see. He's exactly like Tony. *Exactly*."

"What, bossy and pushy and refuses to take no for an answer? Thinks he knows better than anyone else?"

"*And* knows he's charming as hell, too, so he can get away with it," Ash said. "Like Tony, I didn't even hate him for it. I didn't even *dislike* him for it. He was fun to talk to. I just didn't want to work for him. This is where I'm meant to be. You guys are like family."

"Yeah, I couldn't agree more," Ren said. "We're not going to be interested—except maybe to hear the pitch and give Tony shit about it later."

Ash grinned. "Exactly," he said.

"You really think this guy is gonna try to poach all of us?" It would take brass balls to attempt it; but in a different situation, Tony might've done it. Maybe Ash was right and he was actually Tony's long-lost twin.

"I do," Ash said, leaning forward, a gleam in his eyes. "I totally do."

"It would be mean to fuck with Tony like that." Ren had always liked Tony, though half of the time he couldn't deny Tony made everyone a little crazy with all his schemes.

To give Tony credit, they were often schemes that paid off. A few months back, Tony had spearheaded an effort to help Ross without actually looking like they were helping Ross, and in the end, they'd *all* ended up with a significant sales boost.

Waffle Day had not only been a huge success for Ross, but for all of them.

"But *hilarious*," Ash said. "He's always interfering. It would be amusing to interfere with him right back."

It was true.

If you looked up "interfering," in the dictionary, there was Tony's face.

"Imagine when he finds out that the guy recruited Lucas."

Ren chuckled. "You think he will?"

"Undoubtedly. The guy has a fanatical following. Every vegan in Los Angeles knows about his truck. Especially since Waffle Day." Lucas' menu offering for Waffle Day hadn't been the winning entry—everyone had known it was going to be Ross, and he'd deserved it—but the unique way he'd made chicken and waffles had totally changed how both vegans and non-vegans alike thought about fried chicken.

It had catapulted Lucas into being one of the most popular food trucks on a very popular food truck lot.

And that was why this Jonas guy was coming for it.

So many people didn't have the imagination to come up with something new. A food truck lot—that was hardly new and innovative thinking, but Tony had turned their lot into something else. People came not just to get the food and grab a beer, but to hang out. Chat with their friends. Listen to the music.

It was becoming a place to see and be seen.

Tony was strutting around, justifiably pleased at how they were doing, when they were just now approaching their one-year anniversary of opening, but it wouldn't hurt to take him down a peg.

"Imagine trying to poach a guy's boyfriend," Ash said with a laugh. "Tony is gonna lose his shit."

"I'd pay real money to be there when he finds out," Ren said.

"Speaking of boyfriends . . ." Ash said, and Ren tensed.

"And how I'm never going to have one?" Ren finished the sentence for him.

He was not necessarily as convinced as he'd always been—after all, if he didn't want a boyfriend, why was he flirting with Jake?—but he wasn't even close to ready to discuss his evolving opinions on the subject.

Even with Ash, who wouldn't give him the kind of crap that Gabriel no doubt would.

Ash laughed at Ren's comment. "We all know you're not interested in a boyfriend, but I think . . . well, I think Seth might be getting one."

"Oh?" Ren forced his voice to stay casual. Uninterested.

"Yeah, he told Lennox he actually met someone he really likes on that new app. You might not have to worry about him mooning after you anymore. That's good, right?"

"Great," Ren echoed awkwardly.

He did not think it was great.

If anyone deserved to move on first, it was him.

"I know it's been awkward, but if he moves on, the same way you have, it'll make it a lot easier, don't you think?"

"Oh yeah. Much easier." Ren heard the irony in his own voice, but Ash wasn't looking for it, so he just smiled in agreement. And then he couldn't help himself, because something he refused to identify as jealous was spiking inside him. "Seth told Lennox about a guy he likes? Really?"

Ash leaned forward, grinning. "I was downstairs in the office grabbing coffee 'cause Lennox was out upstairs, and he asked Seth if he'd found anyone on that app. I guess they made a profile for Seth the other day. And Seth said *yes*. I couldn't believe it."

"Seth is an attractive guy. Why wouldn't he find someone?" Defending him came almost as easy as breathing. He'd wanted him. Badly.

"Because in all the time I've known him, he hasn't ever been interested in anyone . . . just . . ." Ash hesitated, glancing down at his half-eaten salad.

"Me," Ren finished for him. "He's only ever been interested in me."

"I was just worried, that's all. That he wouldn't find someone. He's a good guy."

Ren nodded his agreement with this assessment, because, well, he *knew* it. He'd known it from the moment they met. Even when he'd hated Seth, he'd still admired him. Still respected him.

"So, you taking a date to Shaw's bar opening this weekend?" Ash said, casually changing the subject, like he hadn't made Ren overthink everything, all over again.

"No," Ren said. He hadn't been able to even *think* about a date after the last pathetically terrible one, and chatting with Jake made the idea of calling someone up to go with him even more unattractive.

He'd go alone, or as a third wheel with Gabe and Sean. They wouldn't mind. *He* wouldn't even mind that much, despite all his whining about their loved-up ridiculousness.

"Ah, well, I'm sure there'll be a lot of cute guys there," Ash said. "You could always pick up someone there."

"I could."

For a moment, he considered asking Jake to go with him. Would he say yes? Or would it ruin whatever it was that they'd started to build?

"Lennox and I are gonna make sure Seth goes," Ash said. Then added, tilting his head thoughtfully, "Or maybe he'll ask that guy he's been chatting with."

"Maybe." *Oh God, I hope not.*

The idea of having to watch as Seth and some other guy flirted with each other—or worse—was abhorrent.

"I'm going to suggest that," Ash said, sounding very satisfied with this.

"Or maybe you should just let him figure out what he wants to do," Ren said. "And then let him do it."

Ash laughed. "When did you get so smart? And at *this* stuff?"

"Uh, maybe because I *don't* get involved?" Ren had no idea if that was true, but he did know, without a doubt, that he was absolutely fucking terrible at *this* stuff.

"Good point," Ash said warmly.

For a moment, they were both quiet, eating their lunches in peace, and Ren thought for a split second that the awkwardness might finally be over.

But then Ash chewed and swallowed. "I have a friend I could hook you up with for the party if you wanted. He's cute. And good in bed."

Before Lennox, Ash had had a series of casual dates and boyfriends, slightly more serious than Ren, but ultimately leading to a long list of guys he could probably call.

Ugh.

Old Lorenzo would have jumped all over that, because Ash had good taste in guys. But Right Now Lorenzo was absolutely not interested.

"Uh, thanks, but I'm good."

Ash narrowed his eyes. "Really?"

"Really."

He picked up the rest of his wrap and gestured to the truck, which had only had a handful of visitors in the last twenty minutes. "I've . . . uh, I've got to go give Gabe some help."

Ash looked momentarily confused, but then the baffled look was gone from his face.

"Okay," he said. "Catch you later."

"Bye," Ren said, and absolutely fucking escaped back to the truck.

When he climbed up the back steps, Gabe was still flicking through sales reports on their tablet. "You didn't have to come back just yet," Gabe said, not looking away from the screen. "It's been quiet."

"Oh, I was done," Ren said, then shoved the rest of the wrap into his mouth, chewing with difficulty.

"Okay." Gabe hesitated. "You okay? You've been acting odd. Ever since . . . well, since you and Seth . . ."

"I don't want to talk about Seth," Ren said with conviction. He'd never actually *not* wanted to talk about Seth before. He'd always hung around, surreptitiously eavesdropping and gathering whatever info he could find. He'd jumped on every opportunity to have a conversation about the man—specifically or tangentially.

"Uh, okay," Gabe said. "Anyway, are you okay?"

"I'm fine," Ren said.

"You seem . . . off."

It was annoying how damn perceptive Gabe was. Probably because they'd spent nearly every waking moment together for the last few years. They worked together, they lived together, went to the bar together, and even though Gabe was fucking terrible at trivia, he'd gone with Ren plenty of times.

"Really, I'm good."

"You want to come with Sean and me to the Fickle Cup opening on Saturday night?"

"Sure," Ren said, and then immediately changed the subject. "Did Tony give his okay to close the lot earlier that night?"

Gabe nodded. "Seven. Gives you plenty of time to doll yourself up for all your admirers."

"Yeah."

"Don't worry," Gabe said, shooting him a quicksilver grin, "you can go with me and Sean, but I won't expect you to come home with us."

"Right. Of course not."

Gabe never expected him to go home alone.

But what if he did meet someone at the opening night party?

What would he do about Jake?

It wasn't like they'd made each other promises. Or they'd even met. But somehow, Ren felt like it would be wrong to sleep with some other guy.

Some other guy that wasn't Jake.

CHAPTER FOUR

"YOU'VE BEEN *glued* to that tablet for the last week. What are you even doing?"

Ren had considered not saying anything to his cousin—if only because he didn't want to draw attention to the fact that he'd been equally as distracted, because he'd spent the last week grabbing stolen moments to chat with Jake.

He didn't know what they were doing, and to his surprise, it turned out that was part of the fun of it.

Neither of them had brought up meeting in person yet. They hadn't even sexted yet, and Ren hadn't once been tempted to suggest it—though he wanted the guy, that much was crystal clear.

He *had* been tempted to ask him for a picture. It was difficult, with Jake's faceless picture, to not insert someone else's face.

Ren wasn't proud of it, but in his mind, when it was just him and his phone in his bed late at night, it was always a certain face.

Seth's face.

He knew Jake wasn't Seth. But they did have some things in common. They both worked in security, and they both owned their own business with their best friend and partner. But that, Ren reasoned, was hardly unusual. After all, so did he.

But he hadn't asked for a better picture, because the last thing he wanted was for Jake to think he was some kind of shallow asshole who only gave a shit about what he looked like.

Okay, maybe at some point, he'd been that guy. But Ren could at least be honest with himself: he'd been evolving from that for years now.

"Are you even paying attention to me?" Gabe barked, and Ren snapped his attention back to his cousin.

Oh, right. He'd asked him about why he'd been staring at the tablet like it could cure world hunger, and then he'd promptly started daydreaming about Jake.

It was a problem.

"Oh, yeah, sorry. I was . . . I've got stuff on my mind."

Normally, Gabe wouldn't have let it go until Ren told him *all* about it, including how he *felt* about it, but when he didn't, Ren felt a thread of suspicion begin to snake through him.

"I've been doing some research," Gabriel said. "Sean was telling me how he analyzes his sales data, and figures out what he should be selling and what he should be dropping off his menu. And I realized, I *used* to do that, all the time, but I haven't since we changed the menu."

Ren nodded. "And?"

"There's a lot we should be changing," Gabe said.

"What?" Ren couldn't believe it. "Our sales are really strong!"

"Yeah, we've doubled our income from last year. Expenses are up—we should also consider raising our prices to compensate for it—but we're still healthy financially. But there's no point in prepping for and keeping items on the menu that don't sell as well as some of the others. We need to focus on our best sellers."

It wasn't that Ren thought Gabe was wrong—but Gabe was *wrong*.

"So, we're selling some things more than others," Ren said, "maybe we need to look at why that is, instead of just getting rid of the dish."

Gabe shot him a look. Patronizing and superior. He'd always had a version of this; being fifteen months older, Ren had always assumed that he couldn't help it. But this new Gabe—confident in his relationship, and in the developing success of their business—had brought many positive changes, and a few negative ones.

Like that he always thought he knew best.

Like that he thought he got to make all the decisions.

Before, it had been different, because Ren hadn't been officially an owner, too, but when they'd changed the name and Gabe had paid Luca back for his initial investment, they'd filed paperwork which meant that they both owned fifty percent of the truck.

Officially, Gabe wasn't *allowed* to make all the decisions.

Of course, he seemed to have forgotten that entirely.

"I think we need to cut the stuff out that isn't selling," Gabe repeated. "Why would we keep it? If we were a brick-and-mortar place, you think we'd keep stuff on the menu that doesn't sell? We're not the fucking Cheesecake Factory."

"We're not the Cheesecake Factory," Ren said between clenched teeth. "And we're not a brick and mortar either, which is why we can do *more*. We can be creative. We can change the fucking menu whenever we want."

Gabe's expression was superior and annoying. He crossed his arms over his chest. "Why are you being so difficult about this?"

Ren glared. "Because you aren't always fucking right about everything. We got into a rut before—*you* got into a rut before. Why do you want to put us right back into that rut? Because Sean said we should?"

"Oh, so this is about Sean, then," Gabe said, insufferably.

Ren hadn't thought so, because he wasn't wrong about what he was saying. Gabe wanted to put them right back where they'd been. Bored as hell, making only Nonna's recipes, because of course those were going to be the bestsellers on the menu. There was a reason Luca managed a whole chain of restaurants based on her recipes. They were delicious and they were dependable.

But was it a little bit about Sean and how Gabe had gradually started to listen to him more and more? How being with Sean had given Gabe confidence—and then *over*confidence?

Oh, yeah, definitely.

"It's not *really* about Sean," Ren said. "But of course it pisses me off when you listen to your boyfriend more than your partner."

Gabe rolled his eyes. "And you call *me* the King of Feelings. You're so bitter that you're alone and you know what? That's on you. You chose that."

He couldn't quite believe that Gabe would say that to him, and yet he could.

"This isn't about that *at all*," Ren spit out.

Nobody could piss him off like Gabriel Moretti, especially when he was sulking over his ideas not being instantly embraced.

"You're just being an asshole because I didn't want to just go along with whatever you want this week," Ren continued. He straightened. "I'm taking my lunch early. Have fun without me."

He stormed out, letting the door slam behind him.

He was angry, yes, but he was also leaving because he knew himself—knew *Gabe*—and they'd keep trading barbs until they landed one that really stung.

They didn't fight much, but they'd done it enough times that Ren knew he had to walk away now, before it got worse.

Worse, he wondered as he stalked over to his regular picnic table, *than the worst fight you guys have ever had?*

Flopping down onto the bench, he pulled out his phone.

Jake worked with his best friend. Surely that got heated, too, sometimes.

Ren: **I'm going to kill my cousin.**

It shouldn't have been amazing how quickly Ren had become the one person that Seth couldn't stop talking to.

After all, he'd wanted to talk to the guy from the very first moment they'd met, when he'd stuck his head out of the food truck he owned with Gabe and the amusement in those bedroom eyes had pinned him to the spot.

For the last few mornings, as soon as his alarm went off, he rolled over and immediately checked his phone. He'd never enjoyed being an early riser but the Navy had convinced him that while he'd never *like* it, it was a better way to live.

He'd gotten out of the habit when it came to the ridiculously early hours, but he still got up earlier than most people.

But Ren was up even earlier.

"Food service," Ren had explained when he'd asked the day before why he always seemed to be up before Seth. "It's a brutal industry. Long hours."

Seth knew it. He'd learned more about it during the whole mess with Ash and his father and Aaron, and realized that drug use in restaurants was usually for one purpose and one purpose only: to make sure they could keep working the same insane hours.

For a split second, he nearly told Ren that he understood, but he was supposed to *not* be giving himself away, and Ren was smart.

Too many coincidences and he'd figure out the truth before Seth was ready for him to.

They chatted in the mornings, sometimes, but usually during Ren's lunch break in the early afternoons, and *always* in the evenings. It had been less than a week and they already had a routine.

Sometimes they would talk about nothing, the everyday minutiae that made up their day. Sometimes about things that were more serious.

Ren: **How'd you get into security?**

Seth: **I was in the military, actually. When I was discharged, it seemed like the most obvious thing for me to do. The only thing I knew how to do: protect people.**

Ren: **You really are a big, strong hero, aren't you?**

Seth: **I'm not a hero.**

Ren: **The people you protected and the families of the men and women you saved would probably have something to say about that.**

Seth: **Probably, but if I think that way, I'm going to get lazy and sloppy.**

Ren: **Somehow I doubt that very much.**

Seth: **Well, why did you end up becoming a chef?**

Ren: **How do you know I'm a chef?**

Seth: **You work at a restaurant?**

Ren: **Doesn't mean I'm a chef. Chefs are formally trained. I'm definitely not formally trained.**

Seth: **So where did you learn how to cook?**

Ren: **My grandmother, actually.**

Ren: **A cliche, I know. But everything I learned, I learned from her first. She's why I do what I do.**

Seth: **I'm sure she's very proud of you.**

Ren: **She tells all her friends at the retirement home about me and my cousin, so I think so.**

He'd considered asking Ren to meet him at the Fickle Cup opening night party, because there'd be plenty of friends there, if things got awkward or difficult. But he'd decided against it.

Seth told himself it was because it was too early. They hadn't even been talking for a week. After a *long* time of not dating, of only fucking, Ren might not be ready for that yet.

But that didn't mean, Seth told himself firmly as he finished typing up the proposal for the Protectorate's new clients, Benji and Diego Schmidt, that he could keep daydreaming and letting Ren distract him until he slacked off.

What he needed was to get his head on straight and focus on this proposal. Benji and Diego were both famous from their stint in the band Star Shadow, but had hit a new level of fame with Diego's solo album, chock-full of intense love songs that he'd dedicated to his husband and bandmate.

It had also unfortunately led to a rise in threatening social media followers, some of whom had even become stalkers.

Benji and Diego were close friends with their other client, Landon Patton, a pop star who'd endured his own run-in with a dangerous stalker the year before, and he'd recommended Seth and Lennox's company to deal with the problem.

Doing more celebrity security was good for business.

Very, Seth thought as he looked at the bottom line of the proposal, *very* good for business. But it did add stress.

He and Lennox agreed that he would take Benji and Diego on if they signed, and Seth wanted to make sure that he didn't let them down.

His phone dinged again. He'd kept meaning to turn the notification sound off. Lennox—who was over at his own desk—glanced over, a knowing smile on his face, but he didn't say anything.

He probably didn't have to.

All Seth had told him was that he'd met someone.

He'd neglected to mention that the someone was actually Lorenzo Moretti.

Ren: **I'm going to kill my cousin.**

Seth stared at the screen of his phone, wondering what Gabe had done now.

Then he remembered that he wasn't supposed to know that Ren worked with his cousin. Just in time.

Seth: **What's going on with your cousin?**

Ren: **We work together, not sure I told you that, but we do, we own a food truck together. And he wants to streamline the menu, while I'm thinking we should add some of our rotating specials to it, permanently.**

Ren: **We bicker, yeah, but we almost always agree on everything to do with the business, and it's weirding me out that we aren't seeing eye to eye on this.**

Seth: **Remember when I said taking celeb clients on made me nervous? It was my partner's idea, and I didn't**

like it then. Don't like it much now, but I can admit he was right.

It was inevitable that he'd worry that he was giving away too much about what he did; that Ren would connect the dots and figure him out. But then they lived in LA, and security firms—especially security firms that specialized in celebrities—were a dime a dozen.

And what if Ren found out?

Yeah, he wouldn't be very happy about Seth's deception. But they'd forged a genuine connection, which was all Seth had ever wanted.

A chance to talk to the guy who'd leaned out of the food truck that day and turned Seth's world upside down.

Ren: **How did you figure out who was right? Because Gabe's usually fair, but he's not listening. He's just being dismissive and it's pissing me off.**

Seth: **He'll listen.**

He'd replied fast, without thinking, because this was *Gabriel* and like Ren had said, Gabe might tease the shit out of Ren, but they clearly cared so much about each other.

That had been evident, right from the beginning.

Ren: **You seem pretty sure.**

Seth could see the suspicious tilt of Ren's head, as he stared at his phone, like he was there.

Seth: **It's hard, when you both care so much. Give him some time to cool down. Give yourself some time to cool down.**

Ren: **Yeah, that's not half bad advice.**

Seth: **Having a business is a pretty personal thing. It's okay that you both give a shit, you know?**

Ren: **How did you get so damned smart?**

Seth: **It's because I'm old and wise.**

Ren: **No way you're old.**

Seth: **What if I was? What if I had gray hair and a limp and needed to take something to get it up?**

Seth could feel the hesitation on Ren's side, even though he couldn't possibly see it.

Could feel Ren working through the possibility that maybe Seth was more than he'd said he was.

Ren: **You spar and weightlift and you've got a limp? That's impressive.**

Seth laughed out loud, and Lennox looked up again.

"So, you gonna tell me about this guy?" Lennox finally asked.

Seth had to give him credit for waiting almost a week before asking.

"What do you want to know about him?" Seth said.

He typed back a really quick message to Ren.

Seth: **You caught me.**

Ren: **I think I have.**

He wasn't wrong.

But then Ren had captured him six months ago, and had never let go. Or maybe that was Seth, who'd refused to let go of *him*.

Either way, they were irrevocably tied together, and they kept twisting closer and closer.

"Who is he? What's his name? What does he do?" Lennox asked. Three questions that Seth couldn't answer without giving away the truth.

He took a deep breath.

"It's . . . well, you actually know him." Maybe telling Lennox would be good practice for telling Ren.

"You did not," Lennox said, dark eyebrows drawing close together in a disapproving frown. "You absolutely did not."

"I didn't *mean* to," Seth said with an embarrassed shrug. "I signed up on the app, and there he was."

"And he doesn't know it's you," Lennox stated rather than questioned. Like he already knew how stupid Seth was.

He'd always been stupid over Ren.

That had never changed. Not in six months.

Maybe not ever.

"Ren," Seth said, because even though Lennox *knew*, it felt good to have his name in his mouth again, "Ren doesn't know it's me. He thinks it's someone named Jake. But Jake also works in private security, also owns a business with his friend. I haven't . . . I didn't lie."

"Except by omission," Lennox said. Then leaned back in his chair. "He's going to freak out, when he finds out."

"Because he will," Seth said, saying it before Lennox could. "Yeah, I know he will, and yes, he will absolutely freak out."

Lennox had a shadow of a smile on his face. "Because you've won him over, and he never intended to be won over."

"That was the idea, anyway," Seth said, scrubbing a hand across his jaw. "But now I'm worried it's gonna backfire."

"As in, leave you more crazy about him than ever, and make him pissed off at you?"

"Uh yeah," Seth said. He should be used to Lennox's bluntness after all this time; he usually *enjoyed* Lennox's bluntness.

But then it wasn't usually directed at him.

"He wouldn't appreciate this, but you know it's true: he didn't leave you much of a choice, did he?"

Seth considered this for a moment.

Considered Ren's last message.

You caught me.

I think I have.

"The key is going to be telling him in a way that doesn't piss him off, makes him realize that it was . . . well, that it was a romantic gesture."

Lennox laughed then. "And you think that won't piss him off? Ren isn't exactly the romantic gesture type."

"No," Seth said. "But maybe he should be. Everyone should be at least once, shouldn't they?"

The door opened and David walked in. "Everyone should what?"

David Webber was one of their newer employees—but Seth had known him for ages. They'd been on associated teams, deploying from the same base, often drinking at the same bars *off* base. Then Seth had been discharged, and David hadn't, and they'd lost touch with each other, like most friendly acquaintances once the one thing holding them together ended.

But then a year ago, David had shown up in LA, lost, and looking for work. Seth and Lennox had taken one look at the guy, who was clearly struggling with the same problem they'd had when they'd left the Navy—the completely foreign lack of structure in civilian life—and it had been a no-brainer to hire him.

Eleven or so months later, he was much steadier. Had found a girlfriend he was crazy about. Bought a motorcycle that Seth liked to tease him about because he drove it so goddamn fast.

But he was happy and relaxed now in a way that Seth recognized, intimately.

Some guys resented the hell out of the military for running every bit of their lives.

Other guys got used to it, and couldn't handle it when they got out.

"Everyone should indulge in a romantic gesture every once in awhile," Lennox said, shooting a smile in Seth's direction. "What do you think?"

"Romantic gestures?" David rubbed his jaw. "How do you think I got Bianca to go out with me?"

Seth laughed. "We've been wondering the same thing."

"I just dropped by to bring my reports in," David said, sitting down at one of the desks and laptop stations that functioned as drop-ins. The only guys who had permanent desks were Lennox and Seth. Everyone else mainly stayed in the field. There were some days Seth was pretty jealous of that, because paperwork could *suck*. "Everything was calm last night. A few teenagers throwing shit, but a growl stopped them in their tracks." He grinned. "That was the most fun I've had in ages."

"I bet," Lennox said. "And you made the rounds at Food Truck Warriors, too?"

"Lennox wants to make sure his boy is nice and protected," Seth teased.

"Hey," Lennox said, without heat, "your guy is there too, now. You want David to cut his rounds short?"

Seth thought about this for a second—though honestly it wasn't much of a debate. "No," he said. "No."

"Though," Lennox added in a teasing voice, "maybe we should have David around when Ren finally finds out what you've been doing with him."

David shot him a knowing look. "You fuckin' around with Ren, still?"

"He is. Stupidly," Lennox said.

"First off," Seth drawled, "I'm right fucking here, and second off, if it works, it's not fucking around."

Lennox did not look convinced, however.

And he'd have felt a lot better about it, but the concern Seth spotted in his expression mirrored the worry he couldn't quite dismiss, sitting uncomfortably at the bottom of his stomach.

The next day, Ren did not feel any calmer.

Maybe it was because Gabe kept acting like they hadn't just had an argument the day before, the worst fight they'd ever had as business partners—the worst fight they'd ever had *period.*

Or that he kept talking about Sean and the changes he was making to his own truck, changes that mirrored what Gabe wanted to do with theirs.

Maybe Gabe's opinion, while different from his, wouldn't have bothered Ren so much if it didn't feel like a copy of Gabe's boyfriend's opinion.

Like somehow, Sean had stolen away a part of Gabriel, a part that Ren was never going to get back, but now he was intruding in something that had always been about the *two* of them.

"You're being really quiet," Gabe said as they walked back home. Ren never hoped that Gabe would go spend more time at Sean's, but it turned out that the couple had decided to meet at the new bar for the opening. So when they closed up the food truck for the night—early, per Tony's message to the owners' group chat—Gabe and Ren had left for their loft apartment together.

"I'm not being quiet," Ren said. Though he knew Gabe wasn't wrong. He hadn't been talking much—at least not to Gabe he hadn't. He *had* been talking to Jake.

Gabe didn't reply, just shoved his hands into his pockets.

So many times over the last twenty-four hours he'd considered asking Jake to meet him at the party.

What had stopped him?

Not Jake.

Ren was incredibly charmed by the man. Intrigued and interested, on a whole different level than he'd experienced in a long time. Maybe forever.

But what had stopped him wasn't Jake at all, but Seth.

Ren knew Seth would be at the opening night party.

It felt mean in a way that Ren had prided himself on never being, to bring a guy he was actually really, truly interested in to a party where Seth would be present. Even if Seth had a guy that he liked, that he was bringing too.

He wasn't going to flaunt his date in front of Seth's face.

Maybe they hadn't worked out. Maybe Seth had never agreed to come to his bed. But that didn't mean that Ren didn't give a shit.

He hadn't been able to give Seth what he wanted. He still didn't know if he was going to be able to give Jake what *he* wanted.

But he wasn't going to mix the two.

So he'd be going to the party tonight, as a third wheel, *again*, with Sean and Gabe.

Normally, he wouldn't mind, but tonight, he was still pissed off at Gabe.

They climbed up the stairs to their loft, and Gabriel unlocked the door.

Ren had looked forward to this evening for awhile. He considered both Jackson and Shaw to be good friends, especially Shaw these days—and Shaw's boyfriend, Ross.

This was a moment of triumph for both of them, but especially for Shaw, and he didn't want to mar it with his bad mood.

Maybe he needed something to soften his sharper edges. They felt so much sharper, today. He stalked over to the fridge, and pulled out a beer.

"You gonna get me one?" Gabriel asked from behind him.

"Are you going to be an asshole?" Ren asked archly, not turning around.

Gabe's sigh echoed through their place.

"I'm not trying to be an asshole. I'm trying to make good decisions."

"Well," Ren said, shutting the door with a decisive click, "so am I." Gabe could get his own fucking beer.

"Yeah, but you're being stubborn." Gabe shot him a reproving look as he opened the fridge himself, pulling out a bottle and opening it using the opener magnet on the freezer.

"Because you've never been stubborn in your whole life," Ren said. "Remember when you said you weren't in love with Sean? Remember when you said you'd never, ever change the name? When you told Luca to fuck off?"

"I *did* tell Luca to fuck off," Gabriel said, sipping his beer and ignoring the other two points, which absolutely illustrated just how goddamned stubborn he was.

"Yeah, but it didn't stick," Ren said. Not like he'd ever believed it would. Gabe was loyal, bone deep, to his family. And Luca was his brother and the leader of the family.

"With you either," Gabe said with a smile.

"I just wanted to steal his manicotti recipe," Ren pointed out. Though Gabe wasn't wrong. Despite Luca's overbearing nature, he meant well.

Also, the manicotti was so goddamn good, Ren could've cried if he hadn't gotten the filling recipe.

He still wanted to turn that into a sandwich. If Gabe would let him.

Fuck Gabe.

"Okay, so I'm stubborn. You're cut from the same cloth, so if I'm stubborn, so are you." Gabriel sounded so reasonable Ren wanted to get him yelling again.

"I never said I wasn't." Ren *knew* he was.

Gabriel sighed. "What I was saying yesterday was that we *always* intended to start with a wider menu and narrow it down, once we figured out what worked and what didn't."

"But it all works," Ren claimed.

Gabe shot him a look, and it shouldn't have hurt, but it did. "There're some things that aren't selling as well. You know that. It's wasteful to prep for so many different kinds of dishes. You know that too. It's time and it's energy and it's money."

"Yeah," Ren said, hating how sulky his voice sounded. "Doesn't mean we can't adjust them to make them better."

"We'll see," Gabriel said, and Ren *knew* he didn't mean to be patronizing.

But well, sometimes Gabe couldn't fucking help himself.

Ren drained the rest of the beer. "I'm going to get in the shower," he said.

"You meeting someone at the party?" Gabriel asked, like they hadn't just been fighting.

Ren wanted nothing more than to say *fuck it* to the party, but this meant so much to Shaw—and by extension, Ross—and he was their friend. He couldn't skip it, just because he was in a bad mood.

"No," Ren said shortly.

He was wishing again that he didn't give a fuck about Seth, that he *could* be meeting Jake there, and something good might come out of this after all. But he couldn't change that, same as he couldn't change the way Gabriel always thought he knew best.

On the way to the bathroom, Ren pulled his phone out of his pocket, and typed a quick message to Jake.

Ren: **Guess I still haven't cooled down enough. I haven't stopped wanting to wring Gabe's neck.**

Jake answered back almost immediately.

Jake: **You're both passionate about the business. It's not all that surprising. Did your grandmother also teach Gabe how to cook?**

Ren shut the door behind him, and leaned against it, squeezing his eyes shut. Hating that Jake *knew* him, even though he couldn't possibly.

How had he known that Gabe, almost two years older than him, had always gotten permission to stir, his short stature boosted with a little worn three-legged stool, while Ren had always sat on the counter, Nonna between them.

She'd taught them both.

And when Gabriel had gotten sick of Luca being the overbearing older brother, and had left Napa and the family chain of restaurants, Ren had never hesitated. Of course he'd gone with Gabe.

He'd never considered staying, not for his own family or for anyone else.

Because where Gabe was, that was where he needed to be. Where he *wanted* to be.

It had been good, *great* even, until Sean had shown up and puffed Gabe up with all these ideas that *he* knew best.

The food truck belonged to both of them.

Ren had even convinced him to change what they were doing, had come up with the new name, the new concept.

They'd been doubly successful since.

But Gabe had conveniently forgotten that part of it. What made Ren more annoyed than anything was that it was just like Gabriel to forget that anyone but he and his boyfriend existed.

Ren's fingers hovered over the keyboard on his phone.

He typed out the message one letter at a time, slowly.

Do you want to meet me at a party tonight?

For a long moment, he stared at the words.

And then he erased them, one letter at a time, too.

He didn't want to use Jake as a prop, just because he was in a bad mood over Gabriel's bullshit.

Instead, he said: **Yes. Which is why I can't really hate him.**

Jake: **You guys seem close. You're gonna figure it out.**

Ren didn't have Jake's faith, but maybe he'd borrow it, just for tonight.

CHAPTER FIVE

"THE PLACE LOOKS GREAT," Gabriel enthused, pulling Shaw into a quick hug, and then Jackson. "It's gonna be a huge success."

Ren followed suit, hugging both of them. "Anything we can do to help, just let us know," he said. "Of course, you already have a ringer in your back pocket," he added, in a teasing voice, referring to Ross.

Maybe he and Gabe were fighting, and he'd told Jake—and Ren knew Gabe had told Sean, because Gabe told Sean everything—but they'd never dare show anything but a united front in front of their friends.

They'd come to the Fickle Cup opening night party in an Uber in almost complete silence, but the moment they'd gotten out, Ren had found himself smiling and chatting with Gabe like nothing was wrong, and his cousin had followed suit.

If he was going to keep up the pretense, he was going to need something stronger than a beer. He eyed the bar out of the corner of his eye as Shaw went into proud boyfriend rhapsodies about the new menu Ross had designed for the bar.

"And wait til you try the stuffed mushrooms," Shaw finished up, beaming proudly.

"Stuffed mushrooms?" Gabe sounded skeptical, and it annoyed Ren that he knew exactly what his cousin was thinking.

Stuffed mushrooms weren't exactly fresh thinking, but then, it was Ross. He could work miracles with anything.

Shaw wasn't wrong about that particular fact.

"We'll have to give them a try," Ren said, patting Shaw on the arm. "Now I'm sure you're super busy, so we're going to get out of your hair and grab a drink."

"Enjoy yourselves," Shaw said, "and thanks for all your support."

Shaw turned away to greet some more newcomers, and he and Gabe wandered over to the bar.

"I want to know what Ross did to stuffed mushrooms," Gabe said as he looked at the chalkboard menu, scrawled artistically next to the gleaming glass shelves of liquor bottles behind the bar. "Whatever it is, it's sure to be brilliant."

"Of course it is," Ren said. Nope, he was not bitter at all. He loved Ross. He loved Shaw. He had no problem acknowledging they were really good at what they did. But it would be nice to be given credit for his *own* little share of brilliance, instead of having Gabe trying to dismiss it all the damn time.

"You sure you're okay?" Gabe said, turning towards him.

"I'm fine," Ren said. "Totally fine." He leaned over the bar. When he'd looked in the mirror before they'd left the loft, he'd known he looked his best. But from the way the bartender's eyes met his, Ren *knew* he looked his best.

"Oh, hey there. How's it going? What can I get you?" the bartender asked, walking over immediately.

Ren could feel Gabe's eye roll, but it wasn't like he was going to complain that being with Ren usually meant they got great service.

"I'll have the house old-fashioned," Ren said.

"Good choice," the bartender said, smiling at him. Then he turned to Gabe, the brightness of that smile dimming just a bit. "And you?"

And okay, Ren could acknowledge a lifetime of being second fiddle could make Gabe a little bitter himself. But then he'd met someone he really loved, who loved him back.

That had given him confidence; unfortunately, now it was that same confidence that was wreaking havoc on their normally good-natured partnership.

"I'll have a beer, uh, I guess that IPA on the end," Gabe said, gesturing to the last tap handle on the right.

The guy went to get their drinks, and Gabe turned to Ren. "Don't you dare complain that the attention gets old," he said, a grumpier edge to his voice than normal. "You enjoy the attention. If you didn't, you wouldn't be all trussed up in your James Dean chic." Gabe gestured again, this time at Ren's outfit.

Tight black jeans, black boots, and a paper-thin white t-shirt, all topped off with his favorite leather moto jacket. Gabe liked to call it his James Dean chic, and normally, it was funny. But tonight, Ren wasn't laughing.

"Trussed up? I'm not a chicken about to be roasted," Ren pointed out.

"Is this for anyone in particular or just to make the bartender pant after you?" Gabe asked. "Or maybe Seth?"

"I don't care about the stupid bartender," Ren said, ignoring Gabe's jab about Seth, though now *his* voice was grumpy. He hated fighting with Gabriel, mostly because it never happened.

Also because they knew each other way too well, and knew just where to stab for maximum effect.

Gabe sighed. "I'm sorry, okay? I don't want to fight with you."

It was so like what he'd just been thinking, but Ren wasn't surprised.

"You calling pax?" Ren arched his eyebrow.

"Tomorrow, we'll go over the menu, make some decisions. I think we can both get what we want," Gabe said.

The bartender arrived again, setting their drinks in front of them on the shining, polished bar.

"No charge," he said, winking. "Open bar tonight, for the opening party."

Gabe grumbled something about overhead, but Ren shrugged. He didn't mind paying for drinks, though *not* paying for his drinks was nice too, though hardly unusual.

Ren stuffed a five-dollar bill into the tip jar, and took a sip. It was a good drink, but then Shaw had been a bartender for a long time, and he wouldn't suffer idiots pouring behind his bar.

He spotted Sean before Gabe did, as he weaved his way through the crowd.

It was hard to be annoyed with him—or with his cousin—when Sean's expression was so soft and happy, and when Gabe spotted him? He just fucking *beamed.*

"Hey," Gabe said, gathering his boyfriend into his arms. "Isn't this place great?"

"I wouldn't expect any less," Sean said. Turned his head slightly. "Hey, Ren, how's it going?"

"If you're asking if Gabe and I are still fighting, I don't think so . . ." Ren wrinkled his nose. "What do you think?" he asked Gabe.

"I never wanted to fight in the first place," Gabe said, self-righteous as always. Ren rolled his eyes.

"Yeah, we'll hash it out tomorrow," Ren agreed. Not intending to give any further than he wanted to.

"Good," Sean said, smiling warmly. "I'm glad to hear it."

The thing was, Ren didn't even dislike his cousin's boyfriend. In fact, he'd *always* liked Sean.

"Come on, let's get a drink, and see if we can find Ross and some of those mushrooms," Gabe said. More to Sean than to Ren, which didn't surprise him at all. He'd known coming with them would feel a little like a third wheel. But there were tons of people here that he knew, from the Funky Cup to the Food Truck Warriors. There were Alexis and Jackson and Ross, over in the corner, with Tony and Lucas, and Ren swore he heard Chase's booming laughter, trickling down the staircase that led to the rooftop bar.

He'd probably be up there with Tate and however many Riptide players he'd brought with him for the evening.

Ren could join any of those groups, and they'd welcome him, because they were his friends, too.

But then when he turned to pick up his drink and head over to one of them, out of the corner of his eye he saw a guy, standing by himself by one of the high-top bar tables.

Ren almost turned away, because of course he wasn't really alone. Lennox and Ash would show up, and he'd have people to spend the evening with.

He didn't need to rescue Seth.

He was into Jake; *very* into Jake.

But somehow his feet carried him over there anyway, drink in his hand, and heart in his throat, remembering the last time they'd spoken, over a week ago, when Seth had told him that sleeping together would be a very bad idea.

It wasn't any more of a good idea now, Ren knew that.

Yet there he was, tipping his drink towards Seth—towards Seth's identical drink, sitting on the table in front of him.

"I didn't know you liked old-fashioneds," Ren said.

Seth didn't look upset that he'd come over. Didn't look like he wished Ren would leave immediately.

Maybe if they couldn't sleep together . . . they could be friends?

Ren dismissed that ridiculous thought almost immediately.

You couldn't be friends with someone you wanted so badly you burned with it.

"There's a lot you don't know about me," Seth said.

It was honest, like so much of what Seth said, and it might've even been a bit mean, but there was a soft regret in his eyes now. Like that was all he'd wanted—for them to know each other.

"You say that like I didn't try to get to know you." Ren grinned, and the softness in those gray eyes, such a cool contrast to Seth's auburn bright hair, sharpened a bit.

Seth leaned forward, elbows on the table. "You're right," he said. And his voice was gravelly deep, like he was thinking about it right now.

Lifting his drink to his lips, he tried to wet his suddenly dry mouth, but several gulps later, the strong alcohol beginning to swim through his system, Ren couldn't help but wonder if that hadn't been a tactical mistake. The bone-deep pull he felt towards this man was still there. And now, it was *worse*, exacerbated by the booze he'd drunk.

He put his mostly empty glass down. "I think if we both agree I'm right about most things, we'd be better off."

"Sure," Seth said.

Ren tossed the rest of his drink back. Met the eyes of the bartender, and lifted his glass. The guy was eager, like a puppy. Even though Ren was already over here, flirting with someone else.

Or trying *not* to flirt with someone else.

Because that would be a waste, wouldn't it?

"And," he said, "what I think is that we should be friends."

Seth looked skeptical. "Really? You have friends? Just friends?"

Ren shot him a glare. An Italian-flavored glare that cut most everyone else down to size, but on Seth, it just glanced right off him. "Of course I have friends."

"Of course you do. Like the bartender over there, falling over himself so he can get you a fresh drink," Seth said with amusement.

"I didn't encourage him." Ren heard the frostiness in his voice, but the truth was, his insides were on fire.

It would be so easy to lean forward and just . . .

Yeah, he wasn't doing that.

They were trying to be friends.

Kissing your friends was generally discouraged.

A waiter brought over his new drink. Set it in front of him.

"Here's the thing," Seth drawled, the Southern edge back in his voice, and Ren was reminded, viscerally, of how much he'd wanted him the first time they'd ever met. "You don't *have* to encourage them, because you look like . . . well, because you look like that."

"Look like what?"

It was stupid to ask. It was probably the booze talking.

Seth chuckled under his breath. Sipped his own drink. "You *know* what you look like."

"Yeah, but maybe I want to know what *you* think I look like," Ren said flippantly.

Seth sighed.

Set his drink down with a click onto the table.

For a second, Ren thought he'd pushed too far. Before, every time they'd gotten to this point, they'd run right up against Seth's ironclad self-control.

But this time, he didn't walk away.

He didn't tell Ren this was a bad idea.

"You look like the sun setting over the ocean, like the edge of the Blue Ridge Mountains against the sky, like a fire crackling in the night, with the stars spread out above me." Seth's voice was solemn and earnest—but the fire he'd mentioned was burning in his eyes.

Ren's fingers tightened on his glass. His mouth felt dry again, but he didn't drink, because the booze was swirling through his system, erasing the part of him that kept echoing Seth's own words.

This is a bad idea.

He cleared his throat. "That's not . . . I didn't expect that. The Blue Ridge Mountains?"

Seth looked almost embarrassed. "I grew up there, in Asheville. And sometimes the sky is so blue, and they're so dark, you can't look away."

"That might be the most unique compliment I've ever received. And the stars?"

It was Seth's turn to gulp his drink. And even though in the six months he'd been watching him, Ren didn't think he'd ever seen him order a second, he lifted his finger to the waiter.

"They're so bright, in the darkness." Seth's voice sounded short, nothing like the dreaminess that had infused it before.

It suddenly occurred to Ren that continuing to subject himself to this—subjecting *Seth* to this—was cruel and unusual punishment.

Why had he come over here again, when there were so many other people he could talk to?

"I don't suppose we can really be friends," Ren said with a regretful sigh.

Seth laughed, shocking and bright. "Did you really think we could?"

Ren lifted his glass, which to his surprise, was actually empty again. "Might've been the booze talking."

The waiter arrived then, with two more drinks.

Ren really knew he should slow down. Especially if he kept standing here with Seth.

"Thanks," Seth said to the waiter, sliding a bill across the table towards him. "And some food maybe?" He glanced up at Ren, who knew exactly what he wanted to try.

"The mushrooms," he said decisively. "I heard the stuffed mushrooms were really good."

The waiter tucked the money into a pocket. "I'll see what I can do," he said briskly.

Seth's expression was brimming with amusement when he turned back to Ren. "Mushrooms?"

"Do you not like mushrooms?" Ren wondered.

If Seth didn't like mushrooms, then *yeah*, dating him definitely would've been a disaster.

That was also probably the booze talking.

"I love mushrooms. Not as much as old-fashioneds, or fires under the stars," Seth said, "but they're pretty lovable."

"We'll see how lovable Ross' are," Ren said, leaning forward, his eyes meeting Seth's. He ignored the clang of warning in the back of his head.

What were they doing?

Getting drunk together and sharing a plate of stuffed mushrooms?

Still not sleeping together?

Ren decided that it didn't matter what they were doing, because he was enjoying himself.

And if the way Seth was smiling was any indication, he too was enjoying their time together.

But then he'd known it would be like this, hadn't he?

Of course he had.

Ren pushed that thought aside with another long gulp of bourbon.

"If Ross' mushrooms are like his fried chicken . . ." Seth's voice was worshipful, and Ren was surprised at the jealousy that flared deep.

He didn't have a great poker face at the best of times, but after two and a half drinks, *strong* drinks, Ren could only imagine how transparent he looked.

Seth grinned. Like he'd read the thoughts right off his expression. "He's from South Carolina. It's a little like coming home, to eat his food," he said. "But don't worry, I like yours plenty."

"What's your favorite?"

Even though Ren already knew.

He knew every single thing Seth had ever ordered from the truck.

Creepy? Or observant? Ren wasn't sure which it was, but he hadn't been able to help himself.

"I think I'm pretty partial to the Thai meatball crunch wrap," Seth said casually. Like he couldn't get the exact same thing at Sean's truck—but he never had.

He'd always come to Ren and Gabe's truck, and he'd always ordered the same thing he'd ordered that first day.

Nostalgia? Blind hope that the outcome might change? The fact that the wrap was actually delicious?

Ren wasn't sure which reason it was—or maybe it was a combination of all three.

"That's a good one," Ren said.

The waiter appeared then, with the plate of mushrooms.

They looked standard. Ren stared at them a little closer, dipping his head. "They look . . . they look like stuffed mushrooms?" he questioned, confused.

Seth smiled again. "Were they not supposed to look like stuffed mushrooms?"

"They were. But it's Ross. He's . . . well, you know how he's apparently a genius."

The liquor flowing through his system had apparently also decimated his brain-to-mouth filter, and that bitterness he tried to ignore and tried to forget was unmistakable.

"And you're not?"

"I . . ." *Fuck it*, Ren decided, and picked up a mushroom, putting the whole thing in his mouth.

It was just like Ross, to make a stuffed mushroom that looked just like every other stuffed mushroom on earth, but that tasted like a flavor explosion.

"You're really good at what you do, too," Seth said.

"Goddamnit," Ren exclaimed after he'd chewed and swallowed, heat still lingering on his tongue. "He is such a fucker."

"Ross? I guess he pulled off a miracle, after all?"

"There's chorizo in there, it's spicy, and it's . . . well, I'm not sure what else, but it's delicious. I think that's Manchego, too, and not mozzarella."

"What's Manchego?"

"Spanish cheese. Spanish chorizo, too, I think, and some kind of spicy . . . well, whatever it is, yeah, he's brilliant." Ren rolled his eyes. "If I didn't love him, I'd hate him."

"Opposite sides of the same coin," Seth said, picking up a mushroom. "Love and hate, they're both forms of obsession."

Maybe, Ren thought as he sipped his drink, he hadn't been crushing on Seth—*past tense*, because he had Jake now; *Jake, who he hadn't thought about in at least an hour, now*—maybe he'd been obsessed.

Maybe it had been mutual.

Maybe it was *still* mutual.

"But," Seth continued, "going back to the genius thing. Do you really think you're not as talented as Ross?"

"Or Gabe?" Ren retorted. "Gabe sure thinks *he's* the genius."

Seth's eyes went wide and he set his drink—mostly drunk now, Ren realized; he wasn't the only one who was feeling the effects of the bourbon—down. "You do not fucking believe that."

"No, but *Gabriel* believes that," Ren complained. "We both wanted to get out of the rut, right? We were bored, and so we did whatever we wanted, and okay, maybe he's right, some of the stuff we make doesn't sell as well. But that doesn't mean we should just *give it up*."

"Is that why you and Gabriel are fighting?" Seth asked.

How did he *know* that?

It was infuriating, and a little bit flattering.

Okay, a lot flattering.

At least if Ren was using the arousal burning in the base of his stomach as a measure.

"How did you know we're fighting?"

Seth rolled his eyes. "You two are normally inseparable. You walked in and you were . . . on different wavelengths tonight. Maybe not everyone would've noticed. I bet nobody else *did* notice."

Ren leaned forward. This close, he could pick out every shade of gray and green in Seth's eyes. "But you noticed."

"I notice a lot of things . . ." He trailed off, not quite finishing the sentence.

But did he have to?

Ren already knew what he'd meant to say, before he'd decided it was a terrible idea.

I notice a lot of things about you.

The liquid in the glass in front of him had already begun to loosen his tongue, but the cumulative effect of this conversation finished the job.

"I knew about the wrap," he said. "That it was your favorite."

Seth raised an eyebrow.

"I notice a lot of things about you, too," Ren said, after deciding, what did it matter if Seth knew?

Their self-control was shot. Maybe this was the night it would finally happen, and then this obsession would end forever.

Just in time for him to move on with Jake.

Seth swirled the remaining bourbon in his glass. "These are pretty strong, aren't they?" he asked wryly. Even though he clearly knew the answer to that particular question.

"Yeah," Ren agreed. "Let's have another round."

Seth popped another mushroom in his mouth. "Is that a good idea?"

"I don't know about you, but I'm tired of considering only good ideas," Ren said conspiratorially.

Even though he wasn't exactly the poster child for smart, reasoned decisions.

But Seth? That guy was brimming with them.

Seth's expression was thoughtful—too thoughtful—as he finished his drink.

He was still thinking. And Ren? Well, he was never good with thinking with anything but his dick, but his dick was *definitely* making decisions right now.

Shrugging off his jacket and setting it on the back of a nearby chair, Ren leaned forward. He knew how good he looked.

From the way Seth's pupils dilated, he knew, too.

"What's the last good idea you had?" Seth asked, his voice low, teasing.

"A week ago, when I thought we should have sex," Ren said.

"And you still think we should?"

"Well, *duh*," Ren said, chuckling. "Am I dead? Of course I want to have sex with you."

Seth looked surprised; which was strange. How could he have thought that Ren didn't want him anymore?

"But . . . aren't you pissed off at me?"

"For saying no? If I was pissed off, I wouldn't have come over, would I?"

Seth blinked hard. "Okay, fair enough."

"Now," Ren said, "let's get another round."

CHAPTER SIX

SETH WASN'T SUPPOSED TO know exactly what was bothering Ren—they'd talked about it briefly when he was himself, but Ren had shared a lot more with "Jake."

It was very stupid to be jealous of himself, but he was.

But because he was also Jake, it wasn't surprising to see Ren drinking more than he normally did.

The argument, ongoing for almost two days now, with Gabe would really bother him.

And, Seth thought as he watched Ren grab two more drinks for them, maybe he was even a little bit conflicted over Seth versus Jake.

For a second, he considered telling Ren the truth now. It would solve a lot of their problems. But after three old-fashioneds, he could tell Ren was more than a little tipsy—and heading towards just plain drunk.

It would be a terrible idea to tell him now.

His reaction wasn't guaranteed. He could still be really pissed off at Seth, and adding alcohol to that mix could make for something explosive.

It could be some really hot sex, *finally*.

Or it could be a fight that they couldn't come back from.

Seth decided not to take the risk.

"Here you go," Ren said with a flourish as he set a fresh drink down in front of Seth. A drink that he already knew he'd just be carefully sipping. He rarely drank more than one, and he'd already had two—and it seemed like Ren was going to have plenty for both of them, and Seth intended to keep an eye on him. Which he couldn't do, not properly anyway, if he was drunk himself.

"Thanks," Seth said warmly. "You want the last mushroom?"

"What a silly question," Ren teased.

"Oh! Are those the famous stuffed mushrooms?"

Seth tore his eyes away from Ren's mesmerizing dark gaze, only to glance up and see Gabe and Sean standing there.

"They are," Ren said primly, straightening. Seth found himself already missing the entrancing, flirty version of Ren that he'd been enjoying. He'd gotten a bit of it as Jake, but never in person, and never as strongly as this. He'd never have been able to resist, no matter how good his self control, if he'd had to deal with this version of Ren.

But, he reminded himself, he had to.

He couldn't sleep with Ren before Ren knew the truth. That would be one hundred percent guaranteed to piss him off, *and* for good reason, because it would be wrong.

Plus, if he was going to finally get Lorenzo Moretti into bed, they were both going to be fully sober and able to enjoy every single bit of the experience.

"And," Ren added, slapping Gabe's hand away as he reached in to grab the last mushroom, "that's mine, not yours. Go get your own."

"Maybe I will, I just wanted to know if they were any good."

"Of course they were," Ren said. "Ross made them."

"We can get our own plate of them, right?" Sean said, and glanced over at Seth, a wealth of feeling in that one look.

It was definitely not easy on anyone when these two argued.

"I'm sure you can," Seth said. Ignoring the way that Ren and Gabe were glaring at each other, their argument becoming less about their food truck and more a standoff about a single stuffed mushroom.

"Come on," Sean said to Gabe, "we can go order some food at the bar."

"You can have this table," Seth said, an idea blossoming in his mind. "We were just about to dance anyway."

He'd never gotten the chance to dance with Ren before—though he wasn't much of a dancer himself, he'd always regretted that he'd turned him down before he'd gotten even a single chance to get close to him—and this would also prevent Ren from downing his next drink like the bottom of his glass held the secrets to the universe.

"We were?" Ren questioned, looking surprised. Probably because they *hadn't* been about to. But he was definitely edging past tipsy and into drunk, and Seth was beginning to see that a drunk Ren was also a pliable Ren.

"We were," Seth said firmly, walking around the table and reaching for his arm. Didn't overthink, and let his fingers slip down lower, until he was holding Ren's hand.

He'd never imagined that they'd do this.

Or that Ren would allow it.

But the way Ren was gazing up at him said he'd allow it, and so much more.

Seth's heart beat a little harder as they walked to the dance floor, even as he tried to keep his breathing even.

"I like this," Ren said, eyes fluttering closed as he plastered his body against Seth's.

And *oh*, Seth liked it too. He knew he would though; he'd known from the first moment he'd looked up into Balls & Buns and seen Ren's dark, amused gaze.

He squeezed Ren's hand and settled the other at his hip, the curve of it warm in his palm. "Me too," Seth confessed as they began to move together to the music.

He wasn't sure Ren heard but then he felt Ren's hand, and it wasn't just warm, it was burning hot, settling at his neck, his fingertips toying with the short ends of his hair.

"You shouldn't have cut your hair," Ren said, his eyes flickering open, an earnest look in them. "I liked it long. I wanted to tug it." And like Seth hadn't understood what he'd *really* been talking about, added: "In bed."

Seth swallowed hard. "Maybe that's why I cut it."

Oh, Lorenzo was potent like this.

Potent and dangerous and all too aware of how much Seth wanted him.

Could probably *feel* how much he wanted him.

But even if Seth's dick hadn't been hard against the zipper of his jeans, and pressing into his own hip, Ren would have known.

Seth hadn't exactly been subtle.

Restrained and maybe a little too controlled, but he'd never hidden how much Ren did it for him.

The problem with Jake was that now Seth *knew* Ren, so much better than he had before, and now with everything on the line, he was suddenly terrified he was going to lose him.

"No, that's not why you cut it off, though I'm sure you'd like me to think so," Ren teased, wiggling even closer, and Seth's blood pressure spiked when he felt *Ren's* cock, just as hard as his own. Maybe dancing together had been a really, really bad idea.

His amusement was mesmerizing—Seth couldn't look away.

"Why do you think I did?"

"You probably thought it was efficient or some bullshit like that," Ren said. How was he so charming, even when he was telling Seth that he was full of bullshit?

Seth didn't know, but he wanted to wipe that smile off Ren's face.

With his mouth?

With his cock?

Want rolled off Ren's skin. Seth could feel it, like it had form and shape and he could reach out and touch it.

Did he feel this way about Jake?

Maybe Seth should care, but since he was Jake *too*, the booze had wiped away every bit of his hesitation.

"Definitely some kind of bullshit," Seth agreed.

Ren's fingers dug into the fabric of his shirt, probably leaving marks.

That's how sex between you would be, the voice he kept trying to ignore told him, *you'd be all marked up and you'd feel it later, and you'd love every moment of it.*

But that's all he'd have.

The marks.

He knew that he couldn't sleep with Ren. Not when it was just sex. And that was what Ren was trying to do right now, because he didn't know he was Jake, too.

He thought Seth was just Seth, the guy he'd been trying to eradicate from under his skin for months.

Ren's hips tilted closer, and there was the shine of triumph in his eyes when Seth's pulse thudded harder.

He thought he was going to win, like this was all just a game.

"Lorenzo . . ." Seth murmured under his breath, and he thought he'd been too quiet, under the insistent bass thump of the music, but Ren's head tilted up.

Eyes glued to his mouth.

In a moment, maybe less, Ren would lean in and try to seal the deal.

"You're the only one who ever calls me that," Ren said, amused and fond. "Why is that?"

It was complicated; like so many of the other things associated with Ren.

"Maybe because I'm the only one," Seth said. He pulled back, ignoring the way his body screamed out at losing the press of Ren's body against his. "I need some air. Do you need some air?"

Ren's eyes gleamed. Dark and mysterious and yet not so mysterious after all.

He thought Seth was trying to get them alone.

"Let's go to the roof," Seth said before Ren could suggest somewhere more private. He tugged him away from the makeshift dance floor and towards the winding metal staircase that led to the rooftop bar.

"Really?" Ren sounded skeptical, but he was still following along easily enough, his hand loosely tangled in Seth's.

"It's supposed to have an incredible view of the city lights," Seth said.

"Ahhhh, *romance*," Ren retorted knowingly.

The irony, Seth thought as they climbed the staircase, was that he'd been trying to *avoid* romance.

He'd heard the noises filtering down from the rooftop earlier, and he figured there'd be a lot of people up here, now that the sun had fully set.

And it turned out he was right.

As they emerged onto the rooftop, it was easy to spot the group of Riptide players, with Tate in their midst, along with Alexis and Jackson, and Sean and Gabriel. Tate's sister, Rachel, and her girlfriend, Harmony, were tucked off in the corner, a fuzzy blanket wrapped around their shoulders. Similar blankets were rolled up in wicker baskets. The lights up here were subtler than the ones that crisscrossed the patio at the Funky Cup, tucked underneath the bar, and underneath the ledge, so the view, with its sparkling view of Los Angeles, could be seen more easily.

There were plants dotting the space, as well as some low couches and chairs, and a long bar along one side.

That's where everyone was currently congregated.

"Hey, it's Ren!" Chase, Tate's boyfriend and a wide receiver for the Los Angeles Riptide, called out. "And Seth! You guys are just in time."

"For?" Ren enquired as they walked towards the group.

Seth had fully expected that in the sight of so many people they knew that Ren would drop his hand.

But he was gripping it just as tightly as he had downstairs.

"We're doing a round of celebration shots," Chase crowed. He gestured to the bartender. "Pour two more, please, we've got some more friends."

The bartender smiled, probably certain that she'd be getting an enormous tip from the popular and wealthy football player, and poured two more from the tequila bottle in her hand.

"Hey, let's go," Ren said, gesturing to the group, and that was when he dropped his hand.

It's all good, you already got more than you thought you would.

But it still stung, no matter how many platitudes Seth told himself.

Seth had no intention of taking the shot—he'd had plenty already—but there was no way he was stopping Ren, who with everyone else, chimed in when Chase raised his shot glass to, "The second-best bar in Los Angeles!"

Seth's hand was still loosely circling the base of his full shot glass. Maybe nobody would notice if he never drank it? But before he could decide, Ren leaned over and plucked it out of his fingers and downed it too.

Ren's eyes were glazed now, the alcohol catching up with him, and yeah, he was definitely going to regret that second tequila shot in the morning.

And you won't be there to see it.

But Jake could be, or at least his words might be.

For the first time, Seth realized he didn't really know what the fuck he was doing. Ren might accept Jake, but he was never going to accept that Seth *was* Jake.

He turned to go, but Ren caught his elbow.

"Where are you going?" he demanded.

"I . . ."

Ren frowned, his expressions exaggerated by the booze swimming through his system.

"You're not leaving, are you?" Ren suddenly looked very concerned.

He should leave. It would be smarter than to watch Ren drown the rest of his hopes in liquor.

But instead, he shook his head. "No, I'm not going anywhere," Seth said.

On Ren's other side, Sean was leaning against Gabriel, and he was giggling. Gabe's eyes met Seth's and there was a definite kind of commiseration there.

"Hey," Gabe said to Sean, "you and Ren hold up this bar, okay? I'm gonna talk to Seth real quick."

Seth already knew what Gabe was going to ask before he drew him apart from the group, leaving his drunk boyfriend and his drunk cousin on their own.

Probably to drink more, because Seth had learned the hard way that having a few was a good reason to convince yourself that you needed a few more.

It was why he rarely had more than one.

"I'm going to have to figure out how to get Sean *and* Ren home," Gabe said, "and I'm not exactly sober either. Could . . . could you deal with Ren? Take care of him?" There was a hopeful look in his eyes. Like he hoped that maybe they'd fuck each other out of their systems.

Yeah, Seth had been hopeful of that once, but that ship had long sailed.

"You want me to take Ren home?"

"When he wants to go, yeah," Gabe said. "Is that okay? I kind of assumed . . ."

"It's not . . . it's not like that," Seth said, hating how he stuttered over the lie. *He* wasn't exactly sober either. And not just from the booze.

"Well," Gabe said, "that *is* what it looks like, at least from this angle. But if you don't . . ."

"I'll take care of him," Seth said firmly.

"Oh good." Gabe patted him on the arm. "I appreciate it, man."

"You're welcome."

When they drifted back to the group, Sean and Ren were laughing together, along with Alexis and Tate.

Ren's eyes met his, and he actually looked happy to see him again. "Oh, good, you didn't go anywhere," he said.

"I wouldn't," Seth said.

Ren slid a hand around Seth's waist and tugged him closer. Too close. His gaze was mesmerizing. "I was just thinking . . ." he said, speaking slowly. "That maybe we should go."

"We will, in a bit," Seth said. He hoped that Ren might sober up before that happened.

He'd be less pissed that Seth would be leaving him alone in his bed, in that scenario.

"Then get me another drink, will you?" Ren's voice had dropped, like he was telling Seth a secret just for the two of them, and his lips barely brushed Seth's ear. He had to hold back the full-body shudder as he felt them.

"Sure," Seth said.

The bartender smiled at him when he said what he wanted. "Your boyfriend's cute," she said, as she poured the two drinks he'd asked for.

"He's not my boyfriend."

She raised an eyebrow. "Sure looks like it from here. He can't take his eyes off you."

Yeah, unfortunately, that was entirely mutual.

"It's . . . well, it's complicated."

She winked at him as she set the drinks down and he stuffed a twenty-dollar bill into her tip jar. Too much, maybe, but she'd earned it, dealing with this crowd tonight. "Then maybe you should uncomplicate it."

But he knew he wouldn't be as he brought the drinks back to where Ren stood with their friends.

Ren took a sip and his face contorted in betrayal. "Water?" he hissed.

Seth shrugged. "You said you wanted a drink."

"You knew what I wanted!" Ren looked like he couldn't believe it.

"Water now, drink later," Seth said and Ren rolled his eyes but he took a long sip out of the glass.

The water sobered up Ren some, but then Chase drew everyone back to the bar for a final shot, and there was no way that Seth could stop it.

That meant that by the time Seth and Ren walked out of the front door together, Ren was leaning most of his weight on Seth's shoulder.

Definitely not a bad thing, if they were really going home together.

And from the handsy way that Ren kept shoving his fingers into the back pockets of Seth's jeans, he definitely thought they were.

There was a taxi at the curb, idling and waiting for anyone who needed it, and Seth, who'd planned on finagling Ren's address out of him so he could call an Uber, decided to just take it.

Seth helped Ren pour himself in, and then the driver turned his head towards them. "Where to?" he asked brusquely.

"Lorenzo," Seth said, turning to the man next to him, his head lying on the back of the seat, a vacant smile on his face. "What's your address?"

"Address?" Ren's grin widened. "We goin' back to my place?"

"Yes," Seth said impatiently.

Ren tucked a hand behind Seth's neck and tried to tug him closer.

Seth decided he was lucky that Ren hadn't decided to go for his dick yet.

"Address . . . huh," Ren drawled out.

The driver made an impatient noise, and Seth knew they only had a few moments before he gave up on them and ordered them out of the cab—and now that Ren was sitting down, getting up again was going to be difficult.

So, instead, he gave his own address to the driver.

He could always get Ren home tomorrow, and pour him into his bed. The couch in his living room was plenty comfy and it wouldn't kill him to sleep on it for a night.

It would be so much tougher to *not* spend the night with Ren, even if all they did was sleep.

Ten minutes later, the taxi pulled up to his address.

"What?" Ren said, suddenly becoming aware of what was going on. He stared out the window at the house. "Where are we?"

"We're going to get you into bed," Seth said, shoving some cash at the driver, and wrapping a hand around Ren's shoulders, tugged him out of the back seat of the cab.

"Bed?" Ren said, his eyes perking up.

Shit, that was clearly the one word he shouldn't have said, because while he was halfway hanging out of the cab, Ren decided it was a perfect time to go for Seth's cock.

"Oooph," Seth said as Ren's fingers brushed the front of his jeans, and even though he'd been soft just a moment ago, all it took was a possibility of Ren touching him, and he was hard as a rock.

Ren's fingers slid down, cupping him, his teeth gleaming as he smiled. "Oh, yeah," he said, "let's go to bed."

Double shit.

"Come on," Seth said. He twisted his body, trying to move away from Ren's hand.

He'd feel his hot palm pressed every time he closed his eyes, for a very long time to come.

That would have to be enough for now.

"Oh right," Ren said, laughing now, "you like your privacy."

"Yeah, let's not get arrested for indecent exposure," Seth grumbled as he finally tugged Ren free of the cab.

"Indecent exposure," Ren parroted back as they walked up the front walk to the door of Seth's house.

It was a small bungalow, cozy and quaint. Seth had loved it from the moment he'd seen it, and he'd spent all of his savings from his years in the military to buy it, the year he'd gotten out.

"Yeah, well, we don't need that on top of everything else," Seth said, typing in the code to the front door lock, balancing Ren with his other hand.

"What's everything else?" Ren wondered, as Seth gently pushed him into the open doorway. "Is this your house? Did you bring me to your house?"

Seth chuckled under his breath at Ren's questions, all running together. "Yes," he said. "Come on, this way. The bedroom's over here."

"I didn't know . . ." Ren said, "I didn't know we were still . . ." and the hope in his face as he tilted it up towards Seth took his breath away.

"We're not. You're . . . going there by yourself. To sleep it off."

Ren shot him a look full of promise. "With you?" he asked, biting his bottom lip, clearly trying to look inviting on purpose.

But Ren never needed to *try*. He was inviting when he was just standing there, looking blank-eyed.

Seth chuckled under his breath. Amused—but not really all that amused at all. "Not with me," he said.

"You're being so mean," Ren said, pouting adorably.

It was proof of how far gone Seth was, because he'd never found pouting in any way or form adorable before.

"I'm being realistic," Seth said, ruthlessly pushing down his feelings as he guided them both towards the master bedroom.

He'd been doing it for long enough that it felt like second nature, but it felt so much harder than normal with Ren.

Ren had been weaseling his way under his guard for six months now, and he'd been good and entrenched, even before the Jake experiment.

"So," Ren said, leaning against the doorframe, probably trying to look seductive and accomplishing the task surprisingly well considering how much he'd had to drink, "this is your bedroom."

"Yes," Seth said shortly. Tried to see his room through Ren's eyes.

The reclaimed wood furniture that he'd found in a little shop tucked away in a corner of Los Angeles, with its simple lines, and the dark green bedspread, smoothed out from when he'd gotten up this morning.

Everything was tucked away and neat, and had its place.

Everything except Ren, with his sensual eyes and his full bottom lip, teasing him.

"Looks nice," Ren drawled out, gazing around, and Seth knew the moment his eyes fell on the bed, because they fucking *lit up*.

"Get comfortable," Seth said firmly, "I'm going to get you some water and some aspirin. You're gonna need it."

"What, you don't want to watch?"

Seth turned away, so Ren couldn't see the naked hunger that he couldn't hide.

Of course he wanted to watch.

He wanted to do *more* than watch.

But it wasn't happening tonight, so he pushed away from the wall where he'd been standing, observing as Ren walked over to the bed like he owned it.

Owned *him*.

"I'll be right back," he said briskly.

Hoped, as he grabbed a cold bottle of water from the fridge and found the aspirin in one of his kitchen cabinets, that when he returned, Ren would be tucked away between the sheets, removing the temptation of him from reach.

But when he walked back, he saw Ren had switched on the lamp on the nightstand, filling the space with a soft, warm glow, he'd taken off his boots, and pulled off his white shirt, unbuttoning his jeans partway.

He was the picture of debauched elegance, all warm skin and dark eyes and flawless, slim muscles.

Perfection.

Seth bit his bottom lip so hard he tasted blood. The pain helped jerk him back to reality, away from the fantasy where he went over to Ren and kissed him and did everything to him that he'd fantasized about for six months.

"Come on," he said, "get in bed. You're dead on your feet."

"Not *that* dead on my feet," Ren teased. "Why don't you come over here and find out?"

If he took one step closer, Seth was afraid he'd take a dozen. But his fingers slipped on the condensation of the water bottle, and while he wanted him *badly*, he also wanted Ren to be okay in the morning.

If he didn't drink more water, he wouldn't be.

It was just a few steps to put the water and pill bottle on the nightstand, but they still felt perilous, and after he set them down, Seth escaped right back to the safety of the doorway. "If you need anything," Seth said, ignoring Ren's suggestion, "I'll be right outside, on the couch."

Ren frowned. Like he didn't quite understand. It could've been the booze, or it could've been so much more than that. Seth guessed it was the latter. After all, how could someone come to care for you if you never gave them the chance to.

"You could've made me sleep on the couch, if we weren't sharing the bed," Ren said.

"I could've, but what kind of man would that make me?" Seth said. "The couch is fine, anyway."

Ren didn't say anything, just looked thoughtful.

It was far easier to deal with than the seductive version of Ren.

"Goodnight," Ren said softly.

"Night," Seth said, and closed the door behind him, literally *and* metaphorically.

But the way Ren looked so confused, like he hadn't expected Seth to do something as simple as offer his own bed even though they wouldn't be sharing it, haunted him as he grabbed a water for himself, and found a blanket in the closet.

And as he arranged himself on the couch—which *was* pretty comfy, that was the one requirement Seth had made when he'd bought it, because Lennox had spent plenty of nights on it—he couldn't stop thinking about what Ren had said.

For someone as brilliant as Lorenzo Moretti, it seemed impossible that he could see himself as only good for one thing.

Maybe it wasn't so much an ingrained belief that Ren held, but a habit that died hard.

CHAPTER SEVEN

THE VERY FIRST THING Ren was aware of was that something horrible and unpleasant had just died in his mouth.

Then, it was the pounding in his head, right on beat with his heart.

He was also not in his own bed.

That much he knew.

The only question was whose bed he'd ended up in.

Ren stuck out a hand and felt the cold side of the bed. The uninhabited side of the bed, because it wasn't just slightly warm and cooled from an absence.

It had never been warm at all.

It hurt to even *try* to think, but Ren ruthlessly pushed his thoughts back to the night before. His ongoing argument with Gabe. The old-fashioneds he'd drunk. The old-fashioneds he'd drunk with *Seth*. The way they'd danced together. The hungry look in his eyes. Hot eyes, despite their cool gray color.

He remembered a cab ride. He remembered flirting as hard as he'd flirted in his whole goddamned life.

Seth had brought them to his house.

Then had he ended up in what had to be Seth's bed, *alone*?

It hurt even more, but Ren pried his eyes open, flinching against the morning light filtering through the blinds on the right.

And then they opened even wider, dismissing the pain as insignificant, because they'd landed on the one thing that might shock Ren more than waking up in Seth's bed alone: the Picasso print hung on the opposite wall from the bed, staring right at him.

Knowingly.

Because that was the same goddamn print that was behind Jake's picture on the Flaunt app.

He recognized it immediately because he'd stared at it so many times, hoping that he might see more, might *see* Jake.

Now, Ren realized, he'd seen Jake all along.

Because Jake was Seth.

Anger surged through him in a sickening wave.

Or maybe that was the nausea from his hangover.

Either way, he wasn't going to stay here a moment longer in Seth's bed—without Seth—because the guy had not only lied to him, he'd fooled him, and probably fucking laughed at him too.

Because he'd clearly known just who Ren was, and he'd pursued him anyway, even though Ren had made his feelings clear from the very beginning.

Ren pushed the sheets and blankets aside, scrambling out of bed. Out of the corner of his eye, he saw the half-drunk water and the bottle of pills that Seth had set there the night before.

How he'd been so fucking confused why Seth was such a good guy. A guy who gave a shit.

Shoving his feet into his boots, Ren grabbed his shirt and put it on.

He'd been wrong. Seth didn't give a shit. He'd been playing Ren this whole goddamned time.

He'd been working an angle, even though it was an angle that he knew perfectly well that Ren didn't *want*.

He stomped over to the doorway, and pulled open the door. It was a small bungalow, very similar to Jackson's, all done in clean lines and elegant, understated colors. The couch was empty, and Ren stood there for a second, anger and nausea roiling inside him, and wondered if he should just leave.

No.

He was going to give Seth a fucking piece of his mind first, and tell him, finally, to leave him alone.

As Seth.

As Jake.

As whoever the fuck he really was.

Then Seth came around the corner, with a cup of coffee in one hand, and a smile on his face.

Like he'd been happy because he'd finally manipulated Ren exactly where he wanted him.

"What the fuck," Ren spit out.

The smile disappeared.

"What's wrong?" Seth asked, setting the mug down carefully. "I was just about to bring you some coffee. Are you okay?"

"Am I *okay*?" Ren scoffed.

"You're not okay?" A crease appeared between Seth's brows, and in another life, Ren would have been tempted to lean forward and kiss it away.

But that had been a momentary insanity and Ren was cured of it now that Seth's lies had been exposed.

"I am *not* okay . . ." Ren paused. "Did you think I would be, *Jake*?"

For a split second, Seth looked confused, like he wasn't sure what had given him away, and then Ren watched as realization dawned.

"The Picasso," he said slowly.

"The Picasso, you *fucker*," Ren flung at him. "Were you laughing at me the whole time? Pretending to be someone else?"

"I never laughed at you." Seth's voice was solemn. "I just wanted to talk to you. And for the record, I'm sorry I lied, I didn't *want* to lie . . ."

"Oh, but I forced you to," Ren said. "I get it now. It's all *my* fault, because I wasn't going to give you what you wanted, so you planned a way to steal it instead."

The guilt on Seth's face should've made him feel better. But somehow, that sick feeling in Ren's stomach worsened.

"That's not how it was."

"It's how it feels," Ren retorted. He took a deep breath. Getting angry—getting so angry he shouted and swore—would just prove to Seth that he gave a shit. And he didn't. Not any longer.

It didn't matter that he'd started wondering if he could care about Jake.

It definitely did not matter that he'd begun to think he already cared about Seth.

Nothing mattered anymore.

This was the reason why Ren took what he wanted and always left after.

The *after* the after was messy.

Too messy.

"Now," he said, enunciating each word carefully, "I would like to get home, and to never, ever see you again. I know that's asking a lot, since Lennox is your best friend, so I'll settle for you never saying another word to me, and never, ever looking my direction again."

Ren would have to be a lot more hungover to miss the tremor as it passed over Seth's face.

"I'll drive you . . ." Seth hesitated. "I guess I won't."

"No, you won't," Ren said, and picked up his coat, and turned and walked to the front door, jerking it open and slamming it shut behind him.

The sun was painfully bright, but the hurt felt good as Ren stalked off Seth's property, and then pulling his phone out of his pocket, opened a mapping application.

Seth only lived a few blocks away from the loft that he and Gabe shared. It would take longer to wait for an Uber to show up at this hour than it would be to march his ass home.

"So be it," Ren huffed under his breath as he double-checked the directions, and then, ignoring the pinch of his boots, started off towards the loft.

Ren had just finished his second double espresso of the morning when the front door to the loft opened and then closed behind his cousin.

"Oh, you're here," Gabe said brightly as he walked into the kitchen towards the espresso maker. "I texted you earlier, did you get it?"

"Yes," Ren said shortly.

He was still trying to decide if he was more pissed off or more humiliated. Or both, maybe.

"I just wanted to make sure you got home okay, no need to be pissy with me."

"Why, because you were so busy trying to take care of Sean that you just *left* me with that guy?"

Gabe turned around from the espresso machine. "*That guy*? You mean, the guy you've been crushing on forever? You seemed plenty happy to be left with him last night."

"That was last night," Ren said tightly.

Gabe's expression morphed from confused to concerned. "Did something happen between you two? Was he . . . he didn't . . ."

"He didn't do a single thing," Ren said. "That wasn't the issue. The issue is . . ." He hadn't had any intention of telling Gabriel what had happened this morning. Partially because he was still annoyed at how his cousin had just pawned him off on Seth, and partially because the realization that Seth had betrayed him was still so raw, Ren wasn't sure he could get through the telling of it.

But now, inexplicably, the other stuff, the stupid business stuff seemed to matter less, and all Ren wanted was a hug and to tell his best friend why he was so goddamned pissed off.

"What's the issue, then?" Gabe asked, coming around the kitchen counter to stand in front of where Ren sat, at one of the barstools.

"I signed up for that app, right, like you encouraged me to do," Ren said with a resigned sigh. Gabe slid onto the stool next to him, his espresso forgotten. "I started talking to this guy. And yes, I know, I usually would've suggested we meet right away, and then we'd have had sex, and it would've been fine, probably, or good, even, but I didn't. I . . . I just talked to him. For over a week."

"You liked him," Gabe said, condensing down all of Ren's confused feelings into one damning sentence.

Ren wanted to say no, of course he hadn't *liked* him, but he couldn't. How could he, when every cell in his body was screaming *yes*?

"Okay, fine, I liked him," Ren admitted. "I did. And then this morning, I realized that he wasn't Jake, like he'd said he was. He was never Jake. He was Seth, this whole time."

Gabe looked shocked. "What?"

"He was Seth. He was never . . . he was never who he said he was." Though, Ren's uncooperative brain supplied that he was also exactly who he'd said he was. An ex-military guy who owned a private security company with his best friend.

It was exactly who Seth was, and he'd never lied about that.

Just about everything else, Ren thought bitterly.

"Are you sure about that? I can't imagine he'd lie." Gabriel still looked confused. Ren couldn't really blame him, because he *felt* confused.

"Oh, he lied, all right," Ren blustered, because he'd said his name was Jake, hadn't he? He had very specifically, along with nursing his hangover, *not* been going back through every single one of the conversations he'd had with Jake, trying to figure out if Seth had lied about anything else.

Nope, he wasn't going to do it.

The one lie, about his name, that was more than enough for Ren.

"What an asshole," Gabe said. "I can't fucking believe he lied to you about who he was. To get you into his bed? I'm going to go kick his ass."

This was exactly what Ren wanted: a chance to commiserate with Gabe, and call Seth a bunch of names, and then, ultimately, let his anger—and Seth—go.

But hearing the words out of Gabe's mouth wasn't as satisfying as he thought it might be.

"No, God, please don't. Then he'll know just how upset I am." And that was the humiliating topper to all of this, wasn't it?

He'd cared.

He currently *cared*, present tense.

"Seriously, who does that? Just to fool you into bed?"

"He didn't fool me into anything," Ren said, crossing his arms over his chest. Then realized a second later that he was actually *defending* Seth.

What. The. Fuck.

"But you're still pissed," Gabe stated. "Apparently I can't be pissed though."

"No, he's just . . . he's not a bad guy." It was painful to admit it. Not as painful as waking up and seeing that poster opposite the bed, but *close*.

"You're just pissed that he fooled you," Gabe said.

"Well, *yeah*," Ren said. And he was. It was humiliating, just thinking of all those times when he'd thought, *oh, another thing that Seth and Jake have in common*, and not once, not one single fucking time, had it occurred to him that they were actually the same person.

"I think," Gabe said in a contemplative tone, standing and wandering back over to the espresso machine, grabbing the milk from the fridge, "that it's actually kinda romantic. You wouldn't talk to him, no matter what he did. So he figured out a way to talk to you."

"Don't," Ren said. "Just . . . don't, okay? I know you love being in love but that's not me. That's never going to be me."

But he'd defended Seth, hadn't he? He'd insisted that Gabe not kick his ass.

Not that Gabe probably could.

Gabe came back to him, stirring his coffee. "Maybe, maybe not," he agreed. "But you're something, aren't you? Or else you wouldn't be so angry."

Angry.

Hurt.

Humiliated.

He was all of those things. And Ren realized, hating every moment of it, that maybe his cousin wasn't wrong. Old Ren would have shrugged this off and moved on to the next cute guy.

But there was no way he was getting over this. Not anytime soon. He was going to be pissed for awhile; he could feel the anger, the way it had settled into his bones.

Nobody knew how to do pissed off better than Italians.

Gabe pissed him off sometimes, but he hadn't been close enough to anyone else for them to truly bother him.

And he was definitely bothered by Seth.

"I hate you," Ren said mildly. "I really hate that you said that."

Gabe laughed. "Figured it out, didn't you?"

"How can I trust someone who *lied* though?"

"It's not easy, but you can do it. Maybe Sean never told me he was someone else, but he never told me about this huge part of his life before he came here, he never told me that he was married before. Or that his husband died, and he was still mourning him."

Ren sighed. "Why do I think that you're going to tell me exactly how I'm gonna forgive him for this simple, no-big-deal lie of telling me he was someone else?"

"I'm not," Gabe said, chuckling. "I can't. You've gotta figure that part out for yourself. But maybe start with . . . maybe you're not so pissed that you never want to talk to him again."

Except, that was exactly what he'd just said to Seth.

I'll settle for you never saying another word to me, and never, ever looking my direction again.

"I'm guessing," Gabe continued, "from your suddenly guilty expression that you already told him to fuck off."

"Of course I did. What else was I supposed to say? I woke up in his bed . . ."

"Wait . . . *what*?" Gabe interrupted him, a shocked expression on his face. Suddenly angry all over again. "He slept with you? While you still thought Jake was a different guy?"

"No, no . . ." Ren paused. "I . . . I don't think anything happened? I thought it would. I thought . . . I couldn't have forgotten . . ."

"You were drunk, but you weren't *that* drunk," Gabe teased. "You'd have remembered."

"I either forgot, or he didn't . . ." Ren hesitated. He'd never have forgotten kissing Seth. Which meant that they hadn't.

The alternative was even worse than Seth lying: that Ren had finally gotten a little taste of what he'd been dying for and it had just *disappeared* in a fog of booze.

But he *could* remember them getting close more than once. With all that liquor in him, he'd never have resisted. Not when what he'd wanted for so long was within his grasp. And Seth?

He'd been drinking too.

Not as much as Ren.

But enough.

They must've kissed, and Ren *must've* forgotten about it.

Fuck.

"If it's possible, you look even more pissed than you did five minutes ago," Gabe pointed out, clearly amused.

Which . . . that was fine, Ren supposed. He deserved it, for all the shit he'd given Gabe over the beginning—okay, and the middle, and the current state—of his relationship with Sean.

He absolutely deserved every second of the wry amusement in his cousin's voice.

"There's no way I could've forgotten, but I *must* have," Ren said, scrubbing a hand over his face.

"Yeah, I don't think you've ever slept chastely in someone else's bed before," Gabe teased.

Another comment he totally deserved.

Because it was true.

"Ugh," Ren groaned. "What am I gonna do?"

"You're not going to like it," Gabe said, patting him on the back, reassuringly. "But I think *you* might have to actually go grovel."

Ren's head whipped up and he glared at his cousin. "Grovel? Me? *Why*?"

"You did tell him to fuck off, didn't you?"

"Yes." Ren hesitated. "Not in as many words. But yes."

"And now you want to take it back. You don't want him to fuck off." Gabriel waved a hand. "Some groveling is probably going to be necessary to perform a complete reversal."

"I . . . don't . . . *grovel*," Ren enunciated each word clearly, just so there was no mistake.

Gabe laughed. "So what, you thought you'd just show up and he'd be so grateful that you aren't pissed anymore that everything would go back to normal? What *is* normal? Is that even what you want? I thought you wanted to get over the guy. Move on to someone else."

"Yes," Ren said through clenched teeth. He hated that Gabe was right; he'd expected exactly that. "And that was when . . . well, when I thought I was moving on to Jake."

"But now Jake is Seth. And you aren't over him at all."

Ren refused to acknowledge *that*, and he slid off his stool, heading to the espresso machine. Somehow his head was pounding more than it had this morning.

"What *do* you want?" Gabe asked. Continuing to be a massive pain in Ren's ass. "You can't go over there and say, *whoops, never mind, I might've overreacted*, and not have any idea of what you want."

"Why not?" Ren challenged.

Gabe sighed. "Well, of course you could. But this changes things, doesn't it? You want to fuck him, rather desperately, and you also like him. Or you liked Jake."

"I still don't know whether he and Jake are really, well, the same," Ren argued. Even though he already knew they were.

Ren had said it himself. Seth was still a good guy, and he had his version of honor. Even if he was going to go out of his way to tell Ren he was someone else, he wouldn't have lied about *who* he was.

"Really?" Gabe sounded skeptical. "He doesn't sound like the catfishing type, honestly."

"Well," Ren said, adding hot water to his cup, lightening up the espresso only the tiniest bit, "he *is*."

Gabe had the fucking nerve to laugh. "Maybe don't lead with that when you're groveling."

"I'm not groveling," Ren argued. "I have zero intention of doing any groveling."

"He may not want to see you, if you don't," Gabe said.

This was so patently ridiculous, that it was Ren's turn to laugh.

Which *hurt*.

"Yeah, I'll take my chances," Ren said, and then drowned the rest of his Americano. "I'm gonna take a shower."

"Just in case . . . *what* . . . you don't have to grovel at all, but he grovels for *you*?" Gabe said, following Ren towards the bathroom.

Instead of answering, Ren shut the door in Gabe's face. He could hear him laughing on the other side as he flipped the shower on.

The thing was, he couldn't even conceptualize Seth groveling. Either Seth *or* Jake—and why was he still thinking of them as two separate people anyway?

Neither of them would grovel then, and that was fine. Totally one hundred percent okay.

It was unsurprising, maybe, but guilt gnawed at Seth all day. From the moment that Ren walked out of the bedroom, betrayal written all over his beautiful face, to when he scrubbed the stove, scouring the already clean surfaces like he could scrub away all his remorse, to scrubbing the toilets, regret bubbling up inside him like vomit.

He finally dumped his rubber gloves in the cleaning bucket and tucked it away in his tiny little laundry room, and headed towards his bedroom to change for a run.

But he stopped in the doorway, brought to an abrupt halt by the sight of the bed, sheets and blankets still rumpled from when Ren had slept in it the night before.

Maybe if he'd known that it would all blow up in his face, that last night was his only chance, he wouldn't have let Ren go to bed alone.

No, he still would've.

Ren was drunk.

He'd never have taken advantage like that.

Seth turned towards the closet. After he got back from his run, he'd wash the sheets and the blankets, erasing Ren's presence from his room and his bed, and he'd try to get over it.

Maybe he would. Maybe he wouldn't.

But whichever he ended up living with, he knew that Ren would never forgive him.

He'd humiliated him.

Fooled him.

Lied to him.

Seth yanked off his t-shirt, deciding that maybe he didn't deserve to be forgiven. He'd only wanted to get to know the man, to get a chance to woo him without all the rules that governed Ren's normal hookups.

He'd wanted a different way in, and it was almost worse that it *had* been working. Otherwise Ren wouldn't be so fucking pissed off at him.

But that didn't make him feel any better.

Not when his chances were lying shredded in a heap on the bedroom floor, and Ren's words were still echoing in his ears.

I'll settle for you never saying another word to me, and never, ever looking my direction again.

It wouldn't be easy, but Seth had already done enough shitty things, so he'd do as Ren demanded, and even though his gaze always felt magnetically drawn to him, whenever they saw each other, he'd do his best.

Maybe it would even begin to hurt less if he could pull it off.

Seth strapped on his phone holder, shoved his feet into his running shoes, and took off. He started slow, warming up, but the sedate pace wasn't blocking out or quieting the screaming guilt in the back of his head, so he pushed harder and then harder still, sweat beginning to drip down his forehead as his feet hit the pavement.

But no matter how far or hard he ran, muscles tensing and tiring, he couldn't shut out Ren's words—or the anger Seth had seen in his eyes.

His breaths were coming in big, painful gusts as he finally rounded the corner towards his house.

He'd been gone for at least an hour, though he didn't have the energy to glance down at his phone and see the statistics for his run.

Slowing down, he pulled off his t-shirt and wiped his face with it, his muscles screaming with exhaustion as he transitioned from the punishing pace to cooldown mode.

He turned the last corner, heading up the path to his front door, and stopped in his tracks.

Ren was sitting on his tiny front porch, dressed in dark jeans and a plain gray t-shirt, hair perfect, and shadows under his eyes.

"Hey," he said, standing up as Seth just stared at him.

Acutely and stupidly aware that his t-shirt was dangling from his fingertips, his skin burning under Ren's potent gaze.

"I'm sorry, I'm not sure what I'm supposed to do," Seth said, his tongue clumsy and thick in his mouth. "I thought I wasn't supposed to talk to you—or even look at you ever again."

"I did say that, didn't I?" Ren sighed.

Seth put his hands on hips. "Yeah, you did. And I probably deserved it."

"Did you?" Ren hummed to himself, like he was still trying to decide. "I'm not sure you did, though I was plenty pissed. Pissed *and* humiliated."

"I wasn't laughing at you. Not once. That's not what . . ." Damn his words, he was terrible with them normally, but after that kind of insane run he'd just put himself through, he couldn't figure out what he was supposed to say or do.

He'd never imagined that Ren might come back.

"I know," Ren finished for him. "I know. I wouldn't let you talk to me." His smile was wry. "I didn't see the point."

Seth stared at him. Just a second ago, he'd been exhausted. But now, his fingertips were tingling and hope began to re-bloom, deep inside him, making him feel alive again.

"Do you see it now?"

Ren shrugged. "I don't know."

It wasn't the answer he'd been hoping for, but it wasn't *no*, either.

"I liked Jake," Ren continued thoughtfully.

"*Liked*," Seth said, not bothering to hide his bitterness.

"I don't know how much of you is Jake and how much of you is Seth," Ren said.

"Yes, you do," Seth said bluntly.

Ren rolled his eyes, but he hadn't moved any closer and there was an uncertainty in his eyes that Seth had never seen before.

He didn't know what to do.

Well, that made two of them.

He took a deep, shuddering breath, fingers clenched hard around his sweaty t-shirt. "Why are you here?" he asked.

Maybe the only way to convince Ren of what he believed Ren already suspected—which is that the only thing he'd lied about was his name—was to be one hundred percent scrupulously honest going forward.

Seth could do that.

"I was confused," Ren finally said. He took a tentative step forward.

"About?"

"You took me to your house, drunk and well . . . I know what I'm like when I'm drunk . . . and . . ." Ren's voice trailed off, like he wasn't sure what to say.

How much to admit to.

"Are you asking how handsy you tried to be?" Seth chuckled. "Plenty handsy, okay? But I'm not a boy. Not like those guys you normally date. I can control myself."

Ren eyed him from head to toe, from his bare chest to the shorts that revealed his legs. "Oh, believe me, I know it. But what I'm asking is what I've forgotten. If I forgot, it couldn't have been very good. Was it not good?"

"Forgot what?" Seth shouldn't have been amused at Ren's confusion, but it was impossible not to be. Not when Ren was normally so ball-bustingly confident.

"I thought we did . . . I have this memory of us . . ." Ren took another handful of steps towards Seth. Apparently not dissuaded by his sweat. "Getting close. Dancing, maybe?"

Seth tilted his head. Wondered where Ren was going with this. "We danced."

"Then we . . . got this close," Ren said, crowding in even closer. Just as near as he had been, the night before. Just as—if not *more*—irresistible. "And then it just goes blank."

Seth told himself not to laugh. This wasn't funny. "You think we kissed and you forgot it."

"Yes." Frustration crossed over Ren's face. "I was in your *bed*. You didn't make me sleep on the couch."

"You were hung up on that last night, too," Seth said. "You kept saying you didn't understand."

"Of course I didn't." Ren rolled his eyes. "So what am I missing? I wasn't that drunk but I must be missing *something*."

"Lorenzo," Seth said, leaning in another fraction of an inch, until their foreheads were nearly touching, "if we kissed, it wouldn't matter how much you had to drink, you'd never be able to forget it."

Ren licked his bottom lip. "Sounds like a lot of promises you're making."

Promises Seth didn't know if he could live up to. Ren had probably kissed a hundred guys; he'd probably had a dozen unbelievable, blow-the-top-of-your-head-clean-off kisses in his life. Meanwhile, Seth hadn't kissed anybody in a year, and hadn't kissed anybody he really liked in so much longer than that. He was trembling, and he told himself it was because his muscles were worn out—but the truth was a lot more difficult to face than that.

"I'm making one promise, and one promise only," Seth said, because this needed to be said, before anything happened. "I won't ever lie to you again."

Ren opened his mouth to say something else and Seth realized, like a shot of lightning to the back of the head, that he was nervous too.

Suddenly it made no sense to stand here, aching for each other and doing nothing about it.

So, Seth did what he always did. He pushed through the nerves and the fear, and tilted his head down, pressing his lips against Ren's.

For a second, that was all it was: his mouth against Ren's, not moving, only touching, because even that mere brush of their lips together was like a cataclysm moving through him. He shivered, or maybe that was Ren, and then Ren's hands were around his neck, tugging him closer, his mouth slotting under Seth's own, like it had been made for him.

In the six months since he'd met Lorenzo Moretti, he'd dreamed about kissing him so many times that he couldn't possibly remember them all. There'd been hot kisses and sexy kisses and kisses that made his dick hard. He'd imagined unexpected kisses, and kisses in the rain. With so little romance in his life, he'd let his mind run wild whenever it thought of Ren, because there was so little chance of him ever getting to enact any of his fantasies.

But never in six months had he imagined such a soft, slow, sweet kiss. That just the soft brush of Ren's incredible mouth would be enough to make him shake. That he'd enjoy it so much just like this that he wouldn't want it any other way.

Then Ren made a little noise in the back of his throat, like he was confused, or maybe just that he was as blown apart as Seth was, and he pulled back.

For a second, Seth was confused too.

What had just happened?

He'd been kissing Ren and then he *wasn't* kissing Ren, and that seemed like the worst kind of development.

"What . . ." Ren had to clear this throat, his voice rough. It seemed impossible, judging from the look in Ren's eyes, that he hadn't been as viscerally affected by the kiss as Seth had. "What are we doing?"

They hadn't so much as brushed dicks. They'd stayed a sedate few inches apart. Nobody had groped anybody, though the thought *had* fleetingly passed through Seth's head that now would be a good time to find out if Ren's ass was a delicious a handful as it looked.

No, it had been unexpectedly chaste.

Mind-blowing. And so fucking sweet. But mostly innocent.

"I thought it was obvious what we were doing. And now we're not doing it anymore," Seth teased.

Ren rolled his eyes. "I mean . . . we still want different things. Why are we doing this?"

Yes, that had always been the problem. Except that Seth was beginning to think it *wasn't* actually a problem.

"I don't think that's true, anymore," Seth said. He remembered how hesitant Ren had been with Jake, how he hadn't been sure *what* he wanted. He certainly hadn't just propositioned Jake, either. He'd *talked* to him. Hung out with him, virtually. Flirted with him. Everything that Seth craved, that he'd never gotten for real.

Ren shot him a look. "Don't . . ."

But Seth didn't let him finish. Ren, he'd begun to figure out, liked to make things difficult on himself. Liked to tie himself into knots when things were really, actually pretty straightforward. Like right now.

"What I mean is that what I want is you. And you're here, so I think the feeling is mutual. We don't have to put any pressure on ourselves. We can just . . ."

Ren looked unimpressed. But that, Seth reminded himself, was the facade. He'd been hurt when Seth had lied to him about Jake. He'd been nervous, right before the kiss.

"We can just *what*," Ren said. "I can't just become a different person. Neither can you."

"If I'd gotten my way," Seth said, dropping down and settling on the front step of the porch, "I'd have taken you out, the first time. Nice dinner, I'd have worn a tie, probably, and we'd have finished the evening at a movie, or a concert, or with a quiet drink."

"And you'd have kissed me," Ren said, hesitating, but finally taking a seat next to Seth. Not touching, but not precisely far away either.

"You've seen yourself," Seth teased. "I'd have kissed you, for sure."

"And? What's the point? You'd have taken me on a big fancy date, kissed me at my doorstep, just like a thousand romantic comedies, and then we'd be *what* . . . dating? You know I don't . . ."

"I know," Seth said firmly. "I know you don't. That's why I won't. Not now. But I wanted to tell you what I would've done, because if I didn't, then you wouldn't understand my compromise."

"Your compromise?" Ren looked suspicious. Like he was waiting for another shoe to drop.

Seth was waiting for it too, except he knew what it looked like, and he realized as he pictured it in his mind that he wanted it more than was probably healthy.

How would he move on if Ren rejected his idea? After he'd already tasted him? Experienced a shadowy possibility of what they could have together when he'd been Jake?

"I just want to hang out with you. No pressure, no expectations. I told you, all I ever wanted was you."

"No strings?"

If Ren didn't think they had any strings tying them together, he was lying to himself, because Seth could feel them tugging at him now, but the idea of them clearly terrified Ren, so he shook his head.

Not a lie, exactly, but a necessary deflection.

"What about . . ." Ren hesitated, worrying his bottom lip again. Seth wanted to lean down and lick it. "What about sex?"

"What about it?" Even hearing him say the word sent a tremor through Seth's body but he kept his voice casual.

"You're really going to make me say it?" Ren looked annoyed. Frustrated.

Sexually frustrated, Seth realized, and then it hit him, sudden and jarring. *He's sexually frustrated because of you.*

"It's better," Seth said mildly, hiding how utterly thrilled he was, how much his pulse had suddenly accelerated, "to be straightforward about these things, right?"

Seth didn't have a moment to brace himself, because suddenly Ren was in his space, and this kiss wasn't sweet or soft. It was hot and filthy, Ren's tongue inside his mouth, nimble and quick and blowing Seth's mind.

And then as fast as it had begun, it was over, and Ren's face was hovering a few inches from his own.

Seth had to look away, because it was too much. Ren far away was a gorgeous sight, but up close, his mouth wet and red from his own, pupils blown in his dark eyes, curls mussed from Seth's hand, he was a fucking masterpiece.

But when he glanced away, the first thing he saw was Ren's hand, and it was trembling.

"Point taken," Seth said wryly. "We're going to have sex, okay? Is that what you wanted?"

"More than once," Ren said with satisfaction, a smile creeping across his features like a cat who'd just won the cream. Like he hadn't practically made a career out of never sleeping with the same guy twice.

"If you want to, sure," Seth said, making a promise to himself that he'd make sure that Ren wanted to.

Ren laughed. "You're terrible at this."

"You're here, aren't you?" Seth said, gesturing around him. "So I must not be so fucking terrible after all."

Ren might have rolled his eyes again, but he also looked so pleased that Seth felt the mirror image of the feeling roll through him.

"I guess," Ren said, standing, "I should give you my number. For whatever this casual hanging-out thing is we're doing."

"Actually, I already have it," Seth said.

"Really?"

Seth could see how Ren was trying to puzzle out how he'd gotten it. "I have the number of every person who works at the food truck lot," he said. "For work."

"And you've never used it," Ren said, a smile breaking over his features. "Not once. Should I be impressed?"

"Yes," Seth said. "Very."

"Well, then, I am. Impressed, that is." He dusted off his dark jeans. "You'll text me, then?"

Seth was pretty sure that Ren hadn't meant to sound so hopeful, but it was there, anyway. He couldn't hide it.

"Yeah, I'll text you," Seth said. He'd promised he wouldn't lie, after all, and he definitely intended to text him.

And more.

"Then, I guess I'll see you around," Ren said, and then he turned and walked away.

Unlike every other time he'd walked away, Seth didn't watch him go with a single bit of regret.

CHAPTER EIGHT

IT WAS LATE AFTERNOON, the weak early spring sunshine dotting the tables that were scattered through the middle of the food truck lot.

It was a quiet Monday, and Ren had agreed to look at some of Gabe's data and figure out what they were going to do about the menu for the future.

"You go grab a table," Gabe had said, "and keep an eye on the truck, if anyone actually shows up, and I'll go to the good coffee place."

Ren had raised an eyebrow. "You sucking up?"

"Apologizing for being an overbearing ass?"

"Fair," Ren had acknowledged.

He'd been waiting out here for five minutes now, enjoying the rays of sun, fingers itching to pull out his phone.

To text Seth.

They'd agreed to keep it casual. That, Ren understood. He just didn't understand what casual even meant. It was *not* his usual version of casual, that was for sure, but other than the utter lack of orgasms and only *two* kisses, both of which had kept him up, jittery and frustrated, it wasn't anything else either.

Seth had kept his promise and texted him about an hour after he'd gotten back home. **This,** the text had read, **is me texting you. Hi, Lorenzo.**

Ren had wanted to be annoyed, but he'd laughed, instead. So loudly that Gabe had poked his head into his room and made sure that he was okay.

They'd texted back and forth a little bit, and Ren had saved his number to his phone.

When he'd woken up this morning, his first inclination had been to reach for his phone, and tell Jake good morning.

Except that Jake wasn't Jake, he was Seth, and texting someone good morning wasn't very casual, was it?

So he'd waited.

And he was still waiting.

Monday was their weekly prep morning at the truck, so at least he'd been busy. Then there'd been the lunch rush, and when Gabe had suggested they go over the data, Ren had agreed.

Partially because at least Gabriel had admitted he was an overbearing ass, and also because it would keep Ren's mind occupied and off his phone.

But his fingers were itching now.

Seth *was* Jake. He knew what Jake knew.

He pulled his phone out of his pocket and wrote the text before he could change his mind or overthink it.

Gabe has admitted he's an overbearing ass, and we're going to talk about the menu and possibly whittling it

down. Might want to prepare some bail money.

Seth's response came in so quickly that Ren felt stupid. Why had he been avoiding doing this? He *liked* talking to him, so much. It was stupid to avoid it because he didn't know what it meant. What it meant was that they wanted each other. That wasn't new for Ren, except for the fact that he wanted Seth as more than just a temporary lay.

But maybe Seth was right, and it was still wanting.

I've got you, he said, **but I don't think it's going to come to that. Gabe loves you, and I know you'll wrinkle your nose and disagree, but you love him too. This is just a little bump, you'll get past it.**

Ren smiled. **Why is all your straightforward earnestness so sexy?**

Seth: **I don't know, but I'll take it.**

"I don't think I've ever seen you smile like that."

Ren glanced up and Gabe was there, carrying two cups of coffee, with the tablet tucked under one arm.

"It's just . . ." But Ren couldn't figure out how to explain it because it defied explanation.

"I take it you two made up," Gabe said, sitting down next to him, setting Ren's coffee in front of him.

"You know we did, I told you we did yesterday."

"But there's a difference between *we made up and I'm not going to hate Seth for all eternity* and *we made up and now Seth is the sun and the moon and the stars.*"

"Ew, can I vote for neither of those?" Ren said, taking an experimental sip of his coffee. Rich espresso blossomed across his tongue. Maybe he should regret that Gabe had realized he could be bribed with coffee from the really good coffee place, but if it kept getting him really good coffee, he couldn't.

It worked out as long as Gabe kept fucking up, and Ren didn't see that changing anytime soon.

"Okay, fine, you've made up and you're figuring your shit out. That smile was a little bit more than *we made up and we're figuring our shit out* but I'll give that to you."

"Thanks," Ren said dryly.

Gabe set up the tablet, flicking through several screens until he found the one he was looking for. "This," he said, "is our sales for the last six months."

"Which is about when we changed the name and the menu," Ren said, nodding, staring more closely at the screen than he'd thought he would.

The results weren't exactly surprising. Their number one bestseller was the same thing that had sold well before the name change: their meatball sandwich. It made sense. Nonna's recipes had launched an entire chain of restaurants. And when people thought *meatballs*, they usually thought red sauce and dripping cheese and garlic bread.

But the rest of the top ten was surprising.

"People really like the monthly specials," Ren said, finger resting on the screen. He glanced over at his cousin. "Why didn't you just say that instead of being secretive and mysterious?"

Gabe grinned. "I'm Italian, it's baked into my genes."

"You're an idiot," Ren scoffed. "An absolute fucking idiot, but at least you're my idiot."

"You're not wrong. I *was* thinking the way you were afraid I was, that we should ditch the regular menu items and replace them. But then I thought about it, really thought about it, and you're right. We started doing this food truck thing for flexibility."

"Also," Ren inserted, smiling because he couldn't quite help it, "because you wanted to get away from Luca."

"Yes, I wanted to get away from Luca. If I remember, you weren't his biggest fan, either," Gabe said wryly.

"Fan?" Ren raised an eyebrow. "Frankly, he and the massive stick up his ass both suck. What he needs is to get laid, and often."

Gabe grinned. "Well, Luca is the rest of the family's problem now."

"Thank God," Ren said, meaning it.

"So, back to me actually *thinking*, I realized that you were right."

"Wait," Ren interrupted again. "Did you just say I *was right*?"

Gabe laughed and nodded. "Yeah, and I'm sure you'll never let me forget it."

"I won't," Ren said smugly.

"Anyway, so you were right. We should keep our flexibility. So I thought, let's move some of these to the regular menu, see if they perform as well as when they were the special. If they don't, then instead of doing a permanent menu, I was thinking, we could keep it fresh, keep customers coming back, by creating a rotating menu. Like, change it out quarterly."

"So, like the monthly specials, but a little longer term," Ren said thoughtfully, considering this angle. It would definitely prevent them from getting stuck in any ruts.

"I know you've got ideas. So do I. We should be indulging those, and we can even bring an old special back. Do some social media polls, figure out what people are excited about."

"I love that idea," Ren said. Normally, he might have held back, held how good he thought it was a bit closer to his chest, but today, he couldn't lie; something in the vicinity of his heart was still smarting after their earlier arguments. And to Gabe's credit, it *was* a really good way of combining both the business smarts that Gabe had always possessed with the creativity that Ren valued.

"Oh, good," Gabe said, leaning back and sipping his coffee. "So we're agreed, then?"

"We're agreed." As soon as he said the words, ideas and random snatches of inspiration began filtering through his head. "When do we want to make the change?"

"We'll need to figure out a new signage situation," Gabe pointed out. "And new signage means . . ."

"Ugh, why does Tony get to approve or reject signage?"

Gabe laughed. "Has Tony *ever* rejected a sign?"

"That time that Ash tried to put one up with my phone number and *for a good time, call . . .*" Ren muttered.

"And you should be thankful for that," Gabe said. "You'd have had to change your number."

"Tony just enjoys being the king of his little kingdom way too much," Ren said, because he wasn't going to acknowledge that *yes*, Ash's prank would have sent droves of creepers to his phone, and he should be at least a little thankful that Tony had put his foot down.

"You just don't like anyone who divides our attention from you," Gabe teased.

"That is not even remotely close to accurate," Ren scoffed, even though his cousin was right.

Though, Ren could acknowledge that at least he was less right than usual.

It turned out that having the right person's attention on you was more intoxicating than a whole crowd.

His fingers itched; he wanted to text Seth again. Tell him that it had actually gone pretty well, and that he and Gabriel were solid again. That he wouldn't have to bail him out after all.

That he wanted to see him again.

And not when he stopped by to grab lunch with Lennox, but just the two of them.

He wanted more kisses.

He wanted a hell of a lot more than that.

"So, you going out with Seth again?" Gabe asked, like he knew exactly where Ren's thoughts had gone.

"Again? We haven't been out *once*," Ren objected. "And we're not really going out on a date. We're . . . keeping things casual."

"Oh, just fucking, then," Gabe teased. "I see you won that particular battle."

"Not just fucking either," Ren grumbled.

Gabe laughed. "You should see how annoyed you look. Like a wet cat. It must be fun to meet the one guy on earth who can resist you."

"Not as fun as you might think."

"Well," Gabe said, "I'm going to Sean's tonight, so if you wanted to invite him over . . ."

"You wouldn't complain about all the noise?" Ren said sweetly.

Gabe shot him a knowing look. "Oh, it's cute that you think I worry about noise anymore. I told you, those headphones block it all out. Best investment I ever made, considering I have you for a roommate. Though," he added thoughtfully, "if you've not figured out how to get him into bed yet, maybe it doesn't matter that you'll be alone."

"We'll see," Ren said.

He'd never failed to close the deal when he wanted to —and he *really* wanted to—and even worse, he knew just how much Seth wanted it, too.

He pulled out his phone. **Hey, good news. No bail money required. But I have another request.**

Please come over. Please touch me. I've been waiting for six months, and I'm the least patient person I know.

But he didn't say any of that because that was way too close to begging, and Ren had never begged for it in his whole damn life.

Seth was impressed; Lennox had waited a full morning and part of the afternoon before asking what he'd clearly wanted to ask from the first moment.

"So," he said, leaning back in his chair at the desk across the room, "I saw you and Ren leave the party together on Saturday night. And I didn't hear from you on Sunday."

Seth raised an eyebrow. "Is there a question in there?"

"Of course there is," Lennox said, shooting him a look. "What *happened?*"

"I didn't know we did this," Seth teased, because it was not only satisfying to see Lennox engaging in life this way—after he'd been injured and retired early, he'd been a shell of a man—but he'd have to be dead to not enjoy teasing his best friend. "The whole gossiping thing."

"Blame Ash," Lennox faux-grumbled, even though Seth had yet to see him blame Ash for *anything*.

"So you've got no interest in hearing the dirty details," Seth said. He picked up his phone. "I'll just tell Ash, then."

Lennox made a face. "You're terrible," he said. "I thought you'd be in here crowing first thing about finally winning Ren over, but you didn't even mention it."

"Nothing happened," Seth said, and it wasn't even a lie.

"So you took him home with you and you didn't sleep together?" Lennox sounded like he didn't quite believe it.

"Lorenzo isn't going to sleep with just anyone," Seth said. "He's very discerning."

"He'd have to be, to pick you," Lennox teased.

"He hasn't . . ." Seth paused. He *kinda* had though, hadn't he? He'd had every reason to be pissed as hell, after finding out that Seth had pretended to be someone else, but after calming down, he'd come back.

Not only had he come back to Seth's house, but he'd agreed to the compromise.

"I guess he did pick me," Seth said, hearing the shock in his own voice.

"Guess he did," Lennox pointed out smugly. "So, you gonna take him out? Win him over?"

"Can't," Seth said, and he did regret that. He wanted to treat Lorenzo *right*. Of course, who determined what that meant? As long as Ren understood how he felt about him, what did it matter if they went out to the kind of fancy restaurant that required Seth to put on a tie, or if they just hung out at his house and watched TV?

As long as Ren was happy, it didn't matter at all.

"Then, what's going on?"

"Ball's in his court right now. I told him we could take it more casually, so that's what I'm doing."

"You're going to make him work for you," Lennox said, sounding mystified. "How did you manage *that*?"

"I didn't do anything," Seth said. He hadn't. Not really. Nothing that should've worked, anyway.

"Well, congrats," Lennox said, standing and patting him on the back. "Welcome, the water's just fine over here."

"We aren't in *any* kind of water, yet," Seth said, suddenly worried that the gossip, which would undoubtedly run through the food truck lot like wildfire, would scare Ren away. Just when he'd convinced him that he could give in a little. "And don't tell Ash any differently, okay?"

Lennox shot him a freezing look. "Are you saying my boyfriend gossips?"

"Of course not, I would never say that," Seth said, rolling his eyes. "But it's just casual now. There's nothing to talk about."

"If you think that, you're blind," Lennox said with a chuckle. "Everyone's been talking about you two for ages."

"They're just bored," Seth said. "It'll pass."

"Naw. You two are kinda epic. It's like watching one of those movies on TV that Ash likes so much."

Seth's phone dinged, and it wasn't that there weren't lots of people who *could* text him, they just rarely did. The only person who'd been texting him today had been Ren.

Lennox grinned, and Seth realized that his face must have given him away. "See, I told you. *Epic*."

Hey, good news. No bail money required. But I have another request, Ren's text read.

Seth smiled, because he couldn't quite help himself.

I'm glad to hear it, but not surprised, Seth typed back. **What's the request?**

Ren's answer came in almost immediately. **Gabe is abandoning me for Sean, leaving me ALL ALONE tonight. You should come over and protect me.**

Seth: **Protect you from what?**

Ren: **Monsters under the bed, of course. And there might even be a few in the closet.**

Seth chuckled under his breath. He knew what Ren was asking, and why he wasn't just coming out and *asking* for it.

After all, he was the one who'd put the restrictions on whatever they were doing.

You want to hang out tonight? Or you want me to defend you against all the big scary monsters?

Seth felt excitement begin to creep up his spine. He knew exactly what Ren wanted. What he was hoping for.

And it wasn't like he didn't want to have sex. He *did*. Especially with Ren. But after six months of believing that he'd only get one chance—one night—with Ren, it was hard to adjust his thinking.

Ren himself had said that they were definitely going to be doing it more than once, and despite his previous lifestyle, Seth had never assumed he was fickle. Ren would make a decision and stick to it.

Maybe he should just let Ren seduce him. It would be fun. It would be undeniably very good. They'd both enjoy themselves a lot.

But what if the tension between them was what kept Ren interested, and once that was gone, his interest faded along with it?

It wasn't logical, but then not much with the heart—or a guy's dick—was.

Ren's answer was straightforward enough. Just like the man himself.

I don't know if you can protect me against the monsters underneath the bed if you're not IN my bed.

Touche, Seth replied, **but why don't we start with the monsters under the couch and we'll go from there?**

Ren: **I suppose I could be persuaded to start there.**

Seth: **I can be pretty persuasive.**

Ren: **Isn't it supposed to be me persuading you?**

Seth: **Maybe we can persuade each other.**

Ren: **I like the sound of that.**

Seth: **Your place, then?**

Ren: **You know where it's at?**

Seth: **Had your phone number, didn't I?**

Ren: **You're a regular creeper, aren't you? Do you know my address, too?**

Seth chuckled under his breath. **No. Just a completist. I'll ask Lennox for your address. You live with Gabe right? He picked up Gabe once.**

Ren: **Pragmatism should not be this sexy. You could patent this and sell it as an aphrodisiac.**

Seth: **Somehow I doubt we're going to need any aphrodisiacs.**

In fact, Seth was already pretty sure that it was going to be hard as hell to resist Ren tonight. He could always change his mind. Or maybe his dick would take one look at Lorenzo, and decide for him.

But Seth was already pretty sure that he could resist most of what Ren might throw at him. Especially if it meant that he could have Ren for more than just one night.

Maybe for forever.

Ren: **You're right. But yes, I do live with Gabe. Except, BIG REMINDER, he will not be around tonight.**

Seth rubbed a hand over his face.

He won't have to use his special noise-canceling headphones to block out our TV noise, then, Seth responded.

Ren replied back. **You're no fun. Maybe I'm gonna have to persuade you to indulge in a little fun.**

Seth wished he could sit here and text all day. But he had to finish proofing this second proposal, and get it off to the Star Shadow guys. They'd liked his first one, but they'd offered a few suggestions of their own, so he'd made changes.

I could do with a little fun, Seth texted back, **but I draw the line at a lot. Got to get back to work, so I can see you tonight.**

Ren's answer came in immediately. **8 PM sharp,** he texted, **and don't keep me waiting.**

CHAPTER NINE

"I DRAW THE LINE at a *lot* of fun," Ren muttered to himself as he got up off the couch at the knocking on the door, remembering Seth's message from earlier in the day. "Unbelievable."

He already knew that Seth was going to make him work for it.

He wasn't even particularly upset by that fact.

He could take it slow.

Theoretically.

The truth was, he just didn't want to. He'd had a taste, *finally*, and now he was primed and ready for more. He wanted Seth under him and on top of him and next to him, and in every single goddamn way that mattered.

If they had to pretend to watch a movie first, chastely sitting next to each other on the couch for two hours to get there, Ren was willing to do it.

He was a little afraid of just how much he *was* willing to do to get there.

Glancing over at the mirror next to the door, Ren gave himself a quick once-over.

His hair was perfect. His face . . . well, that was usually perfect by default. His plain white t-shirt didn't do anything to detract from it. He'd almost considered wearing his tightest, skinniest jeans, but at the last second, decided that while he *was* desperate, he didn't have to look that desperate.

Instead, he'd put on a pair of jeans with an ugly tear at the knee. They'd been a pair of his favorites, and he hadn't wanted to throw them out, so he'd kept them for quiet nights at home.

Just like this one.

And hey, maybe Seth had a secret kink for exposed knees.

He pulled open the door.

Seth was standing on his front stoop, wearing an olive-green utility jacket, and a pair of jeans. He *wasn't* hot. He just wasn't. Except no matter how many times Ren told himself that, that *zing* that went up his spine—excitement mixed with hope and attraction and a desperation to *know*—always happened anyway.

His fingers tightened on the edge of the door.

"Lorenzo," he said, drawling out his name so that it contained far more than the normal three syllables. "Good to see you."

"Come on in," Ren said, and couldn't help his intake of breath when Seth took a step forward, right into his personal space.

He'd assumed that he'd have to work all the magic he possessed to *eventually* get Seth naked tonight. Maybe

Seth was going to make it easy on him and they'd just get naked right away.

But then Seth stepped right around him, heading from the tiny foyer into the attached living room with its big, comfy couch.

"When are you going to start calling me Ren?" he asked as he followed him to the couch.

Seth shrugged off his jacket, laying it on the arm of the sofa, exposing his chiseled biceps, dotted with freckles.

Because like most redheads, he most definitely had freckles.

Ren had had too many fantasies about pressing his lips to each and every one.

"I like calling you Lorenzo," Seth said. He didn't sit, just stood there, looking at him with those soulful greenish-gray eyes. Ren could never figure out how eyes so cool could feel so warm when they fell on him.

"I hate it," Ren said. Not quite true—but he wasn't going to let Seth get away with it. Of course, he *was* letting him get away with it.

He'd let Seth get away with just about anything.

Except not having sex with him.

"Right," Seth said, and grinned.

Ren had had many men in his apartment to "hang out." But none of them had ever made his palms sweat with just a smile.

"Do you want something to drink?"

"Are you going to have something?" Seth wanted to know.

Ren hadn't really thought about it, but now that he did, maybe a beer wouldn't go amiss. He was nervous, or maybe just excited, and he wasn't used to feeling this way.

"I was going to have a beer. You want one?" Ren said, heading into the kitchen. He liked this loft particularly because all the gathering rooms flowed together—living room, kitchen, dining room. Only his bedroom and Gabe's and the bathroom were separate.

"Sure," Seth said, and Ren saw out of the corner of his eyes as he wiped his own palms on his jeans, as he finally settled down on the couch.

Not on one end. In the goddamn middle. So there was nowhere Ren could sit that wasn't *right* next to him.

Okay, Ren could get behind that.

He grabbed two beers, and after opening, carried them over, setting Seth's on the coffee table in front of him.

But Ren took a large gulp of his right away, before setting it on a coaster, and then settled onto the couch right next to Seth, their thighs brushing together.

He cleared his throat, forcing the tremble in his fingers to still. "You want to watch something?"

Seth smiled, slowly. "I'd like that."

Any other time, with any other guy, Ren would've leaned over and kissed him. Because they weren't here to watch anything other than him.

But Seth really wanted to *know* him. He wouldn't have pretended to be Jake if he didn't.

What if there was nothing for Seth to know? What if he was only a very pretty, but empty vessel? Good only for a night of pleasure, but nothing deeper?

Ren swallowed hard. He didn't really believe that. But it had been so long since he'd had to show anyone anything but the barest sketch of who he was.

What if Seth learned who he was and was disappointed?

"Did you have something in mind?" Ren asked.

"Why don't you put something on that *you* like?" Seth said. "You watch TV, right?"

"Of course I watch TV," Ren scoffed. He grabbed the remote and turned the TV on, switching to Netflix, clicking on his profile instead of Gabe's.

Except . . . then Seth neatly plucked the remote out of his hand before Ren could navigate to something innocuous.

Something that he wouldn't mind Seth seeing.

Like one of those fancy sports documentaries, or maybe even one of those high-brow dramas that he always meant to watch, and never made time for.

"What are you doing?" Ren demanded, trying to grab for the remote, but all he succeeded in doing was closing his fingers around air, and then falling forward, bracing a hand against Seth's chest.

Seth's very, *very* firm chest. Ren wouldn't mind taking some more time to explore just how firm it was, especially without his gray t-shirt on. Again, with any other guy, at any other point, Ren would have distracted him by leaning that last few inches in and pressing his mouth to Seth's.

But kissing, which had begun to feel a little rote and routine, didn't feel that way at all with Seth. It felt precious and hard-won, a promise he didn't want to treat lightly.

Ren didn't know what exactly he was promising, but it turned out that didn't matter.

"Oh, look at *this*," Seth crowed in delight, as he scrolled down, and then over, through Ren's recently watched list. "You like . . . romantic comedies?"

"*Good* romantic comedies," Ren said defensively, even though he knew there were plenty of people—even his cousin!—who would argue that there was no such thing.

When Ren glanced over at him, Seth's expression was amused, but it wasn't clear if he was laughing *at* Ren, or *with* him.

"I don't know the difference," Seth said. "Like what makes a good one? A bad one? An indifferent romantic comedy? Like this . . . what's the difference between *The Ugly Truth* and . . ." Seth glanced at the screen, reading one of the titles there. The last one Ren had watched, incidentally. "*Set it Up*?"

"A lot of things," Ren said between clenched teeth. Why hadn't he just browsed the cable TV, the channels they only kept so that Gabe could watch ESPN and make sure every time he ran into Chase Riley or Spencer Evans, he wouldn't embarrass himself?

No, he'd set himself up for this embarrassing revelation.

"Okay," Seth said, setting the remote down on the coffee table, like it was a peace offering. "I get you probably don't want to tell me."

"You think?" Ren retorted. This was exactly the kind of thing he'd been dreading. But then, if he and Jake had kept talking, he probably would have ended up confessing this particularly dirty secret.

He'd have trusted Jake with it.

He could trust Seth with it.

Taking a deep breath, Ren turned to him. "I know this is probably confusing."

"Confusing how?" And like Ren had hoped, there was no judgement in his eyes. Just curiosity. Like he wanted to know him. *Really* know him. Just like Jake had said he did. Just like *Seth* had said himself when Ren had figured out his deception.

"Well, I don't do relationships, right, and I watch all of these." Ren picked up the remote, and telling himself it was just like pulling a Band-Aid off, began to scroll. "That would confuse a lot of people."

"Lorenzo," Seth said, so patient and kind it kinda broke his heart. "I'm not most people. I know we're still getting to know each other, but you gotta know, that's never going to be me."

His fingers were trembling again, and he pressed them harder into the plastic of the remote. It probably had something to do with the emotion in Seth's eyes.

It seemed particularly silly that either of them had ever assumed they could just "hang out" with "no pressure," because it was *them*.

"Maybe you're not confused," Ren said, "but I want to say this, because I don't always understand it myself. But it . . . it feels good? I like to feel good. These movies, with their optimistic outlook and their makeover montages and the guaranteed happily ever after, they make me happy."

"Okay."

Ren sat there, anticipating more for a long moment, before he realized that there wasn't any more coming.

Maybe that was all that mattered to Seth: that he was happy.

"I haven't ever told anyone this before," Ren said, before he could stop himself. "You're the first."

"Were you going to tell me before I found out?"

"I would've told Jake," Ren said, before he could overthink and *not* mention the elephant in the room. "Not right away, maybe, but eventually. I liked—*like*—him, and I trust him."

The skin around Seth's eyes crinkled when he smiled. "Lucky for you," he said, leaning in, his tone warm and low, "he's here, right now."

"Yeah," Ren said, even though just a few days ago he'd claimed that the opposite was true, "yeah, I think he might be."

Now, Ren thought, *now he's going to kiss you. And it's going to be perfect, just like one of your favorite movies.*

He'd never wanted any of that for himself, before. This was a first. But then Seth was completely unlike any of those other guys. There was something about him—a solid steadfastness—that Ren had never felt before.

But Seth didn't lean in. Didn't kiss him.

Instead, he reached over, and cupped Ren's knee, his palm hot against the bare skin exposed by the tear in the fabric. Ren felt the skin-to-skin contact up and down, from the top of his head, down through his cock, and all the way to his toes.

"Why don't you pick your favorite?" Seth asked. "And you tell me why it's your favorite."

"Really? You want to watch one of these?" Ren told himself not to be skeptical, but he heard it in the tone of his voice anyway.

"Normally, I wouldn't care either way, but if you enjoy them . . ." Seth shrugged. "Makes me want to."

"Okay," Ren said, and before he could change his mind, clicked on the last one he'd watched.

"The difference," he said, as the credits began to play, "between a good romantic comedy and a bad one, is if it's in on the joke. It can't take itself too seriously."

"And this one doesn't?" Seth gestured at the screen.

"Nope," Ren said, and found himself smiling, unexpectedly. Actually excited to watch Seth watching one of his favorite movies.

"So," Seth said tossing a few kernels of popcorn into his mouth, "the terrible boss is a standard romantic comedy thing?"

Halfway through, right when Charlie and Harper had climbed up the fire escape with the pizza and Seth had laughed out loud, completely delighted by the hijinks on the screen, Ren had gotten them two more beers and had popped a couple of bags of popcorn. When he'd returned to the couch with their snacks, Seth's arm had naturally wound around his shoulders, and Ren, who had never been interested in cuddling a single day in his entire life, discovered he actually really enjoyed settling into the warm, cozy side of Seth's body.

"Yes, totally," Ren said. More thrilled than he probably should've been that not only had Seth *not* hated the movie, but had actually enjoyed it enough that he'd wanted to sit here after and discuss it with him.

"And the special joke is that they were both shitty bosses, right?" Seth asked.

"Exactly, though my favorite part is the way Harper plays goofy off Charlie's straight man. Plus they have just dynamite chemistry. You can't fake that, even with a good script. Like Billy Crystal and Meg Ryan? You *believe* that they're meant to be together because they make you feel it. Or when they tried to remake *Overboard*? How did they ever think they could get even close to the way Kurt Russell and Goldie Hawn clashed?"

Seth scrunched his nose. "I don't think I've ever seen that one. I thought I'd seen most of Kurt Russell's movies, but apparently not."

"A Kurt Russell fan, huh?" Ren teased, nudging Seth with an elbow. Seth just chuckled. "I bet he was responsible for your sexual awakening, wasn't he? Was Snake Plissken in all his post-apocalyptic glory the subject of your jerkoff fantasies?"

Seth laughed. "A little bit, yeah," he admitted.

"You'll like *Overboard*, then," Ren said. "We'll watch it next time."

"Next time, huh?" Seth said.

Ren glanced up at him, and felt pinned in place by the heat in his gaze. "Well, uh, I assumed . . ."

"That any man with sense and taste will take as much of you as they can get?" Seth chuckled. "You're not wrong."

"Even though I love romantic comedies and not . . . like serious dramas or silly sitcoms or important documentaries?"

Seth shrugged. "I don't want my idea of you, I want *you*."

Now, Ren thought, *now*, and nearly leaned over and did it himself.

But before he could, Seth removed his arm from Ren's shoulders and sat up.

Ren immediately felt the loss of his warmth—and something else that he couldn't quite name.

"It's late, we both work early," he said, standing up and stretching, exposing a tantalizing little glimpse of bare torso before it was gone again.

Ren had never felt so fucking teased in his whole life. Nobody had ever dared, that much was true.

"You're leaving?" Ren demanded, watching as he picked up his coat and then trailing after him as he walked towards the door. "Right now?"

Seth smiled, like he knew exactly what Ren was so affronted by, and goddamn him, he probably did. "I know you have to get up early. It's late."

"Yeah, I know it's late," Ren said, and pushed himself into Seth's space before he could put his coat on. "Does that really matter when we . . ." He swallowed hard. "When we . . ."

"Don't worry, Lorenzo, I wasn't going to leave without doing this," Seth said, and leaned down, and finally, *finally* kissed him.

It would've been a slow assault on Ren's defenses, except that Seth couldn't have known that Ren's defenses were completely gone already, and that he'd been thinking about it from the moment Seth had come over, over two hours ago.

Or that when their lips finally touched, Ren would feel himself going up in flames like a match touching bone-dry kindling.

He poured himself into the kiss, framing Seth's face, fingertips stroking the soft scruff of his beard, tongue stroking in and out of Seth's mouth, until it felt like he could feel the beat of his pulse in his head and his heart and definitely everywhere else.

"Goddamn it," Seth muttered savagely, and then Ren found himself pushed against the door, and this time it was Seth losing himself to the fierce power of it, grinding their hips together with a fluidity and a confidence that left Ren weak-kneed and his cock as hard as it had ever been in his entire life.

This was the passion he'd known was buried inside all that easy, casual frankness—the complicated fire that burned deep inside Seth that he hid from the world.

Except he couldn't hide it from Ren anymore. Ren had always seen it and now he could finally *feel* it.

Seth slid a hand down his back, and right over the curve of his ass, biting down on his bottom lip hard enough to draw blood, and *oh*, that was both unexpected and unbelievably sexy that he could get rough when he got riled up.

Because Ren intended to rile him up plenty.

But before he could, suddenly he was gone.

For a single second, full of blind hope, Ren believed that he'd be back and maybe he'd be naked, but when he finally gave up on *that* and opened up his eyes, there was a wry tilt to Seth's red, swollen lips and he was unfortunately still completely clothed.

What was it going to take for Ren to get this man *naked?*

"I . . ." Seth flicked out his tongue and tasted the blood on his bottom lip. Okay, they'd both gotten a little rough. But there was only so much teasing and tantalizing that Ren could take. Not when he knew exactly what he wanted. "I suppose that was inevitable, wasn't it?"

"A long time coming," Ren agreed. Already knowing—and hating—that in a minute, Seth was going to be leaving out the front door.

Without Ren.

It was infuriating and frustrating and Ren *almost* respected the guy for his determination.

But nobody was more determined than Ren when there was something he wanted.

"I can't even say I regret it." Seth's voice was low and rough. "Only how hard it's going to be to leave, now."

"Then, don't." Ren stayed pressed against the door. Knowing that if he reached for Seth again and he still walked away, his pride would definitely be stung.

But he knew how he looked. Cock hard against the zipper of his jeans, hair mussed, lips red and wet from Seth's own.

Not many men could leave him like this, only partially debauched.

But the fact that Seth could?

Definitely a good *and* a bad thing.

Because when he gave in, finally, it was going to be the best sex of Ren's life.

He already knew it.

And that sharpened the edge of anticipation even keener.

"You know I should, that I have to," Seth said. At least he sounded as regretful as Ren felt—and as horny, too.

"Yeah, but I wouldn't be me if I didn't try to convince you to stay," Ren said.

Seth laughed. "Don't worry," he said, reaching for him, and to Ren's surprise, pulling him into a surprisingly tight hug. A *sweet* hug. A hug that Ren enjoyed almost as much as the hot-as-fuck make-out session against the door. "Don't worry, you made it plenty tough on me."

"Thanks, I think?"

Seth let him go, and this time Ren didn't try to stop him as he shrugged on his coat, and unlocked the door.

"I'll talk to you tomorrow?" Ren asked. Hearing the hope in his own voice.

"Absolutely," Seth said, and even though he was halfway out the door, he leaned in and gave Ren one more taste of what he wasn't going to be getting tonight.

The kiss was short and fierce and like Seth's hug, surprisingly sweet.

Like it wasn't just a goodbye, but a hello, too.

It was only a short walk home from Ren's loft, but to work off all the sexual energy they'd generated together, Seth knew nothing else would do but a hard, punishing run.

You could just go back there and tell him you changed your mind, his brain supplied unhelpfully. *Pin him to the door again and kiss him until neither of you can stand up.*

He could—and it was inevitable that he *would*, at some point.

When it felt right, he added, thinking as he walked down the street that he ironically sounded a lot like one of Ren's romantic comedies.

His phone buzzed in his pocket, and he pulled it out, glancing at the screen. It could be Lennox—checking in to see how their "hangout" went—or it could be Ren.

Seth knew he was falling in deep by just how much he'd wanted it to be Ren.

And here I thought, the message read, **that I was the biggest cocktease on the planet.**

Accompanying the text was a picture that made Seth—with his ironclad nerves—nearly fumble the phone and come to a complete stop in the middle of the sidewalk.

It was a selfie, with Ren lying, shirtless, in bed, his olive-toned skin glowing with the dim light against the white of his sheets.

It could've been a happy accident that the photo cut off right where Seth wanted to see most—right where the sparse trail of dark hair started right under his belly button, a punctuation in his toned stomach—but Seth knew it wasn't.

The message though truncated, was clear enough.

Seth bit his bottom lip, tasting blood again.

Because it wasn't the expanse of skin that had him so tempted. No, it was the look in Ren's dark eyes, the fucking *yearning* in them.

What was he doing, turning away from that?

He hesitated, almost deciding to go back.

If anyone was going to get Lorenzo Moretti off tonight, it was definitely going to be him.

And yet, Seth thought of the way he'd opened up to him, even if he hadn't exactly wanted to at the beginning. If they'd spent the evening in bed, he might know what made Ren moan and then scream, but he didn't think he'd have learned what made Ren *happy*.

Maybe, eventually, when they finally burnt the sexual energy out of their bodies, but with how all-consuming it felt, Seth wasn't sure they'd be getting there anytime soon.

No, he decided, no matter how impossible it felt, it was right to wait.

Until the time felt right.

Still, his fingers shook as he texted Ren back.

It was looking at that goddamn picture—it was like looking at the thing he wanted to see for the rest of his life.

Somehow I doubt there's any more teasing happening.

Ren didn't answer right away, and by the time Seth reached his house, he was a shaking, horny mess.

It wasn't like Seth didn't objectively know that Ren got himself off.

But he was doing it *right fucking now*, and it took all the self-control Seth had not to turn around and go help him.

He typed in the wrong code to the front door twice, and then took a deep breath, and finally got it right, shutting it behind him with a pained exhale.

Shedding his jacket and then his shirt as he moved through his house, he barely made it to the edge of his bedroom, bracing himself against the doorframe, before he was unzipping his pants, groaning as he palmed his cock.

Just the pressure of his hand where he needed it so badly was enough to send a pulse of pleasure zinging through him.

Seth's head thumped back against the doorframe, and he finally let his mind go.

Ren . . . lying in his bed.

Ren . . . laughing.

Ren . . . kissing him.

Ren . . . touching him with those dark eyes, full of lust and passion and affection.

It might have been embarrassing how quickly it took, with the right motivation, for Seth to hit the edge, his hand working his cock in slow insistent pulls as he imagined that it wasn't his hand at all that was tugging him inexorably towards orgasm.

Then his phone dinged again, and he fumbled with the hand that wasn't occupied, and the picture—just the fucking picture—that Ren sent, was enough to send him right over.

Ren lay in bed, in the same position as before, but now his eyes drooped, sleepy with satisfaction, and oh yeah, there was definitely come splattered up his chest.

A text came in right after it, right as Seth was hovering right on the cusp of coming his brains out, and he absolutely shouldn't have come that hard from just a message.

But it was Ren—so much fucking Ren—condensed into one sentence.

In case you need some extra motivation, he said.

Lights flashed behind Seth's eyes, and the phone dropped to the ground as he shuddered through his orgasm.

It wasn't quite the afterglow he'd have experienced with Ren, lying in that bed with him, but Seth made himself clean up anyway, throwing on a pair of loose pajama pants. He picked up his phone and it wasn't hard to figure out exactly what he wanted to say in return.

Next time, he typed, **we do that together.**

Oh, Ren replied instantly, **you want me to come over tomorrow morning? Show up in your bed, while you're still half-asleep? Or join you in the shower?**

Ren . . . wet and slick . . . pressed up against the tiles . . . oh, Seth liked that idea a lot, and he had every intention of fulfilling the fantasy sooner rather than later.

A little horny? he teased.

Oh, nothing about it is little, Ren texted back.

Seth's head hit the pillow. He couldn't figure out if he wanted to wring Ren's neck for being such a goddamn tease, or smile.

Maybe both.

CHAPTER TEN

"HERE I THOUGHT," GABE said when Ren climbed into the truck, carrying two coffees in his hands, "that you'd not only be late, but you'd be *really* late."

"I don't know why you thought that," Ren grumbled, though he knew exactly why Gabriel thought he'd be late today. No doubt Gabe believed that with Ren alone at their loft, Seth would've stayed over.

"Maybe because you haven't ever failed to close the deal before," Gabe teased lightly, taking the coffee Ren offered.

"I closed it," Ren said. "Just not . . . just not like normal."

Next time we do that together.

"Oh? And how is the 'new normal'?"

"Ugh," Ren groaned, pulling on his apron. "Different. Less orgasms than I signed up for. But not . . . not bad. Not exactly."

"Look at you, growing as a person," Gabe said, smacking him on the shoulder. "Truly, I'm proud."

"I hate you," Ren grumbled.

"No, you don't," Gabe retorted cheerfully. "Not even a little bit."

"I hate you even more when you're right," Ren pointed out.

"Exactly. Now, you wanna get started on meatball prep? Or you wanna finish the sauce?" Gabe gestured to where he was stirring the beginnings of their nonna's famous red sauce.

"You're already there," Ren said, heading to the big coolers in the back, filling the enormous metal bowl in his hands with ingredients for their standard meatballs that they used in just about everything.

Ren unpackaged the meatball mix that one of the local butchers ground for them specifically, a combination of beef, pork, and veal. Then, he grabbed a handful of leftover rolls from the day before that he'd specifically left out to get stale, and setting them in a smaller bowl, soaked them with milk.

He was elbow deep in mixing the now wet bread together with an entire crate of eggs when a knock sounded on the front of the truck, where the window was still shut.

"It's early," Gabe said, shaking his head, "who wants a sandwich this early? We're not even open yet."

"Then tell them to fuck off. Nicely, of course," Ren said, mushing together the bread with the eggs. Nonna had always taught him that cooking wasn't a clean task, and at the very beginning, when he'd been young, doing this with his hands had always weirded him out. But now he was used to it, even enjoyed doing it.

Everyone who ate here ate something he prepared with his own two hands. With so much processed, mechanized crap out there today, there was something very satisfying in doing things by hand.

Nonna would be proud that they'd resisted changing anything about her recipe.

"Fine," Gabe grumbled, setting the wooden spoon on the edge of the pot, and instead of opening the window, went out the back door.

A moment later, he stuck his head back inside the truck. "You'd better come out here," Gabe said. They were ominous words, but at least Gabe looked thoughtful instead of upset. So at least, Ren thought, it wasn't *bad*. Not like when Ross' ex-partner had vandalized the trucks at the lot, and then tried to burn it all down by blowing up Ash's truck.

"Give me a sec," Ren said, scraping the bread and egg mixture off his fingers. Once most of it was in the bowl, he headed to the sink, and took his time scrubbing it all off.

Drying his hands on his apron, he picked up his coffee and headed down the stairs, and around the front of the truck. Gabe was standing there with a tall, dark-haired guy in sunglasses and a pair of jeans and a black button-up that looked expensive, like they'd both been tailored to fit him.

He was a good-looking guy, but maybe a little too curated, a little too perfect.

Ren shoved one hand into his pocket and approached.

"There he is," Gabe said, turning towards Ren. His voice had way too much forced cheerfulness in it. Were they getting sued? Was this a lawyer?

He kinda *looked* like a lawyer.

"You must be Lorenzo Moretti," the guy said, extending a hand.

"Ren," Ren said, shaking it.

"Jonas Anderson."

From the over-styled hair to the unyielding handshake, there was no fucking way that this guy wasn't a lawyer.

"Jonas here is opening another food truck lot," Gabe said, tossing Ren a knowing look as they went to sit at the nearest picnic table. "He wants to offer for us to come over to the dark side."

"Oh, it's not *very* dark," Jonas said with a laugh that sounded just a hair too practiced.

Ash had said this guy was a mirror image of Tony—all sheer hustle—and Ren could totally see it.

If the two of them ever met up, and that seemed to be inevitable, because of the way that Jonas kept going after all of Tony's food trucks (and Tony's *friends*), the universe might just implode.

"What is it, then?" Gabe asked, leaning forward, and looking more genuinely interested than Ren had imagined he would be.

After all, they'd known this was probably coming, but Ren had never guessed that either of them would even seriously consider Jonas' offer.

He wanted to tell Gabe that he hadn't needed to interrupt his meatball prep by bringing him out here, that he could've said no just as easily by himself, but maybe . . . *no*, there was no way that Gabe would ever voluntarily leave Tony. Or his boyfriend.

"It's a fantastic opportunity to grow and change your business. For *expansion*."

Jonas was clearly drinking his own Kool-Aid, because his expression was full of excitement. For himself, certainly. But also . . . well, it wasn't *only* excitement for himself.

If he was a shade more altruistic, this would be exactly the pitch that Tony had given them, a year and a half ago.

"I don't know if we're in the market for that kind of expansion," Ren inserted smoothly, trying to stay nice. Maybe they'd need a lawyer someday, because someone tried to sue them over an overcooked meatball or something.

Ren tried to make a habit of never pissing off anybody with money.

Luca, Gabriel's brother, was the sole exception to this policy. Ren lived to make Luca's life a living hell.

"I'm not sure *what* market we're in," Gabe announced.

Ren rolled his eyes. Tony was absolutely going to kill him, and Ren was thinking he wasn't planning on stopping him.

"Well, let me tell you more," Jonas said. He'd caught the whiff of interest in Gabe's voice and his excitement had tripled in the last thirty seconds. "We're going to have a very diverse lineup of trucks . . ."

"All poached from Food Truck Warriors, apparently," Ren interrupted with a wry tone.

"Not *all* of the trucks I've approached are from this lot," Jonas said reproachfully. "And that word . . . *poached*, it's so ugly, isn't it?"

"Or honest," Ren grumbled under his breath.

"A *very* diverse lineup of trucks with the highest culinary pedigrees," Jonas continued like he hadn't just been interrupted. "I'm also gathering together an exceptional marketing team, and putting a lot of money into both marketing *and* advertising. Which . . . nobody is doing here, not at all." Jonas looked particularly smug at this revelation. Ren could just imagine him facing off with Tony. He hoped that when it happened, he didn't miss it. Someone enterprising could probably sell tickets to the inevitable confrontation.

"We do some events," Ren pointed out, wondering how the hell he'd come around to defending Tony, "and of course, everyone here has a strong social media following."

"Of course you do, but you're *busy*," Jonas said, fanaticism glowing in his blue eyes. "If you're paying rent to park at a lot, they should be doing more work *for* you."

Ren rolled his eyes. Didn't even try to hide it.

"You talk to Tony Blake about any of this?" he asked.

"We haven't spoken, but we don't need to," Jonas said with certainty. "His lot doesn't have anything to do with mine."

"Somehow I doubt that," Ren muttered.

"Tell me more about what kind of events you'll be hosting," Gabe said. "We get a nice big crowd on nights with music. The trick to a really successful truck is to not just get the lunch crowd but the dinner *and* the late-night crowd. I can't tell you how many meatball sandwiches we sell to drunk twenty-four-year-olds."

Ren stood by his earlier statement: he absolutely hated Gabe even more when he was right.

"Of course, of course, well, right now we're still in the planning stages, but we'll have a full lineup on the weekends. And the marketing team has been tossing around some brunch ideas."

"Brunch?" Gabe perked up. He loved brunch. It was like Jonas here was speaking his magical language.

"We don't serve brunch," Ren reminded his cousin.

"But you *could*," Jonas said. "Think of the diversification!"

"You ever work in a restaurant or a food truck? A Dairy Queen? A Subway, even?" Ren asked Jonas.

"No, no, I'm a corporate lawyer by trade . . ."

Ren burst out laughing, and Gabe glared at him.

"Lawyers do need to eat," Gabe said.

"Yes, we do, which is why I'm wanting to do something like this. I'm looking to be . . . less of a lawyer, and more of a business owner. I really admire this place, but I think it could be even better. Better run. Better organized. Better advertised."

Oh geez.

Fuck someone else selling tickets.

Ren was going to do it himself.

"An ambitious man," Gabe said, nodding with approval.

"Is there anything else?" Ren complained. "I have prep to do."

"Let me give you my card," Jonas said, flashing his Rolex, tucked just under the cuff of his custom-tailored shirt as he pulled out one of his embossed cards. "Let me know if you'd like to sit down and discuss more specifics."

"Sure, will do," Gabe said, and went through the whole charade of shaking Jonas' hand again, while Ren had already stood up and was walking back to the truck.

Ren barely waited until the back door was shut before he said, as pleasantly as he could, "What the fuck was that about?"

"What do you mean?" Gabe said, staring at the card in his hands like it held the solution for world peace.

"I mean, why didn't you just tell him to fuck off?" Ren said, returning to his bread and milk and egg mixture, which, because he'd had to spend all that time listening to the lawyer-turned-food truck conglomerate bloviating about how great he was, had become over-soft.

He'd add a bit more bread, Ren decided, poking at it. That might help.

"That seems kind of short-sighted," Gabe said with a sigh. "You didn't like him?"

"Do I like Tony?"

"Most days I think you tolerate him?"

"Exactly," Ren said, tearing up another stale bun into small pieces, tossing them into the bowl and beginning to mash them up. "That Jonas guy was barely tolerable even for five minutes. He's smoking too much of his own Kool-Aid."

"Isn't the metaphor *drinking* the Kool-Aid?" Gabe asked with a chuckle, stirring the sauce on the stove.

"Yeah, but not for that guy. He totally would snort it or smoke it or something weird. Just like Tony."

Gabe laughed. "Yeah, I can see that. But seriously, it's a good offer. I'm sure Tony would be angry but . . . I wasn't thinking of leaving here. I was thinking, business is good. Why shouldn't we expand?"

Ren hadn't even considered that, and when he did, he wanted to throw the whole bowl of gloppy bread-milk-eggs at his cousin. "You're serious? You want to split up?"

"I don't *want* to," Gabe said with a shrug, "but we should talk about it. This would be a good way to do it."

"No," Ren said.

"No, like *no this wouldn't be a good way to do it* or *no way, you're cracked*?" Gabe asked.

"You already know the answer. I don't want to split up. I don't care if we could start a whole fucking empire, like your brother."

Gabe chuckled under his breath. "Okay, okay, I get it. No Luca-like aspirations for you, huh?"

"Listen"—Ren turned to him, just so Gabe knew he was one hundred percent deadly serious—"I know the world tells you that you should always be reaching for more, that settling for something that *just* makes you happy is wrong, but it's not."

Gabe settled against the counter, crossing his arms over his chest. "What about Shaw? He opened the new bar."

"And that was right for him. But this isn't right for us."

"You're sure about this?"

"Have you ever known me to not be sure about something?" Ren asked as he poured his gloppy mixture into the ground meat. It was true; he was by far the more decisive of the two of them.

"Yeah." Gabe uncurled himself so he could stir the sauce again. "About Seth. But not about business. Not about the truck. When I told you I was thinking about leaving Napa and starting it, you said, *when can we leave*? And you pushed me to change the name way before I ever did. In fact," Gabe said, huffing with laughter, "you're the one who came up with the new name."

"Yep, I did." Ren ignored the part where Gabe had said he'd been indecisive about Seth. He wasn't, was he? No, he'd just wanted the man on *his* terms. That wasn't being indecisive. That was being the *most* decisive.

"I just don't want us to close ourselves off to the possibilities," Gabe said. "So, think about it, okay?"

"Ugh, I don't need to think about it," Ren said. And then suddenly it occurred to him that maybe *he* was sure, but Gabe wasn't.

Did Gabe want to split up?

Ren opened his mouth to ask and then snapped it shut again, and instead of saying anything else, he attacked the meatball mixture in the bowl.

He didn't like questions he was afraid to hear the answer to.

Now there was this one about Gabe, but last night, he'd wondered, as he lay in bed, unable to sleep even after his orgasm, and overthinking how the evening had gone, that maybe the reason why Seth was reticent to sleep with him was because it *could* be easy for him.

He'd still been picky about guys—he only slept with guys he *wanted* to sleep with—but if he'd wanted someone, he'd never hesitated.

Was that why Seth kept pulling away even though it was clear he wanted Ren as much as Ren wanted him?

Ren folded in a whole bunch of chopped parsley, as well as finely diced onion, into his meat mixture, and began to form balls, hands moving quickly as he laid them out on large trays for storage.

But as fast as his hands moved, his brain was moving even faster.

And he didn't like any of the conclusions he was afraid to jump to.

Where are you at?

The message came through just as Seth parked his car on the street, home from another consult with Diego and Benji, the Star Shadow guys. He'd been planning on going for a run after, and had already told Lennox, as he'd driven home, that he wouldn't be back in the office.

He'd thought he'd take a nice, long run, try to work off some of his sexual frustration—it definitely didn't help that it was self-imposed—and then wander over to the food truck lot for dinner. Maybe see if he could convince Ren to hang out again.

That had felt more casual than texting him today and making official plans.

Official plans to have sex, he reminded himself. *If anything deserves the word official, it's finally getting Ren into bed.*

But it had felt weird for Seth to text Ren and ask, **Tonight?** So he hadn't.

Seth hadn't anticipated that Ren would text him and ask him where he was right at this moment.

Just got home, he typed back once he'd let himself into the house, and headed back to his bedroom to change. **What's up?**

A minute later, there was a knock on the front door. Seth, who'd just pulled off his t-shirt, considered putting it back on, but then as he was trying to decide, the person knocked again, more insistently.

"Fine," Seth grumbled, and headed towards the front door, shirtless.

He pulled it open, and Ren was standing on the porch, looking impatient.

"Hi?" Seth said, surprised to see him. *Good* surprised, yes, but still surprised.

This was a Ren on a mission, though, not interested in small talk, though Seth could feel his appraising, admiring glance at his bare chest as he walked in.

He turned around in the living room, and Seth waited a moment, because there was a determination shining in his eyes. He was here for a reason.

And not for what you think, Seth told his cock, because it now just automatically perked up whenever Ren was around. Half in hope, probably, and half in despair that it would never happen.

"Are you not sleeping with me because I've slept with a lot of guys?" Ren demanded.

That was not the question that Seth had expected Ren to ask—though he hadn't really been sure *what* Ren was here for.

"What?"

"Are you not sleeping with me," Ren repeated, slower, enunciating each word carefully, like he did not want Seth to mistake his meaning even one iota, "because I've slept with a lot of guys?"

"No? I don't . . . I don't care what you've done," Seth said, a little bewildered. "I just wanted to wait til it felt right. I was a little concerned, I guess, because once all this tension was gone, you might not . . ." It was hard to admit this, and harder still to admit it when Ren was looking at him like that. "You might not want me anymore."

"Oh." The wind went right out of Ren's sails and he abruptly sat down on the couch. "Sorry. I just . . . I didn't think that, not really, but . . ."

"But," Seth prompted, going to join Ren on the couch. He put a hand on his knee, and squeezed gently.

"It's not really about you," Ren confessed. "Well, it *was*. I did worry about that, a little last night, but I didn't think so, because it's never exactly dissuaded you from pursuing me before."

"Nope," Seth agreed. "Not one bit. Your past is what it says on the tin: *past*."

"Right, okay, well . . ." Ren sighed. Looked a little embarrassed. "It wasn't really about you. This guy came to see Gabe and me today and made me . . . well, he made me question things."

"Question what? And what guy?"

Ren chuckled. "Don't worry, he's no competition."

"I wasn't . . ." Seth protested, but Ren just grinned.

"Yeah, you were. But it's okay. I . . . I get it."

Seth squeezed his knee again. "Alright. So tell me what happened."

"The guy is Jonas Anderson. He's opening a food truck lot a few blocks away from Food Truck Warriors, and he's been trying to recruit some of the food trucks to join his lot."

Seth raised an eyebrow. "What does Tony have to say about that?"

"I'm not sure Tony knows yet," Ren said wryly. "But, here's the thing: he's like a Tony *clone.* A corporate lawyer, so he didn't grow up in restaurants like Tony did, and he's trying really hard to be all casual even though he's so curated it's *painful.* But that same earnest attitude, *I can do it better than anyone else*, and I *know* better than anyone else, that he absolutely shares with Tony."

"And he wants you and Gabe to jump ship and join him?"

"Yep, and I was totally expecting Gabe to tell him to fuck off, we're happy where we are—because I thought we *were*—but Gabe listened. Actually took the guy's card. Then told me that maybe we should consider expanding."

Ren's voice grew bitter towards the end, especially on the last word, like he couldn't quite bear to hold it in his mouth.

"You mean, splitting up," Seth said softly.

"He didn't see it that way, but yes," Ren said.

"And you don't want to?" Seth asked, even though he already knew. He'd done some long assignments in San Diego, which had taken him away from Lennox and their base of operations here in Los Angeles, but after the last one, he'd told Lennox that even though it paid well, he didn't want to spend so much time away from home again.

They'd let the client go, even though they'd paid well.

Because Los Angeles and frankly, *Lennox*, they were home to Seth.

He'd been looking for a family since he'd joined the Navy—even though he still spoke to his mom occasionally, it was never the same—and he'd found it.

And then he'd found an extended one in the food truck guys.

"Of course I don't want to," Ren said. "We're . . . we're a team. I don't want to be *two* teams. It's already hard enough now that Gabe has Sean. It was just the two of us for so long, and don't get me wrong, I'm thrilled that he's happy, that they're happy together but it's . . . it's not the same."

"Sometimes even a good change, it hurts a little." Like when Seth's mom had met and married Andrew. She'd finally settled into a good life, but by that point, it was too late for Seth.

"Yeah. I don't even like going into the Funky Cup now, and seeing Bryan bartending, and not Shaw. It's not right.

I *know* I can go down to the Fickle Cup and see Shaw anytime I want, but it's the change of it."

"And you guys splitting up, that would be a huge change."

Ren's eyes pleaded with Seth. "You get it, right? And then I thought, what if Gabe really *wants* that?"

"You think him taking Jonas' card and not telling him to fuck off means that he wants you two to split up? Start another truck?" Personally, Seth thought there was no way that Gabe actually wanted that—the two of them were thick as thieves, more than family, but Seth understood the fear.

He'd felt the same, when he'd finally left the Navy. Would he lose this family that he'd worked so hard to find and to build?

For over a year, he'd been at loose ends—worse than that, really—but then Lennox had gotten out, too, and then they'd had each other.

No matter what happened to them, they would always have each other.

"No, that's the worst part. I think he's trying to be nice, but it made me *think* about it, and I don't want to think about it. I want to know the answer and then move on. I was fucking afraid to hear the answer." Punctuating his frustration, Ren stood up and began to pace in front of the couch. "And then I thought about *you* and how I was worried that you didn't want me because of well . . . *me*, and it wasn't a fun morning *or* afternoon."

"You stewed about it."

Ren turned to face him, gratitude written all over his face. "Yeah," he said, "yeah, I did."

"I can't speak for Gabe, but I don't think he wants you gone," Seth said, "and as for me, I definitely do not give a shit if you slept with every single guy you ever met."

"I didn't, just so you know." Ren looked hesitant again. "I wasn't like . . . all over *everybody*."

"I know," Seth said calmly. He'd expected this conversation at some point. Hadn't expected it today, but maybe it was good to clear the air, before they did actually sleep together.

And they were going to.

He wasn't afraid anymore. There was no way Ren was going to sleep with him and then tell him to fuck off. He knew it, deep down, in a place where everything was certain.

"Ugh," Ren said, collapsing on the couch next to him. "Why are you so great?"

Seth smiled, feeling the words echoing deep down. "I don't know, why am I so great?"

"When we met, I did not expect that you would be so easy to talk to," Ren said, and suddenly he was *right* there, pressed against Seth's side, his hand resting on his bare chest. "Or that I would want to *talk* to you."

Seth couldn't stop his heart from beating a little faster. If Ren felt it, so be it. It wasn't like he was holding back—not anymore. "What did you think you wanted to do with me?" he asked.

Ren's eyes glowed. "This," he said, and leaned in, fitting their mouths together.

Ren kissed him deeply, and this time Seth let go and kissed him back, just as passionately, tugging him closer and then closer still, reaching down and tugging his t-shirt off.

Bare skin collided with bare skin, and Seth didn't know if it was him groaning or Ren, but it didn't matter. Ren's fingers trailed over his arms, gripping his biceps, before moving down lower, between them, sliding down his stomach. It felt so goddamned good to be touched—and even better that it was Ren touching him. But just when Ren got to the button on his jeans, he pulled back, mouth red and wet and swollen.

He looked like a fucking masterpiece.

And he was all Seth's.

"Point of no return," Ren teased, a single fingertip tracing a pattern over the hard ridge of his cock, still trapped in his jeans. "You ready?"

"Not like this," Seth said, barely grasping at his own self-control. "Not on the couch."

Ren raised an eyebrow. "Why not on the couch? We're here?" He patted one of the cushions. "And it's plenty comfy. Frankly, we've waited . . ."

Seth didn't let him finish his sentence, instead pulling to the side and then scooping Ren into his arms. He wasn't light—but Seth was used to carrying much heavier weight than him, and it was only a few steps to the bedroom.

"Oomph," Ren said, as Seth carried him. "I didn't expect that." His gaze was sly and warm. "But maybe I should've?"

"Expect the unexpected," Seth teased and set him on the edge of the bed.

Ren slipped off his shoes and Seth did the same, and then they collided again, kissing ravenously, their mouths moving together like they'd been doing this for a hundred years instead of just a handful of times.

He could keep kissing forever, because it was just that good, the best he'd ever had in his thirty-seven years, but they'd waited long enough.

Epic, Lennox had called them, and Seth could feel it, in every touch of Ren's, in the throb of his cock as he knelt lower, to tug Ren's jeans off.

Ren groaned as Seth pulled off his jeans. His cock was hard and straining against the fabric of his black briefs. He looked . . . well, Seth thought if he looked right at him, he might lose the remainder of his self-control and he wanted this to be good. Not just good. Fantastic. Wonderful. Earth-shaking. He'd been thinking about it for far too long for it to be anything less.

"Let me," Seth murmured as he tilted his head down, kissing the ridges of Ren's ab muscles, letting his tongue drift down lower and lower, his fingers pulling down his briefs the rest of the way.

Just like the rest of Ren, his cock was gorgeous. Thick and full and so hard, *for him*. Seth didn't think that sight would ever get old.

When he leaned down and licked a stripe up it, he moaned a little at how good he tasted. That would definitely not get old, either.

Or that apparently Ren was a babbler in bed.

"Please, God, *please*," Ren begged. "Please, please, *please*."

If he'd known that Ren would be this hot and sweet in bed, he'd have never been able to resist, even six months ago.

He let more of Ren's cock slide into his mouth, and tongued the head, loving the way that Ren let loose another string of nonsense pleading.

Learning someone new—what they liked, what they didn't, what really got them going—was always an adventure, but with Ren, Seth really wanted to dig in and settle down, and frankly, never, ever leave.

After another long, lingering suck, he stood, his knees aching a bit in a way that felt unexpectedly satisfying, and slid a hand under Ren, pushing him back further on the bed.

"What?" Ren asked, pleasure fading from his eyes. Which, as far as Seth was concerned, would never do. He leaned over, and gave himself over to giving Ren as much pleasure as he could stand.

He wanted him babbling and incoherent, right on the edge of coming for ages, he wanted him to absolutely fucking lose it when he came.

Ren was in absolute fucking heaven.

Seth was as good as he'd ever imagined, insistent and skilled. Every touch felt like lightning trapped in a bottle, fizzing just under his bare skin.

Just the kissing on the couch had been so goddamned good, and then Seth had shocked and pleased him by picking him up and just *carrying* him into the bedroom.

He'd never expected that. Never thought he wanted it either, but his heart rate had accelerated even more when Seth had done it—and like Ren weighed nothing at all.

And then there was the way he was sucking him down, deep and insistent, like he intended to make Ren lose it. Which he was . . . if only because it felt so good.

Seth slid a hand under Ren's ass and squeezed, trailing his fingers forward, and cupping his balls. Ren arched under his hands, and groaned, unable to keep the sound in a minute longer.

Normally he gave more than he took, and he worried about how the whole choreography of sex would go. Wanted to make sure it was incredible for everyone. But everything happening in this bed felt right and good and Ren found himself letting go of the worries more than he'd thought he would.

Seth sucked him a little deeper, a little harder, tongue wrapping around the head of his cock, the pleasure of it shooting up his spine until he thrashed on the bed.

Ren squeezed his eyes shut, bracing against it, not wanting to come yet. It was so good, he wanted just a little bit more.

Then, like Seth was reading his mind, he slid a finger up higher, pressing it against his hole, just tracing the edges of it and making him shiver.

"Oh, God, *yes*," Ren babbled.

Like he'd been waiting for permission, Seth pushed in slightly, sucking him deep and hard, the thrill of it building through Ren's body.

He heard rather than saw Seth fumble around in a drawer in the nightstand, and then his finger was pressing in, slicker than before, and he was fucking it in and out in a maddening rhythm, just off from his own deep sucks.

It felt fucking great, and then, suddenly, that was an understatement, because a second finger slid in next to the first and Seth pressed against that spot, the one that always made him see stars. Except today he wasn't seeing stars—he was seeing a whole fucking galaxy.

He wasn't sure, with all that pleasure rocketing through him, that he could hold on much longer, but the moment he wasn't sure, the moment it nearly overwhelmed him, Seth pulled back, breathing hard, eyes glassy, and their gazes met and Ren knew he had to hang on for just a bit longer.

Because from the passion burning in Seth's eyes, he was about to get fucked within an inch of his life, and love every second of it.

Seth shed his jeans, and Ren opened his mouth to say something, something clever and witty about how he hadn't even been wearing underwear, and if he'd known that, six months ago, he'd have never made it off the lot without coming in them, but nothing came out. Just . . . nothing. Maybe a lot of begging and pleading. But nothing of actual value.

And miraculously, Seth didn't seem to care. The fire in his eyes just stoked even higher, as he pulled a condom from the drawer and carefully, inexorably, rolled it down his cock.

Oh. Ren realized. *His cock.* He'd finally gotten to see it.

It was long and hard and magnificent, and it was going to feel so good that he could barely wait for Seth to get on with it.

Like everything else, Seth approached him carefully, deliberately, pulling up his leg and positioning, but then as he started to slide in, Ren watched as the world blurred and they finally came together. Seth's eyes snapped shut and his fingers tightened on Ren's skin, and when he was finally totally inside, Ren barely able to *breathe* at that point, he let out a long, strangled moan.

Like he was just about to lose it.

Ren reached up and cupped his fingers around Seth's head, tugging him down, changing the angle of his cock inside of him, nearly making him gasp with the pleasure of it. But that wasn't the idea. He somehow managed to push it aside, and he said, "Let go," and pressed his lips firmly to Seth's.

It was like falling into the middle of a hurricane, except the hurricane was Seth. He was wild but not hard. Passionate but never overbearing. And it felt like it was over in a moment, even though Ren knew that Seth had drawn it out as long as he could, bliss spiraling out and out until he could barely take it any longer, begging and pleading for him to let go.

Then Ren couldn't help it, he just fell.

Hard and fast, and he was coming so hard he swore he'd feel the residuals in a week, as he pulsed up his chest, tightening around Seth's cock, milking it as Seth groaned and followed right after him.

When it was finally over, Seth didn't even fall on him, just . . . carefully settled to the side of him, wrapping a warm, muscled arm around him.

Ren didn't like cuddling after sex, usually, but after sex like that? He would do just about anything, and he leaned into it.

"That was . . ." He still didn't have the words.

"Good?" Seth questioned, pressing his lips to Ren's chest. He felt them burn into his skin. Like a brand.

He'd never wanted to feel marked, either, but he did.

And he didn't hate it.

"Better than good," Ren said wryly. "You know that."

"Oh, I did, but maybe I just wanted you to say it," Seth murmured.

"At least," Ren added coyly, "the best sex I've ever had in the afternoon."

Seth smiled.

It was a slow, private smile. Like it was just for him.

Maybe it was the cuddling. Maybe it was the branding that he hadn't minded. Maybe it was the casual thing that wasn't casual, not even a tiny bit, but Ren knew he was in trouble.

Was this what falling in love felt like?

When one minute the man next to you was just another guy, and the following, he was the one you wanted to tell all your troubles to? When he was the one who made you feel like you'd burn from the inside out if you couldn't have him every single possible way?

Ren had never felt that way before.

He'd never let anyone close enough before.

But Seth, he was there now, and Ren wasn't sure that he could displace him.

Even if he'd wanted to.

"You have to go just yet?" Seth asked.

"I can stay for a minute . . . at least," Ren said. Not wanting to go just yet either. "Gabe's gonna be pissed, but well, he can get over himself."

"I think," Seth said, "that he'll be happy for you."

It was also annoying when Seth was right.

But that didn't mean that Ren liked him any less.

Maybe it even meant that he liked him *more*.

"Then I'm definitely staying," Ren said, and cuddled in closer, pressing his hand to where he could still feel Seth's lips. Right over his heart.

CHAPTER ELEVEN

"THAT WAS A LONG-ASS day," Ren grumbled, collapsing onto the bench of the picnic table holding his cousin, Ash, Tate, and Alexis.

"It wouldn't have been so long if you hadn't played hooky yesterday," Gabe teased.

"You let Ren out of your sight?" Tate asked in a pseudo-shocked voice. "Really?"

"You guys need to hire some help," Alexis pointed out sagely.

They probably did need to hire some help, especially if he was going to continue to sneak over to Seth's for long afternoons spent in bed.

"I'd ask if you believe it but . . ." Gabe said, "Ren said he was taking a, and I quote, 'a quick break for a late lunch,' and came back, looking moony-eyed, three hours later."

Ren felt absolutely zero regrets.

"You were fine. It was a slow afternoon. And I got back in time for the dinner rush," Ren said, taking a drink of his beer.

"*Barely*," Gabe said, shaking his head. "And you didn't even answer your phone!"

"I was a little busy," Ren said.

Tate laughed. "I just bet you were. So, is Seth coming tonight?"

"To the music?" Ren felt a frisson of . . . something . . . it wasn't exactly uncomfortable, but it wasn't *comfortable* either, go up his spine when Tate asked. It was exactly the way Tate would ask Gabe if Sean was hanging out tonight. Or someone might ask Alexis about Jackson.

"Yeah, the music," Gabe said, looking at him like he'd grown three heads.

In everyone's minds, he and Seth were linked now.

It should have made him squirm more than it did. The truth was, Ren didn't know how he felt about it.

"I'm not sure," Ren said, and then, thankfully the subject changed, Alexis starting to tell a story about a customer today who'd ordered fifty gyros for his entire office.

What Ren *did* know was that he liked Seth a whole goddamn lot. He knew he wanted to see him again, as soon as possible. What he wasn't sure about was being the subject of everyone's watercooler talk, and the no doubt endless ribbing that would take place the first time they saw him and Seth together.

When he'd gotten back from Seth's finally, and Gabe had stopped gnashing his teeth and throwing things around, annoyed that he'd been gone for over three hours during a workday, he'd correctly guessed what they'd been up to.

It hadn't exactly been difficult to guess what he'd been up to.

But if Ren had asked Gabe to keep it a secret, he would have.

Morettis, even when they were pissed off, looked out for each other.

He hadn't. It hadn't even occurred to him until later, when he'd seen Ash this morning, and he'd shot him a knowing look and congratulated him.

So, everyone knew.

It was why when Seth had asked him what he was doing tonight, he'd said he was probably just going to go home and go to bed.

And he'd intended to, before Gabe had insisted that he join him for a drink, and to enjoy the music with some of the other guys.

When he'd walked over here, Ren had nearly pulled his phone out of his pocket and told Seth that his plans had changed. That he'd be hanging out here for awhile, if he wanted to join.

He didn't know what stopped him.

They had agreed to keep it casual; they didn't need to see each other every day. The problem was that Ren *wanted* to see Seth. He'd never felt that way before. Once sex was over, he'd always been happy enough to say goodbye.

But he hadn't wanted to yesterday, and he felt the loss of Seth next to him tonight, particularly.

He'd have invited Jake to this without a single thought.

So what was stopping him now?

Ren pulled out his phone, when he heard a voice behind him, light and teasing.

"So this is what going to bed early looks like?"

He turned and Seth was standing there, a grin on his face. Not looking disappointed at all to see that Ren wasn't quite where he'd said he'd be.

Ren shrugged, relieved that most of the group was still occupied with Alexis' gyro story.

"Gabe guilt-tripped me, and after yesterday, it wasn't all that hard," he admitted.

"Not surprised, but I'm glad I came anyway, even though I kind of wanted to sulk at home," Seth teased, sliding onto the empty bench next to Ren. He didn't hug or kiss him but the look in his eyes—that was enough.

Seth was a private guy, and maybe someday Ren would find out why that was, exactly, but he'd never imagined he'd be big into PDA.

"I'm glad you didn't," Ren said, meaning every word of it. He bumped his thigh against Seth's. Felt the reverberation of just that single touch through his whole body. "I was actually just about to text you, tell you to come over."

The corner of Seth's mouth quirked up, and even though Ren was hardly a PDA fan either, he wanted to lean in and kiss it right off Seth's lips.

But if he did, they'd never escape the notice of the rest of the table, who were all thankfully still distracted by the end of Alexis' story.

"I know it's not very casual . . ." Ren trailed off.

"Casual is whatever you want it to be," Seth said. "And I wanted to see you, too."

Ren relaxed. “Oh, did you?” he said, deploying his best flirtatious tone.

The one that never failed to get him exactly what he wanted.

It hadn’t worked all that well on Seth so far, but that didn’t mean he couldn’t try it.

“I thought me asking what you were doing after work was pretty transparent,” Seth said lightly.

“I . . .” Ren dropped his voice so nobody would overhear. “I didn’t know how you’d feel about everyone knowing.”

Seth did not look bothered at all. Instead, he looked amused. Someday, Ren thought, he would stop being surprised by this man. “I assumed they’ve known for awhile,” he pointed out.

“I mean . . .” Ren cleared his throat. When did he become squeamish about sex? He’d never been. Not once. Not even when he’d been a skinny fifteen-year-old virgin. “They know about *yesterday*.”

“And?”

Ugh. Ren felt stupid now, caught out using painfully uncool euphemisms. “Nothing, I just know you like to be private, but this group . . . not much is private with them.” Ren stopped himself before he actually apologized for not asking Gabe to keep his trap shut.

“It’s fine,” Seth said. “I know how they are.”

Seth reached down and set a hand on his thigh. A big, warm hand. A hand that had done all kinds of glorious things to Ren just yesterday. Ren could go for a repeat of more than a few of them. “Seriously,” he said, his tone lowering, his expression sincere, "it's not a big deal. Unless it is for you . . ."

"No, no, of course not," Ren said. Then he laughed. Totally at himself. "God, this is stupid. Why am I being so stupid?"

Seth smiled. "You're not. You don't usually do this kind of thing, right?"

"You know I don't."

"Then it probably feels a little weird. But it's fine. I'm good, you're good."

"Oh," Ren said, leaning in a little closer. "You're definitely good."

Seth's smile widened. "You keep talkin' like that, I'm going to have to show you again."

"No complaints from me." Ren had *known* they'd have sex again. He'd known it before they'd even had sex—he'd even *said* it, out loud—and the actual sex had been so good that he was sure they'd both assumed it, but hearing Seth say it, and saying it himself, really brought the knowledge home.

They were doing this. Whatever *this* was.

"Alexis Constantine Papadopoulos," a voice growled from the other side of the table.

Alexis had just finished telling his story about the huge box of gyros and Tate was laughing, and Gabe was smiling.

The one person who didn't look amused was Tony.

He was standing at the head of the table, and looked particularly outraged, even for Tony.

"I don't think I even *knew* Alexis' last name," Ren said in a hushed whisper to Seth.

"I did," Seth said. "But not his middle name, that's new."

"That's because you're obsessed with all of us," Ren teased. "Most of all, me. I bet you know *my* middle name."

"Domenico. Maybe we should all be calling you Dom instead of Ren," Seth said with a grin.

"Tony, what's going on?" Alexis asked, confusion knitting his brows together.

"What's going on?" Tony threw his hands up dramatically. "What's going on? How can you ask me that?"

Everyone—but especially Ren—always said that Gabe was the most dramatic. He liked to call him the King of Feelings to piss him off especially, but the truth was, Tony got into his feelings even harder than Gabe.

And he was definitely in his feelings right now.

"What's going on?" Lucas popped up behind Tony on cue, as if he knew his boyfriend was on a rampage and he'd arrived not to stop him but to watch.

"He," Tony said, pointing right to Alexis, "got *poached* and didn't even tell me!"

"Oh, *that*," Alexis said, rolling his eyes. "He wasn't really serious. In fact, he was kind of . . ."

"He's not the only one," Tate inserted wryly. He glanced around the table, and yeah, a lot of them were nodding.

In fact, *all* of them were nodding.

"What?" Tony's voice was strangled. "You *all* got poached and *nobody* told me?"

"How did you find out?" Ash wanted to know. "I didn't tell you because I knew you'd freak out. And yeah, there's definitely some freaking out going on."

"You, I don't want to hear from you," Tony said, pointing fingers again. "And for the record, the only one who told me was *Jackson*, and it wasn't even on purpose. He thought I already knew!" He shot a dirty look at Alexis, who looked a tiny bit ashamed. "He wanted to know what I was going to do about this guy who was trying to poach all my food trucks away from me! And I could just sit there and question him stupidly, wondering what the fuck he was talking about."

"None of us even considered it, that's why we didn't tell you," Tate said, so reasonably it almost sounded true.

Almost.

"Well, Gabe took his card," Ren said.

"What?" Tony faux-gasped. And yeah, he was totally usurping Gabe's throne right now in a major way.

"Not *seriously*," Gabe said, shooting Ren a glare. "Not on purpose!"

"Oh, yeah, it *accidentally* fell into your pocket," Ren said.

"Someone," Tony said, flopping onto a seat at the head of the table, "get me a goddamn beer and tell me what's going on. Who is this guy? What does he want?"

"He's . . . well, he's . . . *you*," Ash said apologetically.

Tony squinted at him. "What the hell does that even mean?"

"It means that he wants what you already have," Tate said. "The guy's some corporate stiff, he's got money, clearly, but he's just trying to buy what we've built, from the ground up. I told him he could forget about it, that it would never work, but I've never seen anyone more determined." Tate paused, hesitating. "Except for you, Tony."

"Oh great," Tony said, taking the beer that Lucas handed him, leaning into his boyfriend's embrace—no doubt Lucas was trying to be supportive but Tony had found a captive audience and there was nothing he enjoyed quite as much as that.

"Yeah, he's kinda your clone. Except that he's rich. Tacky rich," Ren said. "And he's a *lawyer.* A corporate lawyer to boot."

"What is a corporate lawyer doing trying to run a food truck lot?" Alexis said, clearly mystified. "I definitely got that he had money—he kept upping the offer, and the marketing and ad dollars he was going to invest—but I thought he must be some kind of corporate developer. He doesn't even own restaurants?"

"Nope," Gabe said. "He's probably never been in a kitchen in his whole goddamned life."

Tony set the bottle down on the table with a thump. "I can't fucking believe this," he said. "And Jackson said the lot he wants to open is close, like *right* here? Why didn't we know about this?"

"Probably because we don't know who owns all the property around here," Lucas said in a soothing voice. "And it doesn't matter if he does. We're firmly established, after only a year. There's nothing he can do to hurt us, babe. You know that."

Tony sighed, and leaned into his boyfriend's embrace. "I want to believe that. But he clearly has a fucking lot of nerve, because he tried to poach all of you."

"And we all told him to fuck off," Tate said.

"Except Gabe, apparently," Ash inserted with a sly grin. "Why was that, again? I don't think we heard *why* you listened to him?"

"He wants to give me something I don't even want," Ren said with an exaggerated eye roll. "My freedom, apparently."

"Like either of you could ever work for that guy," Tony said.

"Why shouldn't we have another truck?" Gabe objected. "Alexis has a whole *fleet* of them."

"Because Alexis isn't going to work for the enemy," Tony grumbled.

"No offense," Ren said, "but I don't want to be Alexis."

"No offense taken," Alexis said gravely, inclining his head. "Some days, I don't really want to be me either."

Tony turned to Alexis. "You really didn't want to park *any* of your trucks at his lot? My . . ." Tony hesitated, like he was tasting out the word, and he didn't particularly like it. "My copycat?"

"His name is Jonas Anderson," Lucas inserted and the whole table went silent.

Tony opened his mouth and snapped it shut again. "He tried to poach *you*," he stated, rather than asked.

Lucas looked sorry—that Jonas had approached him or that he hadn't told Tony either, Ren wasn't sure. Relationships, they could be a minefield of things you should be sorry for that you weren't, and things you *were* sorry for you didn't have a chance in hell of preventing. It was one of many reasons why Ren had never gotten seriously involved with anyone.

But Tony and Lucas? They were the backbone of Food Truck Warriors.

It shouldn't have hurt *Ren* that Tony was looking at Lucas like that.

But it did.

"He has a lot of fucking nerve," Tony mumbled. Looking more upset than dramatically angry now. "My *own boyfriend*."

"Maybe he didn't know we were dating," Lucas said. He leaned into Tony, lowering his voice. But they could all hear, because they were all listening. The blessing and the curse of this group. "And if I'm being honest, he knew I wasn't going to take it."

"But he made it anyway," Tony said. "And you didn't tell me."

"I love you, of course I didn't tell you. The man isn't an actual threat, but I knew you'd worry about him like he was."

"Later," Tony said succinctly. "We'll talk about this later." He turned to Alexis. "Back to this rich asswipe, *Jonas*, none of you really wanted to go with him?"

"We're happy here, Tony, you know that," Ash said.

"Yeah," Tate agreed. "Sales have been good. We're stronger together than apart, and I think we're all smart enough to know that. It doesn't matter the money he's promising, or the ad dollars or whatever. I don't need that."

"None of us do," Gabe said. "Unless"—he paused, glancing over at Ren, who couldn't hold back his eye roll any longer—"you want to . . ."

"For the final time," Ren said between clenched teeth, "I am not going *anywhere*. You'll remove me off our truck and stick me into a new one over my dead body."

Gabe laughed. "Okay, I guess that's your answer."

"Yes," Ren said, "I thought about it, and that's the conclusion I came to. Took about five seconds."

Seth squeezed Ren's knee. "Less, maybe?" he pointed out softly. And Ren knew he was thinking of the afternoon they'd shared yesterday, of the way he'd confided his feelings about Gabe and the business they shared. It should've made Ren itchy.

And it didn't.

Not in the way he expected.

Instead of making him want to run, he itched to take Seth's hand and find a dark corner they could make out in.

Gabe's expression softened. "I love working with you, too, cousin."

Ren shouldn't have been relieved, because he *knew* it. They'd been together through thick and thin. He'd never regretted his decision to follow Gabriel down to Los Angeles, and not only because he didn't fit in at home, in Napa. It was because they'd always had each other.

Lovers could come and go but family was *forever*.

"Is this the kind of thing you'd take care of for us," Tony wondered, directing his question to Seth, who looked surprised that he'd just been pulled into the discussion.

"Take care of . . .?" Seth asked.

"Find out who he is, what he wants, *exactly*," Tony said. "And clearly I'm not going to be able to pay him to go away, but maybe we can come to some kind of agreement."

"You want me to dig into him and find some leverage so he'll stop bothering you," Seth said.

"That would be fucking fantastic," Tony said enthusiastically.

"I think I can manage that," Seth said, amused. "But I'll definitely be drawing a line at more."

"Oh," Tony said, waving his hands. "I'm not asking for a *hit* or something. Or . . ." He glanced over at Ash. "For you to blow up his lot or anything. Nothing like that. He just seems to know *all* about us, and we don't know anything about him."

Seth nodded. "Good to be informed. And if some of that info comes in handy." He paused, grinning. "So be it."

"I like the way you think," Tony said, reaching over and shaking Seth's hand. "Now that that's settled, I'm going to go argue with my boyfriend, and more importantly have some hot makeup sex afterwards."

Lucas laughed. "Awfully sure of yourself, aren't you, babe?"

Tony turned to him, and the look in his eyes was what told Ren that they would be okay. "Always," he said to

Lucas. "And even more sure of you."

They disappeared into the night, a series of catcalls following them.

Alexis wandered off next, followed by Gabe and Ash. Probably they were heading to the Funky Cup, to meet up with their boyfriends.

Leaving Seth and Ren alone.

Ren took a long sip of his beer and wondered how soon he could suggest they take off too. His loft would be empty, and Seth had a whole empty house.

It seemed wrong to not take advantage of either one. Besides, Ren was still feeling itchy, and not uncomfortable itchy, but *sex* itchy, crawling up his spine, intensifying whenever Seth laughed or pressed his thigh into Ren's.

"So you're really okay doing Tony's dirty work?" Ren asked.

Because while *yes*, he absolutely wanted to get naked with this man, it was nice to just talk to him too.

"It's not very dirty work," Seth teased, leaning in a bit closer. "I'm sure Tony would like it to be dirtier. But no, I expected him to ask. This guy does know a lot about him. Makes sense for Tony to be informed too."

Ren grinned. "You're going to threaten him, aren't you?"

"Oh, maybe a little bit," Seth said. "But a corporate lawyer won't spook easily."

"You're very good at your job," Ren stated. He didn't know why he hadn't realized it before, but now he did, remembering when Seth was Jake and he'd mentioned the burden of protecting people who were paying him for that privilege.

"And you're good at yours," Seth responded. "I knew it the first day we met."

"I just remember what you said about those guys you were going to protect—you worried about it. You wouldn't worry if you weren't really good at what you do," Ren said.

"I've been protecting people for a very long time," Seth said. "I'd hope that I'm good at it."

And somehow, Ren knew he was both changing the subject and also, impossibly at the same time, telling him something important about himself.

"Since you were in the Army?" Ren asked.

"Navy," Seth corrected gently. "But yes."

Someday, Ren resolved, Seth was going to tell him about his time in the Navy. How he got so good at protecting people. But not tonight.

He finished his beer and set it down, standing up and reaching for Seth's hand. "Mine or yours?" he asked.

Seth grinned. "Which is closer?"

Ren's loft was closer. It took less than ten minutes for them to walk there, and by the time Ren let them in, he was half-hard in his jeans just from the anticipation of getting his hands on Seth again.

He turned to him, Seth's hair still fiery in the dim light of the main room.

"Come 'ere," Seth said, voice rough, and before Ren could think—or *overthink*—he was in Seth's arms, and they were kissing, hot and wild, Seth's tongue brushing against his, reminding of just how good his mouth had been yesterday.

Had it just been yesterday? Ren was so hungry for it, it felt like it had been ages since he'd had sex.

But it wasn't just the sex. It was this fucking man.

Ren couldn't get enough of him.

He pulled away, panting slightly, cock going from half-hard to rock hard. "I need to take a shower," he said. "And then we can do a *lot* more of that."

"A shower, huh? You dirty, Lorenzo?" Seth teased.

Ren fluttered his eyelashes at him. How had he gone from hating being called Lorenzo to loving it when Seth did it? It must be dark magic. "You'd better believe it."

"Then I guess I'd better get in with you," Seth said, and before Ren could open his mouth and stop him, he'd tugged his shirt off, and it was hard to argue with what was in front of him.

Seth's muscles were honed and lethal, and Ren remembered his desire to kiss every single freckle—and there were a lot of those, dotted all over his pale skin, from his gorgeous strong shoulders, to the firm pecs, and down even lower, punctuation marks to his incredible fucking abs.

Ren had admired his self-control that the first time he'd seen Seth like this, after so long imagining how good he'd look without clothes on, he'd *only* kissed him.

But tonight, he wasn't going to only kiss him.

"If you do, I can't guarantee it won't get a lot dirtier," Ren teased, pulling his own shirt off and then, after toeing his shoes off, unbuttoned and unzipped his jeans, letting them fall in place as he turned and headed towards the bathroom.

Any man with sense would follow when presented with what Ren knew was his spectacularly curved ass.

And Seth, well, he had sense in spades, because not only did he follow Ren into the bathroom, but when he pressed up against him, right as Ren reached out to turn on the shower, he was naked. Completely naked. Ren could feel Seth's skin pressed to his own, from head to toe, and his cock twitched.

"You're such a tease, and I fucking love it," Seth murmured into his ear, then biting it softly. He reached around, and pushed Ren's jeans down the rest of the way, and then worked off his briefs, all while nibbling on his ear and neck in a way that was so distracting and consuming that by the end of it, Ren was reduced to garbled moans.

How did this man manage to overwhelm him so completely every time they got naked?

Ren didn't know.

But he also wasn't fighting it either.

"Let's get in," Seth said and gave Ren a little push, following after him, into the hot spray of the shower.

It wasn't a very big shower, but it was big enough.

Of course it didn't have to be particularly large when the moment the door was closed, Seth had Ren pressed up against the cool tile wall, and they were kissing ferociously, Ren going weak-kneed.

And then his hand reached down, just brushing his cock, but he was so aroused, he groaned into Seth's mouth anyway, sure that he was about to get overwhelmed again, in the best possible way. But Seth didn't touch him any harder. Just little tantalizing brushes of those rough, calloused fingertips that he hadn't stopped thinking about since yesterday as they kissed on and on.

Seth's cock was hard and hot against his thigh, and Ren reached for it, ready to do something more than tease, but Seth brushed his hands away.

Ren nearly reached for it again, determined to make Seth feel just as good as he was making him feel, but before he could, Seth distracted him again, closing his fist around his cock and giving it a rough, hard pump.

"Oh God," Ren cried out, burying his head into Seth's shoulder. How had he known he liked it just like that? That he liked it to hurt a little, that it just made the pleasure so much stronger when it had a bite with it?

It was the most relentless, insanely good handjob that Ren had ever enjoyed. Seth worked him up with his big fist, squeezing just the right amount, until Ren was right on the edge, teetering with the pleasure of it, and then he'd back off.

By the time Seth pushed him over, by the time Seth *let* him come, he was babbling and incoherent, mouthing and biting at Seth's shoulder muscle. The orgasm hit him hard, twisting him up inside and then releasing in an intoxicating rush.

"Shit," Ren panted as Seth worked him through the aftershocks. "Shit, fuck, that was so good." He finally opened his eyes, only to see a definite set of teeth marks bitten into Seth's flesh.

He chuckled. "I gathered," he said.

"Sorry," Ren said. Though he wasn't very sorry at all. It had felt really damn good. And now he was ready to return the favor. He reached for Seth's dick, already anticipating how good it was going to taste and feel in his mouth. He enjoyed sucking cock, but he was really, really going to enjoy sucking Seth's cock.

He was hard and slippery, bright red at the tip. Clearly he'd enjoyed giving Ren that orgasm almost as much as Ren had enjoyed experiencing it. As Ren sank to his knees, it twitched in his fingers, and Ren knew he wouldn't get as long as he wanted. No time to savor, not when Seth was this close.

He had a lot of control, but Ren could tell he was already beginning to lose it.

That was a lot hotter than he'd ever thought it could be.

He has it bad for you.

It wasn't the first time a guy had felt this way about him. Ren supposed it probably wouldn't be the last time, either.

But it was the first time Ren felt the echoes of it, too.

He couldn't get enough of this man.

"You gonna look at it or suck it?" Seth asked, his voice low and rough.

Oh, yeah, they were definitely going to have to do this again. Soon, if Ren had any say in the matter.

Ren answered his question by leaning in, wrapping his tongue around the head, and sucking. Seth's fingers dug into his hair, and oh yeah, he liked this too. Then Seth pulled, just a little, and *God*, if he hadn't just come his brains out, he'd be hard and ready to go again with just a little hair pulling and Seth's cock in his mouth.

He took him in a little deeper, sucking hard as he went, and Seth groaned above him, his fingers tightening even more, and yeah, next time, they were definitely doing this *first*.

More precome blurted onto Ren's tongue and he savored it, and what it meant, sliding in even deeper. When he cupped Seth's balls, rolling them in his fingertips, that was the tipping point, because he tensed, and gave a strangled cry, and came.

Ren swallowed, trying not to feel disappointed that it had felt more like an afterthought than a tasty main dish. He really enjoyed giving pleasure. Getting pleasure, too, of course, but part of what he really loved about sex was the give-and-take.

And so far, it had been Seth giving a lot, and Ren taking.

Next time, Ren thought with resolution as he stood and Seth cupped his jaw with one hand, kissing him hard and fast.

The problem was it was so easy to melt under all that passionate onslaught. To be wanted so badly that Seth had worked this hard to be with him. He'd always known that Seth was coolly pragmatic on the outside, and that he had secret fires hidden inside. What he'd never anticipated was that reaching out and touching the fire would burn him so completely, and melt every resolution he'd ever had.

"Let's clean up," Ren said, breaking away from the kiss. "And then I think I promised you *Overboard*, and cuddling."

Seth raised an eyebrow. "Lorenzo Moretti promising cuddling?"

There it was; that same melting feeling that he couldn't seem to control.

"For you, Lorenzo Moretti cuddles," he said, and realized that he meant it, one hundred and ten percent.

Sex had never complicated things before—usually for Ren it *uncomplicated* things—but it was undeniable.

No matter what Seth said, this was no casual thing.

And Ren wasn't even mad about it. How could he be, when it felt so damn good?

CHAPTER TWELVE

SETH WOKE UP WITH a mouthful of hair, and after adjusting so it wasn't tickling under his nose quite so terribly, he thought, *this is pretty fucking great.*

Because he knew, from the moment he'd been conscious, that he was still in Lorenzo's bed.

It wasn't the only place he ever wanted to be, but it was still high up there.

After they'd watched *Overboard*, and cuddled on the couch, Ren had been just about dead on his feet, and he'd hesitated, glancing over at the doorway that Seth knew led to his bedroom.

The look on his face had been thoughtful, almost contemplative, peeking through the clear exhaustion. Then he'd tilted his head, and Seth had known he'd come to a decision.

"It's late," he'd said, "you should just stay." He'd hesitated. "If that's okay with you. I know we said . . ."

"Casual is whatever we make it," Seth said. Of course that was not necessarily true. Nobody would assume that sleeping over was casual in any way, shape or form, but why should they let culture and society dictate what they did or how they did it?

It was between just the two of them. Nobody else mattered.

"Right, yeah," Ren said. He'd looked nervous. Unsure. Despite the certainty of his words. "I want you to stay."

And that was all Seth had needed to hear, and he'd trailed Ren to the bedroom, borrowing a spare toothbrush and then they'd fallen into bed together.

Just to sleep.

Before he'd fallen asleep, Ren had turned to Seth, his eyes dark and serious in his handsome face. "I've never done this before," he said, and Seth had known it, had believed it was true before Ren had spoken the words, but he realized as he heard them then that Ren wasn't talking about some guy sleeping over.

He was talking about all of this.

And it occurred to Seth that he should give his own confession back.

"Me either," he'd said. "Sometimes we bunked together, when we were out in the field, but that was . . ."

"Different?" There was a soft glow in Ren's eyes now, and Seth had known he'd made the right choice.

"Yeah," Seth said. It was more than that, but different also sufficed.

"I'm glad it's you," Ren said, as his eyes fluttered shut, and he fell asleep.

Seth had slept the whole night—which surprised him because it was a strange bed, and while he'd admittedly gotten used to that when he'd been on active duty, he was retired now and he'd gotten a little bit soft, sleeping in the same comfortable bed night after night—and he'd just woken up now as the sunlight had begun to filter in through the shades covering the windows.

Ren was still sleeping, curled on his side, facing Seth, a hand he'd had tucked underneath him when he'd fallen asleep now lying halfway between them. Like sometime during the night, he'd wanted to reach out for Seth, but he hadn't felt quite comfortable reaching all the way.

Seth understood; the situation they were currently in was unprecedented for both of them.

He'd known—he'd *hoped*—that someday he might end up here. But then he'd always assumed that he would fall for someone who was a little bit like him. Someone Lennox-like, maybe.

But Ren was completely and utterly different. He was younger, for one, almost ten years younger, though that wasn't so much an issue as the very differing viewpoints they both shared on love and relationships.

As in—Seth had always imagined that he'd have the latter, and that the former would come.

He'd never imagined that the first would already be firmly entrenched in his heart, by the time they got to the latter.

But he'd begun falling for Lorenzo Moretti from the first moment their eyes had met, and every little scrap and tidbit of information he'd learned from and about the man since then had solidified that he was it.

If it wasn't going to be Ren for him, it wasn't going to be anybody.

Trust Seth to pick the most impossible man to woo.

But he must not be doing too poor of a job, because he was in his bed now, wasn't he? And not just for the convenience or fleeting pleasure of sex.

He was there because Ren wanted him there.

Ren's eyes fluttered open. "You," he said, his voice groggy with sleep. "You're still here."

He'd be here, as long as Ren wanted him to be.

"Yes," Seth said. "Good morning."

"Is it?" Ren yawned, rolling onto his back to stretch.

It was a glorious sight, seeing Ren like this, clad only in a pair of tight navy-blue briefs, all that smooth, lithe muscle on display, and all that fucking skin. Seth let his eyes drift upwards, and tried not to laugh.

His hair, normally tamed into a dark, curly style, was *everywhere.* It explained why Seth had woken up with hair in his mouth, because it had defied even the boundary set by Ren's pillow and crept over, to invade Seth's.

"What?" Ren asked, self-consciously running a hand through his hair.

Seth knew the moment Ren realized just why he was so amused.

Ren's lips compressed shut. He did not look happy.

"I must look ridiculous," Ren mumbled. Probably something that didn't happen often for him.

Seth realized he was seeing the *real* Ren right now, the one who wasn't trying to present the most attractive front he could. And Ren stole a little bit more of his heart.

He'd give it to him with both hands, if he could. But Ren wouldn't take it. Not yet.

"I think you look gorgeous," Seth said, and it wasn't exactly a hardship to roll Ren underneath him, and hover above him. After all he was *still* gorgeous. Wild hair and all.

"It's this damn curly hair," Ren said. He reached up, brushing his fingertips against Seth's skull, at his close-cropped haircut. "Maybe I should do what you did, cut it all off."

Seth didn't believe he'd actually do it. After all, Ren was a little vain. Understandably so, but there it was. "If you want to," he said. And meant it. He'd take this man however he could have him.

Ren shot him a look. "What, like you'd still want me if I was ugly?"

"Absolutely I would," Seth said, meaning that too. "And it's not like you shaving your head would actually make you ugly."

"Okay, fair point," Ren said with a chuckle. "I'll give you that one."

"Oh, you will?" Seth questioned, leaning down and pressing a kiss to the side of Ren's head, right where his curls were wildest. "How generous of you."

Ren's expression turned serious again. "What are you doing tomorrow night?"

"I don't know, what *am* I doing tomorrow night?" Seth teased.

He didn't know what made him so nervous about Ren being serious, but something about it made him edgy and worried. Like if Ren thought too hard about any of this, then he'd come to the kind of conclusion that Seth dreaded.

It wasn't giving Ren any credit—or him, either, for that matter—so Seth shoved the thoughts away. He was with Ren *now*, he didn't need to be second-guessing himself, when there wasn't any reason to worry.

"It's trivia night at my favorite bar," Ren said, "and I think you should come with me."

"What, the Funky Cup has trivia?" Seth was surprised, he thought he'd known the Funky Cup schedule like the back of his hand.

"No," Ren said. His grin was mischievous and a little daring. It made him want to do all kinds of dirty, pleasurable things to Ren. Even though they didn't really have the time. He needed to get home, and Ren needed to go to work. "Don't tell Shaw, and definitely do not tell Jackson—or Alexis, for that matter—but no, the Funky Cup is *not* my favorite bar."

"Because they don't have a trivia night?"

Ren nodded. "I'm picky about them, too," he added.

"I'm astonished, Lorenzo. You? Particular about something?"

Ren smacked him on the shoulder lightly. Then, like he was caught by the feel of Seth's bare skin, his fingers lingered. It seemed like he wasn't the only one who was thinking with his dick this morning.

Tomorrow night wasn't that far away, but it felt like a fucking eternity.

"I like things just so, there's nothing wrong with that," Ren said.

"Well, I'll take it as a compliment."

Ren's eyes were dark—so dark, it felt like Seth could get even more lost in them. "You should," he said.

"So trivia night tomorrow?" he said, and though it nearly killed him, he rolled off Ren. Before his cock decided he should start something that he didn't have the time to finish.

He had a big meeting this morning with the Star Shadow guys, and he couldn't be late. No matter how tempting Ren was.

"Trivia night tomorrow," Ren said. "I usually take an Uber. Leave from the food truck lot."

"I'll meet you there. What time?"

"Eight?" Ren suggested. "Trivia doesn't start til nine, but it's good to get there early, so we can find a decent seat, and also size up the competition."

Seth grinned, already looking forward to learning another facet of Lorenzo Moretti. "So you're competitive, then?"

Ren shot him a look. "We play to win," he said, and oh yeah, that was almost more than his self-control, quickly being eroded by Ren's very being, could take.

He rolled over, and swung his feet down, letting them touch the hardwood floor. "I won't let you down," he said, even though he had no idea if he was actually any good at trivia. But he would be, for Ren.

"I didn't think you would," Ren teased. And then he followed Seth, shifting his body until he was pressed against Seth's back, as he groped on the nightstand for his phone. "You left," he said.

"I gotta get up, get home, get ready. I've got a meeting."

Seth didn't need to look at Ren to know he was currently wearing a pouty expression. It shouldn't have, because he was clear-eyed when it came to Ren and his tendency to be a bit bratty, but it sent a thrill running through him.

Ren wants you.

Ren wants you right here.

"If you get up, I bet you we could share some coffee *and* a nice long goodbye kiss before I go," Seth said.

"Fine," Ren grumbled, but then after the aforementioned coffee was brewing, it was him pressing Seth against the counter to give him a goodbye kiss.

And when Seth finally left, the front door shutting behind him, he couldn't stop smiling.

The next night, Ren waited for Seth outside his food truck.

"What are you up to tonight?" Gabe had asked as they'd finished cleaning up. "Isn't it trivia night?"

"It is," Ren had acknowledged. He'd brought Gabriel before, but while he was painfully dramatic, he didn't have the cutthroat instinct that Ren liked to have in a partner on trivia night.

After all, he always played to win.

Seth was going to be a different story, though. He was smart and quick and Ren could already sense how he might know things that would fill in Ren's knowledge gaps.

And he'd never give any breaks. After all, he'd never given Ren any.

Sure, they were doing this "casual" thing, but deep down, Ren knew they weren't fooling anyone.

Especially his cousin.

"You're taking Seth, aren't you?" Gabe asked.

Ren had nodded, hoping that he wouldn't make a big deal out of it. But Gabe hadn't. He'd merely smiled and said that he hoped they had a good time.

Didn't even waggle his eyebrows suggestively, like he usually did when he thought that Ren might be having sex.

It was hardly the first indication that this casual thing was getting more serious, but it wasn't lost on Ren either.

He didn't know yet what he was going to do about it. After all, at least half of the reasons why things *weren't* casual were his doing. He'd been the one to suggest Seth sleep over. Just because he'd wanted to. The only disappointment had been that the really hot goodbye kiss they'd shared hadn't developed into anything more.

And then last night, he'd been busy, the truck staying open late for a big band that Tony booked, and all he'd had time to do was exchange a handful of texts.

But tonight, he was going to take Seth to trivia night, and then after . . . well, win or lose, Ren always liked to hook up after trivia night. Something about the adrenaline that pumped through him with the competition made him reckless and horny.

Something about Seth satisfying all that tonight made him even more aroused, just by thinking about it.

"Hey."

Ren glanced up and Seth was approaching. He wore a dark green button-up shirt and jeans, and looked so fucking edible that for the first time in a very long time, Ren was tempted to say, *fuck it* to trivia night, and just head to his place or Seth's.

But it had been a very long time since he'd skipped trivia.

He wasn't ready to do it—not for Seth and Seth alone—yet.

Mostly because he was a little bit terrified of what that might mean.

"Hey yourself," Ren said, and this time it felt not only easy but necessary, to fold himself into his arms, tilting his face up for a kiss.

It was not casual at all.

But it felt imperative, and Ren had never been very good at resisting something he wanted—and he really, really wanted Seth.

"You ready to kick some ass?" Ren asked as he pulled away a fraction. A hello kiss was one thing; he was beginning to learn just how easy it was to slide into something a lot more passionate, at least with Seth. And he wasn't sure he was quite ready to start making out in the middle of Food Truck Warriors.

"Always ready," Seth said easily, slinging an arm around Ren's shoulders as they headed towards the sidewalk. "I have a car, waiting, if you're good with that."

"Oh, that's nice," Ren said, surprising at how pleased he felt at the gesture.

This is not a date. This is just . . . a casual hangout.

But Ren was not stupid, and he also didn't like lying to himself.

Okay, this is . . . casual dating. How's that? Does that make you want to run for the hills?

It did not.

It made him want to burrow even more tightly into Seth's shoulder, as they slid into the back seat of the Prius that Seth had reserved for them.

The drive to the bar that hosted trivia night wasn't long. They arrived, Seth finalizing the transaction in his phone as they walked up to the bar entrance.

"You really meant it," Seth said after he finished and glanced up.

Ren pulled the door open. It was always busy on trivia nights, but that's why he liked to get there early. Still, there were only two seats at the bar left, and he grabbed one, Seth taking the other.

"What did I really mean?" Ren wanted to know.

"That you said you liked to find secret spots that you could lose yourself in," Seth said, gesturing around him.

Ren was confused for a split second, and then remembered. Oh yeah, he'd put that in his Flaunt profile, as a thoughtless last-minute addition. Something he wouldn't have normally said about himself, because that was the kind of thing hookups didn't need to know. But he'd done it anyway, because the rest of the list had seemed so . . . banal.

And Seth had remembered it.

"This is totally that kind of place," Seth said.

Ren looked around at the bar, seeing it from Seth's perspective.

From the outside, it didn't look like much at all—a dim, dark, dingy building, with none of the charm that Jackson and Shaw had infused into the very bricks of the Funky Cup. But inside, it oozed it.

The lights were dim and tinged reddish and orange and yellow. Curtains were flowered and fringed, a shawl draped over a lamp in the corner, taking away from the direct light. The walls were papered with years upon years of old music posters, some of the edges peeling and shredding. The bar top was clean but the patina of the wood was dark from use, book-ended with fancy brass fittings, looking like it belonged more in a Victorian horror novel than a bar in downtown Los Angeles.

It was a unique and original kind of place, the kind that Ren had known he'd enjoy from the moment he'd stumbled in years ago, when he'd first come to LA.

He'd always enjoyed trivia, the random and strange collection of factoids unimportant to everyone else, but he'd honed his love of it here. He'd tried other trivia nights, at plenty of other bars, but none of them had ever felt right the way this one did.

"I like the way they run the trivia contest here," Ren said.

It was not all he could have said, but there were some things that apparently he wasn't as comfortable sharing. Gabe probably knew, because he'd come with him a handful of times, but he'd never brought an actual date here.

Not even a guy he'd really wanted to sleep with.

Occasionally he'd *met* someone here that he'd ended up fucking, but the fact that he'd brought Seth felt both like absolutely the right thing to do, and also terrifying as hell.

"Oh?" Seth's eyes twinkled and it was like he *knew* that wasn't all that Ren liked, though he hadn't said anything else.

It should have been annoying, but Ren wasn't annoyed at all.

"Hey, Ren," Jason the bartender said, sauntering over. "What can I get you two?"

"My usual," Ren said. One of the many reasons he liked coming here was that Jason made an old-fashioned just the way he liked it.

"I'll have the same," Seth said.

"You said yesterday you were busy tracking down that copycat guy, yeah?" Ren asked. "Did you find out anything else about him?"

"Jonas Nichols Anderson," Seth said, popping a handful of roasted nuts from the wooden bowl on the bar into his mouth. "A lawyer, as he told you. Made a fortune in litigation, isn't exactly retired now, but he's certainly at a loose end, has been for some time, as he isn't actively listed on any cases I can find. He's basically a figurehead at his firm now."

"So he's bored," Ren guessed.

Seth nodded. "He's owned the property he's converting into the food truck lot for awhile now. From what I can see, he bought it up because he knew this area of downtown was beginning to gentrify, and he wanted in on the ground floor."

"He was planning on sitting on it, and then selling it for a ridiculous price to some developer," Ren observed.

"Yep," Seth said. "His social media isn't as locked down as I'd have recommended if he was a client, so I could glean some from that. He appears to have dated a series of younger guys. Lots of actor hopefuls, a few 'singers.' The latest was a model, but they broke up last year, it seems like."

"Not very surprising, considering this is LA," Ren inserted wryly. He scrunched his nose. "He wouldn't be bad looking, if he wasn't so . . . I don't know . . . *curated*."

"Like he's a museum piece, or a billboard," Seth said flatly. "Anyway, he's at a loose end, and like you said, bored. I have no record of him coming to Food Truck Warriors for the first time, but I'd guess it was sometime last summer, because a month later was when he started traveling around. Lots of big cities. Some smaller ones." Seth nodded to Jason, who was setting their drinks down. "One thing they all had in common though—they all had a major food truck presence. There's even some tagged posts and some pics he took that he posted on Instagram. He was definitely getting ideas."

"All the way back then?" Ren didn't want to sound disappointed but he was.

"You said it yourself; he's like Tony. He sees something, he wants something, he makes it happen. No matter the obstacle."

"Like copying someone else's idea? Like poaching a guy's friends away from him?" Ren could hear how bitter he sounded. He hadn't even thought he *liked* Tony all that much, until someone set out to become a better version of him.

Now he was just outraged and pissed off on Tony's behalf.

"He seems to think the two can co-exist peacefully," Seth said, and Ren would have to be a lot less observant to miss the careful way he said that.

"You talked to him," Ren stated. He sipped his drink.

"I happened to run into him, yeah," Seth said with a grin. "Found out his favorite coffee place, hung out there, bumped into him, got him talking—which wasn't very hard, by the way—and when he mentioned his new project, wondered what was going to happen to that other great food truck lot only a few blocks away."

"And he said he thought we could co-exist?" Ren said with disbelief. "And you think he was telling the truth?"

"He'd have no reason to lie to me, since he had no idea who I was, but here's the thing." Seth took a deep breath. "I'm not sure I disagree with him, actually. Different trucks, different entertainment, and even if it does come down to it, you're far more established, with roots in the community. I'd give Food Truck Warriors an edge all day long."

"Huh." Ren considered this. "Well, I guess we'll see."

"I didn't know him way back when, but has Tony always been this way?" Seth asked, sipping his drink. The man had an appreciation for good bourbon, and it only made Ren appreciate *him* all the more.

"Tony?"

"Yeah. Or did he just wake up one day and decide, *I'm going to be ambitious*."

Ren wrinkled his nose. "Is Tony actually ambitious? I'm not sure. I think he's plenty stubborn, with extra determination to spare. And according to Wyatt—have you ever met his brother, Wyatt?"

Seth shook his head. "Haven't had the pleasure."

"He's crazy busy. Cookbooks and culinary demos, and being married to a major professional baseball player, but well, according to Wyatt, his brother dropped out of culinary school, argued with everyone, lost a bunch of jobs, and only turned his life around when their grandmother died."

Seth actually looked surprised. "Tony did?"

"I know, it's surprising, right?" Ren had been surprised when he'd shared a beer with Wyatt one night, and Tony had somehow come up. "But I don't think it was just when his grandmother died. He changed, too, when he met Lucas."

"You were around then, when they met?"

"Oh, yeah." Ren grinned. "Food Truck Warriors didn't exist, obviously, but Tony and Wyatt's truck was on the food truck circuit, same as the rest of us, and we often ended up working the same festivals and the same blocks downtown, for the lunch crowds. Anyway, when they met, it was like . . . oil and a blowtorch."

Seth raised an eyebrow.

"I knew Lucas." When Seth looked interested—more interested than he had been, anyway—Ren rolled his eyes. "No, we did not hook up. Though he kinda did the same thing I did. Lots of hookups, no relationships."

"And he changed when he met Tony."

"I don't think he . . . *changed* necessarily, he and Tony just realized how good they were together. When you meet someone who fits you like that, who fills in all your nooks and crannies and opens your eyes, I don't think it makes you a different person, but it shows you another way."

Seth reached out and squeezed his knee.

Like he knew what Ren was trying to say.

And just like that, suddenly, Ren realized that he hadn't *just* been talking about Lucas. Maybe he'd been describing himself, too.

Because he hadn't changed. Not significantly.

But Seth *was* showing him a different way.

"Sometimes it's not better or worse," Seth said, with understanding in his gray eyes, "but just different, right?"

"Right," Ren echoed. "Anyway, Lucas had been through a tough time at home, his parents kicked him out young, for being gay, and when Tony fell in love with him, Lucas' story made him want more for the queer community. A place where we could come together."

"Jonas Anderson can't hope to match that kind of emotional dedication," Seth said.

"No," Ren agreed.

"He'd be stupid to even try," Seth added wryly, "except that because he *is* like Tony, he's sure as hell going to try, anyway."

"You're not going to stop him, are you?"

"I don't think I could, but I can make sure he stays inside the boundaries that Tony and I decide on," Seth said. Suddenly his eyes went darker. "I protect the people I care about, and I care a lot about y'all."

"Not just me?" Ren teased.

Seth leaned in a bit closer. Ren wanted nothing more than to close the gap between them, and kiss him again, taste the bourbon and the cherry on his lips. But it was wild enough that he'd brought Seth to trivia night. Kissing Seth here? That was a whole extra level that he wasn't sure he was prepared for yet.

"Not just you," Seth agreed in a low voice, "but you're definitely at the top of the list."

Ren had guessed as much, but it felt so unexpectedly good to hear him say it.

"Now," Seth continued, putting a hand on Ren's knee and squeezing. "Tell me something about this trivia night. How does it work?" He gazed around at the gathering crowd. "Who do we need to watch out for?"

Ren laughed, unexpectedly delighted. "You want me to give you a rundown on our competition?"

"Absolutely," Seth said. "After all, we play to win, right?"

"Right," Ren said, grinning. "So those guys over there all went to Stanford, and came down here to work. This is like the one time they let them out of the office or something. They're smart, but . . . not pop culture savvy? So I can usually get them on the music or movie or entertainment questions." He gestured offhandedly at a group of four younger guys who were gathered in one of the tall booths closest to where Henry was setting up with his clipboard and microphone and tall stool.

Lots of other trivia nights had gone more computerized, but Ren liked that Henry hadn't.

It was one of many reasons why he kept coming back.

"They also like that booth because they claim it gives them advantage," Ren said, rolling his eyes. "They are full of bullshit, by the way. I've sat in lots of different spots and kicked their ass plenty of times."

Seth looked fascinated. "I bet you have. Who else?"

"Hilda and Natalia over there," Ren said, gesturing to a pair of older ladies, "they're dynamite at history. Both massive history buffs, and Natalia writes historical romance novels, which . . ." Ren blushed. He should not be saying all this, confessing all his hard-won secrets, but it felt natural to tell Seth them. "Which are actually pretty good."

"You've read them." It wasn't a question necessarily, but it also held zero judgement. Ren hadn't missed how warm Seth's gaze had gotten. It was setting him on fire, and in a moment, he might be actually forced to squirm on his stool.

"They have a similar vibe to the romantic comedies, you know," Ren said. "I like them. A lot. Especially Nat's."

"Any other regulars?" Seth asked.

"There's me, of course, and it looks like . . . yeah, Jason's wife, Mackenzie, over there." He gestured to a short redhead, wearing a headband like a crown in her curls. "She can be formidable."

Jason leaned over the counter and grinned. "She'd be thrilled to hear you say that." He turned towards Seth, his gaze suddenly speculative. "I don't think Ren's ever brought a date to trivia night before."

"Oh?" Seth looked pleased. Very pleased.

"Yep," Jason said with a knowing smirk. "Don't think he ever has."

"Jason, I'm going to tear up your tip into very small pieces and set it on fire," Ren said between clenched teeth.

Jason just laughed though, because he probably knew the threat was meaningless.

Seth leaned forward, and it was impossible to miss the intrigued questions in his eyes. "Tell me more," he said.

But just then Henry cleared his throat into the microphone and not only saved Ren's life—but probably Jason's tip too.

"I think we're just about ready to get started," Henry said. "Who's in tonight?"

Ren raised his hand and, with his other, reached over and to his own surprise took Seth's hand in his own and squeezed it. "We are," he said.

CHAPTER THIRTEEN

"YOU ARE ABSOLUTELY FUCKING brilliant," Seth said.

Ren wanted to believe that he'd only said that because he was three old-fashioneds in, which was a lot for anyone to drink, but despite the brightness in his eyes, Seth didn't slur a single word, and he'd even come up with the answer to a particularly thorny question about the Waltons TV show that Ren hadn't had a chance in hell of answering.

"Am I?" Ren questioned, grinning at the man next to him.

"Oh, you are, and it's sexy as hell," Seth confessed. A little loudly.

Ren had been called sexy for a number of reasons over the years. Almost every single one had had something to do with the way he looked or talked or smiled or walked. A lot of times they had to do with the way he fucked.

But he'd never had anyone tell him that his intelligence was sexy before.

That they were attracted to his *brain.*

It was surprisingly intoxicating.

"You really mean that," Ren said, even though it was unnecessary to ask, because while the look in Seth's eyes might be a bit glazed, there was truth there, too.

"Oh, I do. You're sexy taking out the trash. And with bed head to rival anyone. But . . ." Seth dropped his voice. "But you're definitely sexiest when you're using that big brain of yours."

Ren felt a warmth that had nothing to do with the two drinks *he'd* consumed.

He was about to lean in and kiss Seth—because how could he *not* after that?—the ultimate *fuck it* to that silly idea that neither of them liked PDA, when he heard a voice that stopped him dead in his tracks.

"I haven't seen you around here lately," the voice said, leaning in closer.

Ren didn't have to turn around to know who it was.

He and Carl had hooked up about a year ago. They'd met after a trivia night, when Ren had been flushed with victory over the Stanford crew, much the same as tonight, and they'd had a very memorable night of sex.

Carl was hot.

Carl was also not very smart, because he'd never figured out that Ren only came here for trivia night. Obviously he'd been looking for him on other nights of the week.

In fact, Ren couldn't deny that he hadn't kept an eye out for him, too. The sex had been *very* good. Good enough that Ren had considered breaking his normal pattern by sleeping with him twice.

But now, with Seth's gray eyes on him, and that warmth in his chest that he didn't think had anything to do with the bourbon he'd consumed, Ren found it hard to even remember why he'd wanted to see Carl again.

Even if he had, he definitely had not wanted to run into Carl now, when he was with Seth.

"Funny, because I come here every Thursday," Ren said with an edge of frost, as he turned around. Hoping that Carl would take the hint and leave him alone.

"Oh." Carl smiled a bit dopily. He was still hot. Tousled blond hair, piercing blue eyes. A build that would give Chris Hemsworth a run for his money.

But somehow, he left Ren completely, utterly cold now.

"Hello," Seth said, leaning around Ren's body. He wasn't big enough to block Carl—a semi truck wouldn't have been enough to block Carl from Seth's view, but Ren had been trying anyway.

"Hello," Carl said, perking up, because no doubt he wouldn't be averse to a two-for-one special, and Seth was *very* attractive. "I'm Carl."

Ren remembered that flirtatious look of his, even though it had been a year since he'd seen it, and he wanted to drop through the floor.

Seth knew that he'd slept with guys. He'd never tried to hide that fact. But it was another thing entirely to be confronted by one of Ren's one-night stands.

And just when things were going so damn good, Ren thought. He wanted to pretend he was baffled by his worry. But he knew exactly why.

Seth was going to get jealous. Seth would get spooked by the evidence of Ren's usual proclivities standing right fucking there. Seth would be less willing to continue their "casual" thing.

He might even lose Seth over Carl's annoying reappearance.

"Hi, Carl, I'm Seth. Seth Abramson."

"I thought," Carl said, turning his head towards Ren, "that you didn't go on dates."

"I go on dates," Ren said defensively. Okay, they were almost always a precursor to sex, but that didn't make them less of a date.

"Let me guess, you two went on exactly one date," Seth drawled. When he was drinking, his Southern twang always came out. Ren had never imagined that he'd find that particular accent sexy, but he wanted Seth to whisper hot, sexy, sweet nothings in his hear in just that voice as he fucked him deep.

He'd hoped that he might get his wish tonight. But now it didn't look like that was going to happen after all. Disappointment surged through Ren.

Fucking Carl.

"We did." Carl smiled. "A very memorable date."

"Actually, that wasn't a date at all. We met here." Ren scrambled to fix this, even though he could see the car crash coming from a mile away.

"And then," Carl said, dropping his voice. This had probably never failed for Carl. He was that good looking. Really, if Jonas was Tony's twin, then Ren could suppose that Carl was his. Just bigger, and a whole lot blonder. "And then we fucked."

"Oh, I bet you did." Seth sounded amused rather than annoyed. But Ren was sure that when Carl disappeared again, that would change. Seth had too much self-control to let something as petty as jealousy show in front of the man he was jealous of.

"How about it?" Carl suggested. "We could always do a repeat." He glanced over at Seth. "With him too, if he's into that."

"He's not," Ren answered for Seth before he could open his mouth.

He didn't know for sure whether Seth would be in for a random threesome, but he couldn't imagine a scenario in which he would be.

Seth's eyebrow quirked up. "I'm not?"

"You're not." Ren made sure his tone invited zero arguments. But this was Seth, and Ren wasn't stupid enough to believe that he hadn't dealt with much tougher shit than a pretty boy attempting to be tough.

You are tough.

Except, comparatively, he totally wasn't.

"Am I interrupting . . . a *date*? An actual date?" Carl grinned like this amused him.

Before, Ren would rather have died than admit that this was more than the casual thing they'd agreed to. But he'd brought Seth to trivia night, hadn't he? And Seth was the first man he'd slept with twice in forever. Never mind how he just fucking liked *talking* to the guy.

It was totally not casual.

"Yes," Ren said. "Yes, you actually are interrupting a date. Seth and I are . . . we're on a date. A real date."

Seth smiled slow and so goddamn sexy that Ren nearly grabbed his hand and led him out of the bar. They didn't need to be here, dealing with Carl. They could be having a hell of a lot more fun someplace else.

"I guess we are," Seth said in that molasses-slow drawl of his. "On a date, that is."

"Well, I'll let you get back to it," Carl said. He patted Ren on the shoulder. "Good to see you again, Ren."

Then he was gone, and Ren tried not to brace himself but it was impossible.

For a long moment, Seth didn't say anything, just looked at Ren. "We should go," Seth said, finally, and Ren felt the words like the death knell of all his hopes.

Hopes he hadn't even realized that he'd had until this moment. But he'd had them—that much was undeniable now.

"Alright," Ren said. Because what else could he say?

Seth threw a few bills down onto the bar, and then reached for Ren's hand, helping him down from the barstool.

It felt almost cruel for Seth to take his hand now, when it might be the last time. But Ren gripped it hard, squeezing it as they left the bar.

Seth didn't let them get very far, and Ren wasn't surprised at all when he pulled them into an alley next to the bar.

"Did you mean it?" he asked, crowding Ren against the brick. He still hadn't let go of his hand—because Ren was holding it so tightly or because he didn't want to, Ren wasn't sure.

"Mean what?" Ren asked, confused.

Maybe Seth was drunker than he'd imagined.

"That we were on a date," Seth said. The look in his eyes was intense. And all of it, every single bit of it, was focused on Ren.

"I said it, didn't I?" It was mean to drag it out this way. Ren wanted to yell at him, tell him to just *say it* and get it over with, but instead they were fucking around with this date bullshit.

"Yeah, yeah you did." Seth scrubbed a hand across his face. "I just . . ."

"Didn't realize that we would be running into guys I'd fucked?" Ren asked bitterly.

It was Seth's turn to look surprised.

No. More than that.

Seth looked *shocked.*

"What?" he exclaimed.

"I'm sure we're going to run into more," Ren said, hating how bitter he sounded. "The list isn't short, so it's inevitable."

"You think . . . you think I'm *upset*?" Seth took a step closer, catching Ren between the bricks and his big, warm body. Ren couldn't help himself—that was the story of his life, wasn't it?—and he instinctively rubbed up against all that warmth.

"I'm not upset," Seth said, and then he was smiling, giddily, almost, and it wasn't because he was drunk. Ren was pretty certain of that. "I'm not upset at all. I'm fucking thrilled. You asked me on a date. A *date.* You never take people to trivia night, but you took me."

"Yes." Ren gazed up at him. "I guess I did."

"No guessing about it," Seth said, and then leaned in and was about to kiss him, just as he'd been craving all night, blood running hot not just from the competition but the fact that Seth had been sitting there, hot as hell and all fucking *his* all night long.

But Ren suddenly pushed him back. "Wait," he said. "No."

"No?" Seth grinned. "Seemed a lot like *yes.*"

"It is yes, you dummy," Ren said. "I'm just confused. You aren't angry?"

"Angry?" Seth looked puzzled.

"Angry, jealous, envious, disgusted, etcetera, etcetera?"

Seth's expression was blank for a moment and then suddenly, he was laughing. Laughing so hard that he threw his head back and just plain fucking *cackled.*

Ren was not amused.

He elbowed him in the stomach. "I mean it. We need to talk about this."

"Well, I think it's pretty simple," Seth said. "No, I'm not angry, jealous, or envious of Carl, if that's what you're asking. And I'm definitely not disgusted."

It was impossible not to believe him. Not when he was staring at Ren with all the truth in his eyes.

He meant every damn word he was saying.

"How could I be?" Seth kept talking, probably because Ren was just standing there staring at him, his jaw slack, half in disbelief, half in a riotous, painfully sharp hope.

"I'm here, with you. He's not. None of those guys are. But I am. And," he added, leaning in another fraction, and *oh*, those lips were so close. There was nothing Ren wanted more than to lose himself in them. "*And*, you said we were on a date. So I can safely assume if this date continues to go well, I'll get another."

Ren nodded slowly, biting his bottom lip. Seth was not wrong. There would undeniably be another date. Ren was kinda counting on it.

"Yeah," Ren said, and he could hear the arousal in his voice. Feel it in his cock, as it pressed against Seth's thigh. He couldn't wait to get home and get naked with him.

"Is that a *yeah*, I'm going to get another?" Seth asked, smiling again.

"Are you trying to bribe me for another date with a kiss?" Ren asked archly.

"It depends on if it's working or not." Seth looked boyishly pleased with himself.

It was a really good look on him, and Ren vowed to himself to put that look in his eyes as often as he could.

Because who was he kidding?

There were going to be a lot more dates.

"Come on," Ren said, pulling out his most seductive voice, the one that had never failed, "let's go home and go to bed."

Ren was always beautiful.

He was an extraordinary amalgamation of colors and features and it *hurt* almost to look at him.

Seth was learning that there was so much more to Ren than the way he looked, but tonight, the brilliance of his mind outshining the beauty of his face.

And Ren like this? Naked out on his bed, on his sheets, lips curved up into a smile, eyes glowing with happiness and with frustrated lust—but also the sheer genius of his mind.

He was so fucking smart, and nobody really knew.

Nobody except *him*.

Seth took a deep, steadying breath.

"What are you still doing over there?" Ren demanded playfully. "And what are you still doing *dressed*?" He'd barely kept his hands to himself on their Uber ride back to Seth's house, and the moment they'd made it to the bedroom, he'd barely been able to tear his lips off Seth's long enough to pull his t-shirt off.

Then his jeans came off, and his underwear, and then he was naked, and holy hell, it was an incredible sight.

Ren hadn't said it, but winning—especially winning trivia night—clearly made him hot. And whatever made Ren hot, definitely made *Seth* hot.

"Maybe," Seth teased, ignoring the heavy ache of his cock, and leaning down on the bed instead, just inches away from the tantalizing feast that was Ren's body, "maybe I want you to work a little harder for it. Can't be giving in too easy, can I?"

"Easy?" Ren arched a flawless eyebrow. "Come over here and I'll show you how much I want it. Want *you*."

Seth slid back an inch on the bed just as Ren reached for him. "Wait," he said, even as his whole body screamed out the opposite.

Ren was warm and naked and *wanting*, his cock hard and red at the tip, the yearning obvious in every line of his body. "We've done plenty of waiting. Take off your clothes, damnit."

"You're beautiful like this, you know," Seth said. He meant it, of course he did, because he'd have to be blind not to see it, but also because he was trying to get his shit together.

It would be so easy to get lost in the pleasure Ren was offering—and he was afraid of surrendering himself to it.

"I'm aware," Ren said, licking his lips. Like he could still taste Seth on them. Seth's blood pounded in his ears.

"You know it, but you know what gets me even hotter than seeing you like this?" Seth asked.

"No, but I have a feeling you're going to tell me."

Ren sounded so disgruntled, Seth almost laughed.

"You, schooling those guys on obscure history points, you answering questions about the Rolling Stones' first album without blinking, you owning everyone's asses because you're fucking brilliant? *That's hot.*"

Ren stared at him for a second, then another. Then a third. The air thickened between them, until Seth thought he might lose control just from the heat in Ren's eyes.

"Are you saying that me being smart turns you on?"

"Fuck yes it does."

Seth didn't have a moment to brace himself before Ren was crowding into his space, kneeling on the bed, and tugging his t-shirt off with trembling fingers, their mouths fusing together. His hands were chilly, but he was overheating, and they felt so good on his skin. So good that he didn't even protest as they descended lower, unbuttoning and unzipping his jeans, tugging them down.

"God bless," Ren panted as he nibbled on Seth's ear, "you and your habit of going commando."

"You like it?"

"God, I *love it*," Ren said and Seth didn't have the heart to bat his hands away when they reached for his cock, doing something clever that felt fucking amazing, his calloused fingertips slipping around the head. "Come to bed."

Seth leaned down and kissed him, poured everything he had into the kiss, every ounce of wonder and amazement and astonishment that Ren was here, and Ren was not only everything he'd dreamed, but somehow, *more*, too.

He was a miracle. His fucking miracle.

Ren groaned into his mouth, his fingers digging into Seth's shoulders, his hips undulating against Seth's, searching for some kind of friction.

He pulled back a fraction, taking in Ren with cloudy, dazed eyes, and red, swollen lips. *Gorgeous*.

"First," he said, his own voice gravelly and rough as he pulled down his jeans the rest of the way, and toed off his socks, "tell me something."

"As long as you keep kissing me like that, I'll tell you anything at all." A smile broke over Ren's face, and he was so perfect it was hard to even look at him.

"Where," Seth asked, "was Pablo Picasso born?"

Ren shot him a look full of disbelief. "You want to do trivia *now*?"

Seth reached down and gripped his cock, holding it tightly, because it was throbbing now, twitching at the little bursts of pleasure he was getting from his own touch. "You want this, Lorenzo?" he asked.

Licking his lips, Ren nodded emphatically. "He was born . . . uh . . . he was born in . . . he was born in Spain. I think." He laughed. "I'm not sure I remember where I was born right now."

"Good enough," Seth said and pushed him back down on the bed, covering his body with his own. He prided himself on his self-control but Ren splintered it like nobody else had. Not just because he was so attractive. Because he was so *Ren*.

Ren gasped as Seth reached down, and wrapped his fingers around his cock, tugging it insistently. "What do you want?" he asked. Tried to sound reasonable, but Seth was pretty sure it came out more like a demand. He was that close to the edge, riding it hard and fast. It seemed inevitable that Ren was going to make him lose even the barest semblance of control.

Ren bucked against him, eyes going dark and blurry. "Fuck me," he murmured, "please fuck me."

Then he turned over, pushing himself up on shaky knees, and Seth's mind whited out entirely.

He knew he'd grabbed lube and a condom from the drawer by the bed, but later he didn't remember fingering Ren until he cried out, fingers digging into his hips, didn't remember putting the condom on, but he must have, because the moment he was sinking into Ren's incredible ass, everything suddenly became very clear, every sensation so bright they were unforgettable.

"God, just like that." Ren's voice was garbled by the pillow he was gripping as he pushed back on Seth's cock, as he gently rocked into him. "God, fucking wreck me."

If anyone was wrecked, it was Seth. He'd never lost so much control but Ren seemed to wrest it away from him as easy as breathing.

"You want it like this?" he murmured, leaning over Ren's body, stroking out slow and unhurried, even as his body screamed for him to take him hard and fast and wild. "Or do you want it . . ."

Seth didn't get the words out before Ren was pushing himself backwards with intent. Fucking himself on Seth's dick.

"Oh fuck, oh fuck," Seth gasped out, because the sensation was so good, the pleasure so intense he could barely manage to hang on.

It was easy to forget that Ren was strong, almost as strong as him, because his body was such a fucking work of art, but Seth remembered when Ren suddenly slumped to the bed, and then wrapping his arms around Seth's shoulders, flipped them.

Seth was so surprised that he couldn't help the moan that was punched out of him as Ren slid back onto his cock, hands braced against his chest.

He was so close to coming, it was all he could do to clench his fingers into fists, squeeze his eyes shut, and hold on for the ride, which was fucking spectacular.

"No," Ren said insistently, and leaned in, riding Seth with a force that took Seth's breath away. "You can't close your eyes or turn away. *Look at me*."

It was too much, like staring into the sun, but Seth opened his eyes, because he couldn't do anything else, not when Ren begged him like that.

"I'm gonna . . ." Seth heard how garbled he sounded, how desperate. "I'm gonna . . ."

"Good," Ren said with satisfaction, and the moment he wrapped his hand around his own cock, pulling it in time with his thrusts, Seth was gone, flying off the cliff, coming in waves of a fierce, possessive pleasure that he'd never experienced. And then Ren was coming too, tightening around him, groaning as he worked himself through it, splattering his come up Seth's naked skin. Like he was marking him. Like he *liked* marking him up.

Seth had had plenty of sex. But it had never felt like this before.

Not ever.

And it had definitely never felt so good as when Ren collapsed onto him, his cheek pressed to his chest, his breathing heavy.

"Oh God," Ren breathed out unsteadily. "That was . . ."

Seth had never pretended to have any words. "Yeah," he said. "*Yeah*."

For a long moment Ren didn't say anything else. And then he spoke again.

"Was it . . . has it . . ."

Seth had a feeling that Ren was stumbling over his words not because all the blood had currently exited his brain but because this was new for him, too.

"Never," Seth said firmly.

Ren sighed. "Me either," he said.

And Seth knew, then, without a doubt, that they'd just reached unexplored territory.

CHAPTER FOURTEEN

SETH DIDN'T THINK HE could be any happier.

The last week had passed by in a haze of bliss. He and Ren had been on two more "dates." One time, on his day off, he'd taken Ren to dinner, and then to meet up with the others at the Funky Cup. The other, they'd shared more popcorn and another one of Ren's favorite romantic comedies. This one was about a guy who owned a chain of bookstores and a woman who owned a kid's bookstore. They'd hated each other until they hadn't anymore.

Ren had given him a knowing look when the part in the movie had happened where it became obvious that even though they did not like each other in real life at all, they'd actually been corresponding online, to their surprise.

"This," Ren said, as they'd cuddled in bed after, "was what I meant when I said you'd *You've Got Mail*-ed me."

"I kinda did, didn't I?" Seth had said, pulling him in even closer. He didn't think he could ever get Ren close enough. Even when he was deep inside, that didn't feel like quite close enough. "Except that we never hated each other."

"I don't know," Ren teased, "I kinda hated you for a bit. I tried anyway, after you told me you wouldn't sleep with me for the *second* time."

"I was an idiot," Seth admitted.

"Totally, but you're my idiot," Ren had retorted.

His claim was still sticking with him days later, leaving him in a haze of happiness that he could only lay at the door of one thing:

He was irrecoverably, completely, utterly, in love with Lorenzo Moretti.

And he was pretty sure that Ren was falling for him too. Of course, Ren might not even realize it, but Seth had already decided that he didn't care.

This was so good, Ren didn't ever have to realize his feelings, as long as things stayed as absolutely perfect as they were right at this moment.

"You're grinning again," Lennox said from over at his own desk. "It's weird. Are you sure you're Seth Abramson and you haven't been body snatched and replaced by aliens?"

"Pretty sure," Seth said. Grinning still.

"Well, I know we're all happy for you," Lennox said.

"I don't know, I think David was pretty pissed at me," Seth said. "I made him stay late last night to file a report even though he was meeting up with his girlfriend."

"He knows the rules," Lennox reminded Seth. "Without rules, we'd descend into chaos."

"Quoting me back at me, I like it," Seth said with an approving nod. "But yeah, he wasn't happy with me. So not *everyone* is happy that I'm happy."

"Ash mentioned how . . . *upbeat* Ren is lately, too," Lennox teased. "I'm sure your permanent grin and his upbeatness have absolutely nothing in common."

"Nothing whatsoever," Seth said. And yeah, okay he was grinning again. Six months ago he'd given Lennox an epic ton of shit for behaving just this way, and now he realized why Lennox hadn't even minded.

It felt too good to care that he was possibly annoying everyone around him.

Lennox's phone rang and he picked it up. "Lennox," he said in a clipped tone into the speaker. Leaving Seth to believe that it had been an unknown number. Probably informing him that his car warranty was about to expire.

"I see. Okay. I will let them know. Which hospital?" Lennox's tone went grave. "Alright. Thank you for letting me know."

He set the phone down with a decisive click and turned to Seth. And Seth realized that he was no longer smiling.

"That was Dave's girlfriend, Bianca," he said slowly, disbelieving. "Dave got into a bad motorcycle accident last night."

"What?" Seth stood. Barely believing what his best friend was saying, even though he knew that Lennox would never lie. And never about something like this.

"Yeah, he's in the hospital. She wasn't sure we'd heard. She said he's got a broken leg, in a couple spots." Lennox let out a sigh, a big gust of shaky air. "He was lucky that one of the shards missed his femoral artery."

"And he was riding his bike? Shit," Seth said. "Shit, shit, shit."

"It's gonna be okay. I said we'd look in on him this afternoon. Is your schedule clear?"

"Yeah, but . . ." Seth hesitated. "I'm not sure he's gonna want to see me."

Lennox shot him a look. "What? Why wouldn't he?"

"I just told you, before she called. He was bitching at me, complaining that he had to fill out the paperwork." Seth stared at the desk, remembering the way they'd bickered about it, how Dave had told him he needed to stop trying to recreate the Navy, red tape and all, in their private company. "He said he was gonna be late. He must've . . . shit, he must've rushed to make it there in time."

"Don't you dare take responsibility for Dave's choices. If Dave could, he would absolutely kick your ass for thinking that way," Lennox said. "And since he can't, I will."

"But . . ."

"No buts," Lennox said inexorably. "We'll go together to see him. Make sure he has what he needs. Reassure him that he's still got a job when he's recovered."

It made sense that Lennox thought of all that stuff. He'd always been exceptional with logistics. In fact, his team had borrowed Lennox from *his* team more than once, when a mission was particularly logistics-heavy.

But Seth had been the leader. He'd been number one.

Which meant all of those guys on his team were under his protection. Then, and now.

"You think I can't see you spinnin' your wheels," Lennox continued, heading over to the coffee station. "Blamin' yourself even though it was Dave's choice to speed. He always drove like a bat out of hell."

"We don't need all that paperwork," Seth said through clenched teeth. "He knew it, and he called me out on it. And I wouldn't listen."

"Yeah," Lennox said. He finished pouring his coffee, and walked over to where Seth sat, leaning a hip against the side of his desk. "You can definitely be a stubborn son of a bitch, that's for sure. But it was important to you. You want things just so. Nothing wrong with that."

"Except when it's a guy under my protection," Seth pointed out, hating the wry bitter edge to his voice. He'd been through this too many times.

Maybe this time Dave hadn't died.

He'd gotten lucky. With physical therapy, he'd walk and fight and ride his bike again.

There were guys Seth had been responsible for that wouldn't ever do any of those things again.

Seth might not have a team under his authority anymore, but that didn't mean he wasn't trying to control everything anymore.

"Dave is his own man," Lennox said slowly. "You made him do his job." When Seth opened his mouth to argue, Lennox held up his hand. "No," he said, inexorably. "You made him do his job. Whatever he did after that, that was on him. You can't be responsible for all of us. Not like before."

Seth could understand the logical thought process and the conclusion that Lennox came to. Could follow every bit of it, one thing to the next, then to the final conclusion. It was sound reasoning. Dave *was* a grown man, who made his own decisions, for better or worse.

But all of the sound reasoning in the world couldn't stop Seth from feeling this way.

He clenched his fists in his lap.

It would make him a coward to not go with Lennox, to not face what he'd done to Dave. Seth braced himself for it.

"I'll go with you," Seth said. "Gotta rearrange a few meetups this afternoon."

"Good," Lennox said, giving him a pat on the shoulder. But Seth could see the concern lurking in his friend's eyes, and knew that he didn't believe that it was settled at all.

He knew Seth better than that.

Seth hated the smell of hospitals.

It was a cliche, sure, but there was no doubt about why that was.

Hospitals—and their unique smell that seeped into your clothes, and sometimes into what felt like your *skin*—always felt like the setting of so many worst situations.

This was no exception.

Dave lay, pale-skinned with dark circles under his closed eyes, on the bed, his leg elevated in a sling, so it would stay immobilized. He was asleep. Drugged, Bianca had said.

"The good news," Bianca said, smiling down at Dave with a love and an affection that Seth recognized now, "is that the doctor thinks surgery isn't necessary. They got everything reset properly without it."

She was older—maybe even older than Dave, with dark red hair, and a kind smile.

He knew that Dave was really fond of her. Wanted to build a future with her.

And what had he done?

Carelessly tried to take it away.

Because of some goddamned paperwork.

"That's wonderful news," Lennox said, reaching out and tugging her into a hug.

Something the Lennox of a year ago would never have done.

But with Seth—and mostly with Ash—he'd learned to become a normal person again.

It was jarring on every level to go from military life to civilian life. It had been even harder for Lennox.

But he'd rolled with the punches and come out the other side.

Seth had imagined that he had too, because things felt so much more in control than they had when he'd first gotten out.

But the rage spiraling through him—the rage he never let anyone else see—told him different.

"I know this is a super stressful situation," Lennox said in a reassuring voice, catching Seth's eye and Seth knew he wanted him to say something, *anything*, but Seth didn't trust himself. Not to say the right thing. There'd been a point when he'd always known what to say, but now that wasn't him, it was Lennox. "But you don't need to worry about the hospital bills or recovery or physical therapy. If you two need *anything*, you know how to get in touch."

A tear dripped down Bianca's cheek. "Thank you. You two mean a lot to him. When he got out, he was a bit lost, he's told me about it, and when he started to work for you . . ." She choked up then.

But Lennox, again, knew what to say. "We understand," he said softly. "We're all looking for what we left behind, when we get out."

He glanced over at Seth again. "And some of us can't quite leave it behind."

Lennox's pointed comments were not only annoying, they were unhelpful. If they'd been alone, he'd have told Lennox just what he thought of his interference.

But they weren't alone.

This should be about Dave, and the horrific injury he'd experienced, not about Seth and his control issues.

Seth cleared his throat, reached out and gripped Dave's hand. "You're gonna be okay," he said, to Dave, even though he couldn't hear him, because anything else was unacceptable. He wouldn't tolerate it. "You promise that you'll call us," he said, raising his eyes to Bianca, "if you need anything. Anything at all."

"I will," she said, sniffing. "I appreciate you two coming down here. I'll make sure to tell Dave that you were here."

"Thanks," Lennox said warmly.

For awhile, right after he'd gotten out, and his life had fallen apart, Lennox had often felt like an approximation of a human. Going through the motions, knowing he should feel this, and say that, but it hadn't felt genuine.

But he'd gotten better. Learned to actually *feel* again. To say what was really on his mind, not just what someone wanted to hear.

Seth knew that he was going to get a painful dose of that kind of honesty when they left Dave's room.

"You need to get your head on straight," Lennox said as they walked to his car.

It was not as harsh as Seth had expected, but because he'd tempered it with kindness, it stung worse.

Seth almost never lied. It was almost never the right thing to be dishonest. But he lied now, anyway. "I'm fine."

"You're not fine," Lennox said, his dark brows coming together as he frowned, clearly concerned. "You should take the rest of the day off. Play hooky with Ren, if Gabe can spare him."

Ren. Seth hadn't thought about him once, not since Bianca had called Lennox.

If he checked his phone, he'd probably see a handful of messages from him. They often texted back and forth during the day, and checking his watch, Seth realized he'd been in a fog for hours. Had he eaten lunch? He vaguely remembered Lennox setting a sandwich in front of him. Usually they talked after lunch, after Ren made it through the lunch rush at the truck.

But they hadn't today.

He hadn't even checked his phone once.

"I don't want to see Ren," Seth said. Another lie.

He did want to see him. Desperately.

But what he didn't want was for Ren to see him like this.

Hurting and angry and full of self-recrimination.

"Now," Lennox said as he started the car, "you're going to tell me that you don't want Ren to see you like this."

"I was right," Seth said through clenched teeth. "You are annoying as hell."

"Maybe." Lennox smiled. "But I'm still right. You should call him. I can even drop you off at the food truck lot."

"I'll take the afternoon off but drop me off at home. Maybe I'll go for a run." Seth would accept that; after all, he wasn't sure he could work today, anyway. Not in his usual, methodical, organized way, anyway. The rest? He wasn't ready to deal with Ren or even the possibility of Ren. Not yet.

He'd go home, try to re-center himself, try to deal with all this *anger*, all at himself for failing Dave, and then maybe when he'd exhausted it, he could talk to Ren.

Lennox shot him a look. "I thought things were going good between you." He paused. "He makes you really happy. I know, because I recognize it."

"And so does Bianca," Seth said.

"Oh for God's sake," Lennox retorted. "You're not to blame, and she certainly doesn't blame you. It was a freak accident."

"Because he was *rushing*."

"Except we don't even know that," Lennox said. "I'm not going to argue with you about this, because you're not listening."

"It would be nice if I could just listen to you and ignore everything else," Seth said sarcastically

He *hated* sarcasm.

Probably because he knew it was always the harbinger of the spiral.

"Maybe it's better that you don't see Ren," Lennox said, making sense for the first fucking time today, "because you're being a stubborn ass, and I wouldn't wish that on anyone, even an enemy."

Seth stared out the window. Wishing he wasn't seeing the ghosts of all the men who'd never be stubborn again.

Lennox dropped him off at home.

He went for his run, punishing his body, and himself, for what had almost happened to Dave.

He's lying in that hospital bed because of you. Because you had to be a goddamn stickler for stupid rules that don't even matter anymore.

They *had* mattered. The rules were what had kept everything and everyone together, in one piece, back when they were in the Navy. They were what had helped Seth return his teammates to their wives and partners and children.

The run didn't help though, not as much as Seth had needed it to.

He'd gotten home, exhausted and aching, and even after a long, hot shower, the thoughts—and the ghosts—wouldn't stop coming. He settled down on the couch, and tried to watch TV, even though the words of the ESPN commentators grated.

It was rare that he drank just to drink, especially alone, because when he'd first gotten out, he'd almost gotten lost in a haze of booze, and he was always afraid of falling back into that hole. But today, there was nothing else that would silence the screaming in his head. Not running. Not a shower. Not television.

Seth hit the power button on the TV, and got up, heading to the kitchen.

He found the bottle in the back of a cabinet, where he'd put it an age ago. There was dust on it, but he unscrewed the top anyway and forced himself to go find a glass.

That would be more . . . controlled . . . he decided.

He would pour it in a glass, and take it to the couch, and sip like a normal person. Even though it was the middle of the afternoon.

Wait.

Seth checked his watch again. Not his phone, because he was a little afraid of what he might have missed, what texts Ren had sent that he'd never replied to. Realized that it wasn't the middle of the afternoon like he'd thought, but it was growing darker.

It was actually past seven.

He hadn't eaten dinner either.

Probably, Seth thought, staring at the amber liquid in his glass as he poured himself a few inches worth, he should eat something.

But instead, he took his drink to the couch, as he planned. Hoped that maybe the booze would drown out the ghosts for long enough that he could focus on something else.

Food, maybe.

Or Ren.

Ren.

The bourbon on his tongue, trickling down his throat, reminded him of the man he loved. Reminded him of the drinks they'd shared together. Of the night that Ren had admitted that he'd brought Seth on a date.

Because the happiness he felt—the lightness, the trust, the *belonging* he'd been chasing for more years than he'd been out of the Navy—that was all Ren.

He nearly went to find his phone, which he'd tossed in his bedroom before his run. At the very least he shouldn't leave all of Ren's texts unanswered.

But before he could decide for sure, there was a knock on the door.

A particularly insistent knock, the persistence easily recognizable.

Of course Ren would come looking for him if he ghosted him.

For a second, for a single moment, Seth considered just sitting here on the couch. Not answering the door. Ren didn't have a key. He didn't know Seth was home.

But hiding, Seth couldn't deny that was the ultimate cowardice, and while he might be more of a fucking wreck than he wanted to be, at least he wasn't a coward.

He stood and went and opened the door.

"What the fuck," Ren said, but between Seth taking a deep breath, ready to try to explain what he could, and him letting it out, his arms were suddenly full of Ren.

"Damnit," Ren said, burying his face into Seth's shoulder. "Damnit, I was worried about you all day."

A pulse of guilt resonated through Seth. "Sorry," he mumbled, "something happened, and I didn't know . . ."

Ren pulled back, a thousand emotions in his dark eyes. "I really hate feeling this way," he said. "I thought I would, and I do, while I fucking love it at the same time—but you can't just . . . leave me alone to feel it, okay? You just can't. Not when you persuaded me to feel it in the first place."

"I'm sorry," Seth said. The words didn't feel like enough, but they were all he had. "Did . . . did Lennox send you?"

"No," Ren said firmly. "I fucking sent myself." Then he took a step back, and Seth watched as his gaze took in the dark living room, and the bottle and the half-full glass on the table. "You're drinking. Alone." He turned to Seth. "You need to tell me what's going on."

"I . . ." Seth took another deep breath and it turned out that didn't help either.

Tell him, a voice inside insisted, and it sounded exactly like Lennox.

He'd trusted Lennox forever. Long before they'd ever left the Navy. He'd relied on him on missions and to help protect his men.

He'd trusted him with his professional reputation when they'd started the business together. And he'd convinced Lennox to trust him, when Lennox had been alone and hurting.

What kind of friend—what kind of *person*—did that make him if he was unable to reciprocate?

"Come sit down," Seth said to Ren. "You want a drink?"

"No," Ren said. The look on his face said it clear enough, *you're drinking enough for both of us.*

"I haven't actually had more than a few sips, yet," Seth admitted. "Sometimes . . . sometimes it helps when the rest of my mind won't quiet. That's why I don't drink a lot."

He didn't say the rest. Wasn't sure he had the courage to say the rest. Who wanted to tie themselves to a man who would have to worry about losing himself to liquor for the rest of his life?

But Ren was smart. And even more, Ren was smart about *him.*

"Because you did, at first, when you got out of the Army, right?" Ren asked, sitting down not on the couch with Seth, but across from him, in the big club chair. He leaned forward. "You are going to tell me that you have PTSD."

"It's the Navy, actually," Seth said wryly. Anyone else getting it wrong so consistently might have pissed him off but Ren's heart . . . well, despite his claims that he didn't have one . . . it was always in the right place.

"And," Seth continued before he lost his nerve, "it's not the loud noise kind of PTSD, at least that's what my counselor said when I got out. It's . . . it's the loss of a system, of a structure. When I was leading my team, I knew if I said something, people would listen."

"And now they just look at you like you're on crack?" Ren asked wryly.

"Yeah, it was . . . it was a really hard adjustment for me. I lost my temper a lot. I drank too much. I made a lot of bad decisions. When Lennox got out, he and I helped each other. Having him around again reminded me that I could build another system. One that I liked just as much as the one I had before."

"So you started your company together."

"Yeah. That's when I found the counselor, too." Seth looked at the glass. The liquid inside shimmered gold under the dim lights of the living room. "I don't want you to think that loud noises set me off. Or that you have to worry about me strangling you in your sleep. Other guys, they absolutely deal with that shit. I just don't."

"What *did* happen, then?" Ren asked. He looked concerned.

And suddenly, Seth hated that he was so far away.

"Can you . . ." He hesitated. "Can you come over here?"

Ren didn't hesitate. He got up and was next to Seth before he could feel shame at asking.

If you can't be messed up in front of him, then you can't be messed up in front of anyone.

Reaching over, Ren took his hand and squeezed it. "You can tell me," he said encouragingly. "I want to know."

Seth's chuckle was dry and rough. "It's not . . . it's not like you're thinking. A guy who works for us got hurt. He's gonna be okay but . . . I don't handle that well. I *didn't* handle it well. Probably because it's my fault."

"How did he get hurt? While he was working?"

"He was running late. Driving too fast, probably."

"Then it's not your fault," Ren said soothingly, squeezing his hand again. "You can't stop the world from happening to people you care about."

"Yeah, except I was the one who made him late." Easy to repeat in a litany in his head, but hard to admit, out loud, to Ren, who knew him as this easygoing guy, who'd never seen him be a stickler for rules that didn't matter anymore.

"And?" Ren raised an eyebrow. "So?"

"I . . ."

"No," Ren interrupted him before he could say anything else. "No. I know it's your default setting to take personal responsibility, and that's like really fucking admirable, okay? I'm sure that you were taught to do it, that it became part of your identity. But this isn't on you. I believe that. But you're the one who really needs to believe it."

Seth sighed. Ren sounded so indignant, and he was ninety-nine point nine percent sure it wasn't because he was mad at him, but because he didn't want him to take bullets that weren't meant for him.

"You sound like Lennox."

"Well, I'll take that," Ren said solemnly. "I know it isn't as easy as saying, *don't beat yourself up*, but, *don't beat yourself up*, okay?"

Seth laughed, not really because it was necessarily funny, but because it was easier than crying.

"I'll try," Seth said, and leaned harder into Ren. Enjoying just the way he felt pressed against him. "Thanks for listening, even if I'm a stubborn ass."

"You're not stubborn, and you're not an ass." Ren hesitated, and Seth glanced over at him, just in time to see him worrying his bottom lip with his teeth. "You're not perfect. But that's okay, because I like you every which way."

It wasn't everything. It wasn't the *l* word that Seth imagined hearing, but it was enough, because the words would be nice, but what really mattered was that Ren had come here for him.

"I like you, too."

I love you, too.

Ren rested his head on Seth's shoulder. "You know, everyone thinks you're so laid-back and relaxed, but I knew better. I knew better the first time we met."

"Really?" Seth was surprised, even though he'd learned long ago to never expect the expected from Lorenzo Moretti.

Ren shook his head. "I saw how much you goddamned cared, right in your eyes, when I wouldn't go out with you. You weren't annoyed or offended or even disappointed. It was a flare of something . . . and I knew then there was more to you than met the eye. More to you than anyone else saw."

"Well, I *was* at least a little annoyed, and maybe a tiny bit offended. Definitely a lot disappointed."

Ren laughed. It filled Seth's heart and his head with joy, and it wasn't enough to push out the self-recrimination, but it made it easier not to focus on.

He didn't need booze after all; he just needed the intoxicating man next to him.

"I was a little disappointed in myself," Ren admitted, and that was it, wasn't it?

It was easy enough to take a look at a guy and think, *this is the one*, and it was another entirely to *experience* what the right guy felt like.

He'd been attracted to Ren from the beginning, but what he'd felt then was like a vague, weak shadow of what he felt now.

And if he was really lucky, then he wasn't feeling this way alone.

CHAPTER FIFTEEN

REN REMEMBERED A TIME that didn't feel so far away when he would've ghosted someone rather than deal with their personal problems.

But with Seth, Ren's first instinct was to do the exact opposite.

He wanted to make sure he was okay.

He wanted him to be more than okay. He wanted him to be good. To be absolutely fucking stupendous.

There was a voice in the back of his head that told him he knew exactly why that was. But Ren was ignoring that voice.

Resolutely.

Instead, he went with Seth the next day after his breakdown to visit Dave in the hospital. Gabe hadn't been very happy when he'd said he'd needed the day off, but Ren had only been halfway through explaining why when Gabe started to dial the temp agency.

"I'm glad you're doing this," was all Gabe would say when Ren questioned him. "It's good to see you like this."

"Caring about someone that isn't myself?" Ren had asked.

Gabe had shot him a look. "You've always cared," he'd argued. "But for some reason you thought it was necessary to hide it. You're not hiding anymore."

Gabe was right; he wasn't hiding anymore.

Not even in front of the other food truck guys.

Tonight, for the staff meeting that Tony had called at the Funky Cup, when Seth had walked in, Ren hadn't even hesitated. He'd walked right over to him and thrown his arms around his neck, hugging him tightly.

Seth's smile had told him just how much he'd enjoyed it.

"So, you guys are together now, like *together-together*," Ross said, a crease forming between his brows as he sat down next to Ren.

"We're . . ." Last time they'd discussed it, they'd both agreed to keep things casual.

Things were not casual.

Ren could say that much with absolute certainty.

But they hadn't discussed the actual verbiage of what the casual thing had turned into, and Ren found he was perfectly okay with that for now.

"You're what?" Ross asked patiently.

Ren liked Ross a lot. Not many of the other guys had, at least at first. He could be bluntly pragmatic in a way that offended some of the others. But not Ren. He liked the honesty. And then there'd been the little matter of Ross having more talent in his pinky finger than a lot of them had in their whole bodies.

But Ren had never been jealous, not like he knew some of his friends had been. He'd been in awe, even after finding out that Ross was just as much of a mess as anyone else.

Now, they were friends.

Friends told each other stuff like this.

Ren hesitated.

"We're figuring it out," Ren said.

"Oh, you don't know," Ross said. Which was exactly why, Ren thought wryly, the other food truck owners hadn't been lining up to be his friend at the beginning.

Ren took a sip of his drink. "You got it," he said.

"Ah," Ross said. Like he was glad he finally understood, because he'd been puzzling at this one for awhile. "Shaw and I were very happy and relieved when we finished figuring it out," he added.

"I bet you were," Ren said.

Ross patted him awkwardly on the shoulder. "You'll get there, too," he said.

"We'll see."

"Is everyone here? Can we get started?" Tony said, breaking away from where he was chatting with Lucas and Seth and raising his voice, so he could be heard clearly in their corner of the Funky Cup patio.

"Yeah, we're all here," Tate said, speaking up. "Please don't tell me we're here so you can gift us with another impossible task and one of your cheap kitchen appliances." His voice was teasing. Ren knew how much money they'd all made from Waffle Day—even if Tate was right and that waffle maker had been cheap as hell.

"Nope," Tony said, grinning. "We're here because of copycat me."

Ren had already known why Tony had called the meeting—it had been obvious when Seth had told him he'd be meeting them there—but he was still surprised.

"What about him?" Gabe asked. "Did you find out some dirt on him?"

"No," Seth said. "No dirt. He's what he says he is, a corporate lawyer with probably too much money and time on his hands. He had a breakup last year, around the same time I think he visited Food Truck Warriors for the first time, and he liked what he saw. Thought he could do it, too."

"He can, if he wants," Tony said, shrugging. "But he can't have any of you. First off, because you're not for sale, and second because we're a team and a family. He can't *buy* that. He can only work hard enough to earn it."

"Exactly what you did," Ash said.

Tony nodded. "We worked hard to create a place where everyone would feel safe and accepted." Ren saw him glance over at Ross. "Sometimes we weren't always perfect at it, but we got there in the end. I can understand, though, the urge to experience something great, something like we share, like we experience every day, and want to replicate it. But even if you want a place, you can't buy it, and you can't steal it. You can only grow it."

"Everyone has to be willing and invested," Lucas said. "And we're lucky enough that you all believed in what we were doing."

"It's because of that, because of *you*, that we've made it through our first year, and been more successful than we ever could've imagined when we started out," Tony agreed.

"So there's no way we can just make him . . . go away?" Ross asked.

"A guy like that? Smart? With money to spare? Who's used to being intimidating and never giving in?" Seth questioned. "Not likely. But I think . . . Tony and I have discussed a few options."

Ren was suddenly intrigued. Seth had told him the other night that he'd made a recommendation to Tony, but that he'd not taken it particularly well.

"Tony's first indication is always to fight," Seth had said, as a movie had played quietly in the background at Ren's loft and they cuddled on the couch, "and I get it, because for a long time, mine was too. When I got out, I wanted to fight everyone who wouldn't listen to me, even though they usually didn't have a reason to."

"But you learned," Ren had pointed out. "You don't do that any more."

"Not often, anyway. And at least when I do, the person I'm fighting is me," Seth had said, chuckling wryly. "But Tony is quick to anger and usually quick to reconsider. We'll see if he does."

It appeared that Tony had reconsidered, because he looked over at Seth and smiled. "What Seth is saying," Tony corrected with a smile, "is that he's brilliant, and we should always listen to him."

"That's the chorus Ren is singing these days," Gabe teased.

Before, Ren was pretty sure he'd have felt humiliated. Ashamed, almost, that he'd ended up like this. But now he just felt proud.

Maybe they didn't have their shit figured out yet, but that was *his* guy up there, being brilliant, and helping out his friends.

How could he feel anything else *but* pride?

"Maybe I should be singing it even louder," Ren wondered out loud.

"I'm not going to argue with any of that," Seth said, and the look he shot Ren was sweet and private and real.

And Ren knew without even being told that he was going to get thoroughly kissed later, and even more, if he continued playing his cards just right.

"So what's this brilliant idea?" Alexis wondered.

"I think we should, barring any lingering competitive insanity, partner with him," Tony said.

A silence fell over the group.

Ren saw surprise on several faces. Disbelief on others.

Gabe, for example.

"What?" Tate asked. "He tried to buy us all away and you want to *partner* with him?"

"He's got money," Tony said. "He said it himself, he's got all these marketing experts lined up. He wants to advertise. But he doesn't have the trucks, not if he's trying to buy you all away from Food Truck Warriors. Besides, we have room for a few more trucks, but we're eventually going to run out of room, and I wouldn't mind expanding."

"Can we trust him?" Alexis wanted to know.

"I don't know," Tony confessed.

"I suggested that maybe before we make him a partner," Lucas said, "that we make him a friend. That's how we all started, isn't it? As friends, first."

Ren nodded, liking Lucas' approach. He was always so level-headed and quietly, smartly capable.

That's why he and Tony made such a power couple and such an incredible team. Tony was all light and fire and electric brilliance, but Lucas was pragmatic and level-headed and figured out how to make Tony's crazy ideas work.

"I had Lennox arrange to meet him here, about half an hour ago," Tony said. "He's inside now, with Lennox."

"Lennox is making small talk?" Tate teased. "Wow, that's something I'd never imagine would happen."

"Hey, he's *trying*," Ash said, defending the man he loved.

"What I'm asking is not if he's uncomfortable with Lennox's version of small talk," Tony said, grinning, "but if we should put him out of his misery and ask him to join us outside."

"To be what? A friend? A partner? All of the above?" Ross wanted to know. Ren thought it made sense that he would want clarification. Ross liked his boxes, and liked to understand where everyone fit into them.

"To be whatever he ends up being," Tony said. "I don't know if he's going to want to partner with us. I don't know if he wants to be our friend. He might tell us to fuck off. That's totally up to him. But I thought instead of intimidating him or threatening him, we should give him a chance. That's what Food Truck Warriors is about, right? A chance."

"Huh, okay, I guess I can see that," Gabe said.

Ren could hear the thoughtfulness in his cousin's voice.

"Before we do it, I'd like to put it to a vote," Tony said. "Because we're a democracy."

"Are we?" Alexis wondered with a teasing glint in his eye.

"We sure are," Tony said firmly. "Everyone in favor of inviting Jonas out to the patio, raise your hand."

After he lifted his own, Ren was not surprised at all to look around and see every owner with their arms up.

"I guess that settles it, then," Tony said, grinning as widely as Ren had ever seen him.

Seth came over to Ren's side, as Tony went into the bar proper to get Lennox and Jonas.

"Did you know it was going to turn out like this?" Ren asked him as he tucked himself into Ren's side, pressing close.

"That Tony would eventually come around to the idea of partnering with him? Hell no," Seth said with a low chuckle. "When I told him the idea, he looked at me like I'd grown a second head. But then two days later he called me and said, what if we ask him to be our friend, first, and I was mind-boggled. But then, that's Tony."

"That's why we love him," Ren agreed.

"Yep." Seth smiled, and there was a quiet happiness to him, one that had only seemed to grow as Ren had supported him and they'd become closer, after Dave's accident.

Maybe they really didn't need to figure their shit out.

Maybe they already had.

Ren leaned in closer. "You were great," he said simply. He wanted to say it, because it was true, and also because even though so many people depended on Seth —both before, when he'd been the team leader, and now, when he helped run their business—he didn't think anyone told him enough that he was great.

Because he was, and because he deserved to hear it about a thousand times a day.

"Yeah?" The corner of Seth's mouth quirked up.

Ren couldn't help but think of what he had before; that he'd been asking to be really, thoroughly kissed.

Just the thought of it made him shiver a little.

"We should sneak out now, before Tony and Jonas collide," Ren said in a low voice. "Sneak out and head back to my place. Or your place. Or any place."

"Any place, huh?" Seth leaned in closer. "If I didn't know any better, I'd think you want me . . . *bad*."

Ren had been playing it cool forever. He knew he was good at it. But here he was, stopping a breath away from Seth's lips, heartbeat racing out of control, cock already growing hard, just thinking about everything they could do if they were alone together, with no way on earth he could possibly resist Seth's magnetic pull one second longer.

But it was Seth who closed the gap between them, covering Ren's mouth with his own, and the kiss was hot and it was also sweet.

It reminded Ren of that first kiss, the one that he'd always expected to be so passionate and fiery, but instead had been soft.

Meaningful.

He pulled away, even though it nearly killed him. "Come on," he said, reaching down and tugging at Seth's arm. "Let's get out of here. I think this guy's gonna be around for a long time, and we can always chat him up later."

Seth grinned. "You think so?"

"There was a point," Ren said, downing the rest of his drink, and standing up, "when I would have fucking sold tickets to Tony meeting Jonas Anderson. Now . . ."

"Now?" Seth prompted.

Ren knew what he wanted to say. *Now I just want you.* But that seemed monumental. The antithesis of any kind of casual thing.

The sort of phrase that would prompt a discussion where they "figured it out," at least according to Ross, anyway.

He wasn't proud of it, but he was a little scared.

This was new territory for him.

So instead of answering, he leaned in again and answered Seth's question and finished his own thought with a kiss that left nothing to the imagination.

On the way back to Seth's place, Ren had formulated a plan.

It was not a very complex plan, mostly because it felt like half his blood wasn't currently residing in his brain—but then it didn't *need* any real complexity.

The plan was simple: give Seth a little of the time and attention and pleasure that he seemed so determined to give Ren every single time they had sex.

They might not have hooked up all that many times, but Ren could already see a pattern developing, and he didn't like it.

Well, he *liked* it. In fact, he loved it.

But there was an inherent selfishness Ren couldn't live with.

Besides, he *enjoyed* giving. And he wanted to give everything to Seth.

That thought was at the forefront of Ren's mind all the way up to Seth unlocking the front door, but the moment they were inside, Seth crowded him against the door, kissing his mouth, his neck, anywhere he could reach.

Ren's head hit the back of the door, losing himself in the feel of Seth pressed against him, around him.

It felt so goddamn good, it was almost easy to just loose himself to the sensations. Which was what had happened every other time they'd had sex.

The thought was like a bucketful of cold water dumped on his head.

Ren gasped—and not in the good way—and wrenched his head away.

"What's wrong?" Seth said, pulling back, a concerned expression blooming across his handsome features.

"Nothing is . . . *wrong*," Ren said, and while he spoke, he maneuvered Seth's body until it was the one pressed against the door. "I just want to try something."

But Seth's concern was morphing into apprehension.

"Try what?" he asked.

It was easy to forget that this was a man who didn't relinquish control easily. He had admitted it himself to Ren not ten feet away from where they stood right now.

Maybe that was the only way he could have sex. The only way he *wanted* to have sex.

Ren could adjust to that, but he wasn't going to let it go without talking it over first. "You always do this," Ren said, pinning Seth's body with his own. Feeling the arousal bloom under his skin as his hips met Seth's hips, their chests pressed together. "Always overwhelm me, always take over, the moment we start to kiss."

"You don't like it." Seth sounded incredulous, which made sense.

Who wouldn't like a guy who lavished attention on your body until you felt like you were being blown apart by how fucking fantastic it was?

"I do like it," Ren admitted. He wasn't going to lie. "But I *like* you. I want to make you feel good, too."

There was a stubborn tilt to Seth's chin. "Making you feel good makes *me* feel good," he said.

"And the opposite is true, too," Ren said. "I want to give that back to you."

This time it was Seth's eyes that slid away.

But Ren wasn't going to accept that. He took Seth's chin with a firm, but gentle grip and pulled it back, so

Seth didn't have a choice but to look at him. "Don't do that," he said. *Begged* more like. "Is this about the control thing? Do you need to be in the driver's seat in bed? Is that what this is? Because we can do that."

"No," Seth said, and his breath was coming harder and faster. Ren could feel it against his face. "No, that's not it."

"Then what is it?"

"You've done this lots of times . . ." Seth trailed away.

"Yes." It was stupid to assume that even though Seth hadn't been jealous, this would never come up again. Yet Ren had begun to assume that it wouldn't. That Seth didn't give a shit.

"I don't care, not the way you think," he said. "I want . . . I want to be more to you than just a guy you remember you slept with."

"You're already more than that," Ren admitted wryly, tipping his head against Seth's. Feeling his warm gray gaze deep down in his gut. It shouldn't have been so easy to admit, but then none of this had gone the way Ren had expected. "You know that."

"It's stupid," Seth muttered. "I'm stupid."

"No, you're not stupid."

He was the opposite in fact.

A thought dawned on Ren as he considered what Seth had said—and what he hadn't. "Were you trying to make sure I felt so good that I stuck around? You wanted the sex to be really good."

"Of course I wanted it to be good," Seth said, and maybe Ren wouldn't have noticed the bluster in his words if he wasn't usually so completely laid-back and authentic.

"You were afraid I'd get bored," Ren challenged.

"Not . . . bored, per se," Seth admitted.

Ren stared at him, thinking. He should have guessed it was something like this, but then Seth had told him about the control he was used to having, the control he still struggled with not having, and Ren had begun to wonder if that need had extended to the bedroom.

But it didn't.

Seth had been giving him a banquet of pleasure every night because he'd been afraid that Ren wouldn't stick around if he didn't.

He'd known, deep down, that Seth had feelings. That those feelings made Seth vulnerable, but he'd never imagined what it would be like to hold someone's heart in your hands.

While he'd never been letting anyone close enough to touch his own heart, Ren had never gotten close enough to feel anyone else's either.

But he could feel Seth's now.

Beating hard and strong against his own.

He reached between them, pressing a palm against it. Feeling it. Understanding what it really meant for the first time.

"I'm not going to get bored," Ren said bluntly. "I'm definitely nowhere near bored." He angled his hips so that Seth could feel how hard he was in his jeans. "I'm just as desperate for you now as I was before we had sex. Maybe more. No . . ." It was hard to be honest, but Seth's honesty deserved his own in return. "No, definitely more. I want you more now, so much more, than I did before. And, what I want tonight is to make you feel good."

Seth bit his bottom lip, and Ren wanted to be those teeth.

"Will you let me do that?" Ren asked.

"A man would be crazy to say no . . . so . . . *yes* . . ." Seth trailed off, but before he could speak again, Ren kissed him.

This was more what he'd expected their first kiss would be: all lush, hot passion, his tongue in Seth's mouth, his hands touching every part of him that he could reach, fingers trailing down his chest, and ending right above the fly of his jeans.

Seth's whole body twitched, like he could compel Ren to touch him where he needed it most. But Ren had finally gotten the ability to do what he'd been dreaming about for six long months, that he'd only gotten little brief tastes of so far, and he had every intention of gorging.

Their kiss grew even wilder, Seth panting into his mouth as Ren continued to touch him, brief, exploratory touches all over his clothes. He'd wanted to know what this muscle felt like, and how this other one bunched when he gripped it. Ren knew he'd spent way too much time thinking about it when he should have been trying to forget Seth, but he'd never done it.

Instead, he'd held on to the idea of him, on this crazy thought that if they just slept together, then he could get him out from under his skin.

But that was never going to work, because now the man was buried so deeply that Ren knew he couldn't evict him even if he wanted to.

"God, *please*." Seth begging was the sweetest thing that Ren had ever heard, and he intended to make him so crazy with want that he couldn't stop himself. He reached over and tugged Seth's t-shirt off.

Ren had seen plenty of guys who spent a fortune of time and energy and money in the gym. Their bodies were hot. But none of them had ever set him on fire the way that Seth's did. He wasn't a boy, he was a *man*, who'd seen war and all its horrors and used himself to protect others from those very same things. He was strong because he had to be, not because he chose to be.

"You gonna just stand there and stare?" Even with the pleading edge to his voice, Seth was still cocky and confident, and Ren had to ignore the rush of arousal that surged through him. His cock twitched, wanting Seth's hands and mouth and all the pleasure they brought.

But they weren't doing that. Not tonight.

He reached out, trailing his fingers down Seth's defined chest, tracing each freckle with his fingertip. Then he leaned forward and followed the same pattern with his mouth, nipping and sucking and licking each freckle, until Seth's breath was labored and his own wasn't exactly steady.

He could get addicted to the taste and the feel of Seth under him.

Maybe he already was.

"You're such a fucking tease," Seth said, his voice low and rough.

"You love it though," Ren retorted lightly, enjoying the wrecked edge to Seth's groan when he finally began to unbutton and unzip his jeans. "You're gonna love this even more."

He still hadn't gotten used to how Seth often went commando, and when his hard length bobbed out from his pants, Ren leaned in and gave it an experimental lick up the side, hearing Seth swear and mutter above him.

"I got you," Ren murmured, and this time let the head of Seth's cock, red and leaking at the tip, slide between his lips, and he gave it a nice, hard suck.

He'd spent a significant amount of times on his knees, because he really enjoyed giving a blowjob. But he'd never gotten so into it, so fast. The last time he'd gotten to do this, in the shower, it had been so quick, but this time around, Ren had intended a much more leisurely, teasing pace.

He let Seth's cock slide deeper, and then deeper still, swallowing convulsively around the remnants of his gag reflex.

Seth's fingers dug into his head, into his hair, and held him there, and *God*, as good as that probably was for Seth, it was even better for Ren. His cock throbbed in his pants, and he considered, briefly, trying to take the edge off, but it turned out that making Seth lose it was making *him* lose it too.

He couldn't touch himself, because he'd come, and he wasn't nearly ready for this to be over yet.

"Come on," Seth said, his voice raw. "Suck me."

And so he did.

It was wet and messy and perfect, and they both moaned as Ren took him deep, again and again, Seth's hands still tight in his hair.

Ren could feel him getting close, his balls drawing up tighter, as he massaged them, slipping a fingertip further back and then further back still, just glancing off his hole.

To his surprise, Seth widened his stance, giving Ren an open invitation. He didn't waste a moment, getting a finger nice and slick and sliding it back, pushing it in just a little as he sucked Seth's cock hard.

He got only a moment of warning, but he knew it was coming, because Seth was like a volcano, primed and ready to explode, and he did, actually shouting as he came, his body tensing and then finally relaxing as he shot down Ren's throat.

Ren slumped down, his knees suddenly aching, and it took him a second to realize that Seth was reaching for him, pulling him up, pulling him up against him, and then they were kissing again, and it was sweeter this time. Softer. Seth leaned down and picked him up, their mouths barely breaking, and he carried him into the bedroom, setting him down on the bed and making quick work of his clothes.

It was Ren's turn to plead. "Please," he said. He'd been holding back, because he'd wanted to do this, but now it was like a fire in his blood, raging out of control, and if he didn't get relief soon . . .

But Seth gave him what he wanted. What he *needed.* He leaned over him, caging him in, never letting him forget who it was that was kissing him, touching him, and his fist closed over Ren's hard cock, giving him exactly the kind of hard, insistent pulls he needed to send him right over into a mind-blowing orgasm.

Ren didn't see where he wiped his hand, but a moment later, Seth was collapsing in bed next to him, their shoulders touching. Ren didn't hesitate, merely rolled over, and settled his cheek onto Seth's broad chest, fingers splayed out across his muscled ridges of his stomach.

"I will fully admit to being stupid about this." Seth's voice was warm and soft above him.

"Good."

"That all you have to say?" Seth sounded amused now.

Ren considered this for a moment. His brain was still recovering from what had felt like the orgasm of the century, Seth's fist having wrung it out of him one perfect movement at a time.

"You didn't ask," he finally said. "You've never asked."

"Asked what?"

"Why I only ever hooked up. Everyone always wants to know, and usually they ask, eventually."

It was Seth's turn to be silent for a few seconds. Then it became a full minute. "I figured," he said, his voice careful, "that if you wanted to tell me, you would."

"Everyone always assumes it's some kind of sad story," Ren said. "Some sob story where I got my heart broken terribly, and I vowed never to love again, or some such bullshit."

"I never assumed it was that," Seth said.

"I know."

It was part of why Ren was so crazy about him. He looked at him and saw *him*. Not some amalgamation of fantasy and imagination.

"All those other guys probably thought they could change your mind. Convince you love wasn't shit, or something like that, right?"

Ren nodded. Then turned, so he could look Seth in the eye. It was important that he see him for this. That they see each other. "There's no heartbreak, no sad story, I just . . . I just didn't want to. I wasn't out in high school, not at first, so those were just hookups. Then when I did come out, it seemed easy—*easier*, anyway—to just keep doing the same thing, just less secretive. And then . . . it just kept being easy."

"It became a habit," Seth guessed.

"It did," Ren agreed. "And then it became just part of who I was. Admittedly, I got a little cynical. Lots of guys say they want more, but they're plenty happy to settle for one night. It's almost a relief."

"But not me," Seth said.

"No." Ren hesitated. "No, you were different. From the beginning, you were different."

Seth smiled, soft and slow and sweet, and Ren's insides twisted up. It should've hurt, it should've felt like a warning, but instead it felt like a benediction.

"I was just me," Seth said.

And that, Ren was beginning to realize, was the problem, and at the exact same time, also the solution.

"Well, thanks for being *just you*," Ren said and pressed his lips to Seth's.

CHAPTER SIXTEEN

"THAT WAS A FUCKING incredible meal," Ren said, leaning back. "I thought, why should we come here and eat, the Funky Cup has plenty good food, but I'd forgotten that Ross did the menu here."

"And, there's this view," Seth said, pointing out the admittedly incredible view of the city from the roof of the bar.

Ren had heard from Ash, who'd heard it from Ross, who'd heard it from Shaw, that the rooftop tables were hard to come by, and that the Fickle Cup had actually started taking reservations for them in the evenings.

But when they'd gotten here for a late dinner, a suggestion that Seth had made two days ago, they'd been immediately whisked upstairs. Which meant that either they'd gotten really lucky—or much more likely, that as soon as Ren had agreed it was a good idea, Seth had called and made reservations.

Not exactly casual.

But then, it felt like not much they were doing anymore could be termed "casual."

Ren *wanted* to be mad about it, but he hadn't actually succeeded in summoning that particular emotion yet.

Instead, he was feeling a whole bunch of other ones.

Ones he wasn't comfortable putting a name on yet.

But, Ren reasoned, he wasn't in a hurry to put a label on anything or as Ross said, *to figure their shit out*, and it didn't seem like Seth was either, so why potentially fuck up a pretty fantastic thing?

"It was a good idea." Ren hesitated. "A great one, actually." It had also definitely been a date. But he hadn't protested once. Not when Seth had suggested it, not when they'd been on it, and not even when Seth had paid for their meal and drinks.

And, he was definitely not going to protest if they went back to Seth's place and ended up having some more incredible sex.

"Thanks," Seth said with a genuine smile. A *happy* smile.

He was happy. Ren was happy.

Another reason why it would be stupid to mess this up.

Ren toyed with the edge of his empty glass. "The view *is* incredible, but frankly, there's another I like better."

"Oh?" Seth's eyes flashed with heat.

"You, naked, on a nice, comfortable horizontal surface," Ren said in a hushed tone.

"I like that idea a lot," Seth said. "A nice conclusion to the evening?"

"Nice?" Ren batted his eyelashes. "Who said anything about me being *nice*?"

Seth chuckled and stood.

Ren was about to do the same when a voice stopped him in his tracks.

"Seth? Seth Abramson?" It was a friendly voice—a little too friendly. A little too *glad*, if Ren had anything to say about it. "I can't believe I fucking ran into you here."

Seth was smiling too. Not as warmly as he'd just smiled at Ren, but when the guy—who was tall, broad-shouldered, with dark hair and nice blue eyes—came over, he seemed pleased to see him.

"Good to see you," Seth said, and they didn't hug. Or shake hands. They just stood there and assessed one another.

This was how Ren knew they'd hooked up.

They'd be a lot more apt to touch each other if the last time they'd touched each other hadn't been during sex.

This wasn't an old military friend or someone he'd known before, back east.

No, this was someone he'd met in LA.

Someone he'd hooked up with.

Ren plastered the friendliest smile he could onto his face and rose. "Hey," he said, tucking himself under Seth's arm. They were not usually this touchy-feely. But Ren didn't even hesitate. He pressed a proprietary hand right over where Seth's heart beat steadily.

"Ren, this is . . ." Seth stammered a bit, which was unusual for him. Unless . . . *oh my God*, Ren realized. He doesn't even remember his name. He had sex with this man and didn't even remember his name.

That was the kind of thing Ren did!

Not Seth.

Never Seth.

If he did, then why wouldn't he have had sex with Ren when he'd propositioned him all those months ago?

"Brandon," the guy said, and reached out, with an understanding tilt to his smile, and shook Ren's hand briefly.

"Nice to meet you," Ren said, barely refraining from baring his teeth at the guy.

It would have been easier if he hadn't been handsome. Or personable. Or they hadn't clearly *only* had sex.

"Well, see you around," Brandon said and turned and walked away.

Finally.

It was probably unfair of Ren to be annoyed, considering the guy had exchanged less than twenty words with them, but *still*.

"That was awkward," Seth said with a laugh. "And not as fun as running into your ex-hookup, who wanted to have a threesome with us."

Ren wanted to be amused, like Seth was, like Seth had been when they'd run into Carl. But he wasn't. He wasn't at all. He felt . . . did he feel *jealous*?

Not once in his life had he ever felt jealous of a lover before. How could he feel jealous, when he'd never gotten close enough to be possessive.

"Yeah, so funny," Ren grumbled. "I don't think he wanted you to be laughing about his threesome offer."

Ren caught sight of Seth's surprised expression right before they headed down the stairs. "Wait," Seth said, hurrying to catch up. "Is everything okay? You're not . . . you're not *mad*?"

"Not mad," Ren said as they walked through the bar and out the front door.

"But you're *something*," Seth persisted.

Ren shoved his hands into his pockets. He knew he shouldn't be *anything*. It was completely unfair that he had hooked up with plenty of guys—guys they were apt to run into, just like they'd run into Carl—and Seth had barely flinched, except to be *amused* that Carl had wanted a threesome. But the moment Ren came face-to-face with one of Seth's hookups, he went all Hulk rage monster about it.

"I'm just confused," Ren finally said. "You said you didn't do hookups. But that was clearly a lie, because we just talked to one of them."

"Actually, I specifically said that I wouldn't do a hookup with *you*," Seth clarified quietly. The amusement had disappeared from his face, replaced by a serious earnestness that made Ren want to squirm.

"Why not?" Ren asked, even though he regretted the question the moment the words came out of his mouth. Because he had a very good idea of what Seth was going to say.

It was the same exact goddamned reason why Ren didn't do this, the whole dating thing, but he was doing it now.

Willingly.

"I knew the moment we met that we couldn't just share a night," Seth said softly. All that earnestness in his gray eyes. Ren was torn between melting and being even more annoyed. "It would never have been enough. You were laughing, at Lennox or Gabe, I don't even remember, but I knew then that I couldn't have just the tiny part of you that you doled out to all those guys, and then move on."

"Oh."

Ren wanted to be pissed off. It would have been the more comfortable emotion.

But he wasn't. Not at all.

He was . . .

Something.

Something he did not want to look too closely at, even though it was currently flashing in his head, lit by bright neon, and nearly impossible to avoid.

"I want to be angry with you," Ren said.

"But you're not." Seth was smiling at him again.

"No, not at *all*," Ren said, and then he was smiling too. Laughing, even. At how ridiculous this all was.

He'd been *jealous*.

"Listen," Seth said, through chuckles, "I do need to say something else serious, if you think you can handle it."

"First, do you want to take an Uber or we can walk . . . it's not that far to my place."

Seth's eyes darkened. "Is Gabe home?"

"I don't think so, but if he is, we can kick him out," Ren said.

"Alright, let's walk. It's a nice night," Seth said, and together, they turned down the next street. It was about a mile and a half to the loft, and Ren's idea had been to work through whatever *this* was, this burning in his stomach, before they got there. Then they could have sex without him being so distracted by it.

By what it meant.

"Spring's nearly here," Ren said. "The one-year-anniversary party is in two weeks."

"Feels like longer," Seth observed, and then paused on the sidewalk, turning to Ren. "I know you don't want to hear this, but I want to say it, anyway."

Ren thought, *then don't say it*, but instead what came out of his mouth was, "Okay, then I want to hear it."

What had happened to him?

He didn't know, and he wasn't very happy about it. But at the same time, he was incandescently, brilliantly, wonderfully happy.

"I never did that many hookups. Mostly . . . mostly I did them when I first came to LA, before Lennox and I started the business together," Seth said. "This isn't supposed to sound like an apology, but it wasn't what I wanted. I knew from when I was young that I wanted a real, solid relationship. One I could count on."

"Why?"

"Why was I so convinced that was what I wanted? Because I never had it growing up. My mom, after she and my dad divorced, she dated a whole bunch of guys. They were always serious, always here to stay . . ." Seth let out a sigh, like he was a kid again, and he'd just been punched in the stomach *again*. "And they never were."

"You want someone who sticks," Ren said.

"Yes."

Can you be that guy?

The answer was painfully simple.

I want to be that guy.

But he'd never done it before.

"I hooked up because I was lost and bored and probably drinking too much," Seth said wryly. "But when I met someone I really liked, I wanted more. That's why I didn't want to just hook up with you."

"I understand," Ren said, and he did. Better than he'd imagined he would.

It hadn't just been Seth being a stubborn ass, the two times he'd turned him down. He hadn't been rejecting Ren, but what Ren was offering.

Of course, if he'd known the truth back then, Ren wasn't sure it would've changed much. He would have still been stuck in his ways—*in your rut*, Ren heard Gabe's voice say in his head—and he would have rejected any serious overtures that Seth might have made.

"I keep trying to think if there's any other secrets you should know," Seth said, with a small smile on his face, "but I think you've managed to wiggle most of them out of me."

"I can think of one," Ren said. "Pineapple on pizza?"

Seth laughed, and slung an arm around Ren, and they started walking again towards the loft. "What do *you* think?"

"I think you're too much of a traditionalist to want anything but cheese and sauce and pepperoni on your pizza," Ren said.

"Maybe if I'm getting a little wild, some mushrooms," Seth confirmed. "And you're the opposite. The wilder the better."

"Don't you dare tell Gabriel about the pineapple," Ren said seriously. "He would probably disown me. But truthfully, it's delicious. I like that sweet and salty combo."

"Yeah, I just bet you do. I can't imagine that at all," Seth said, chuckling.

"I like you, don't I?" Ren said impudently. But he heard the uncertainty in his voice. Seth probably heard it too, but didn't remark on it.

He only retorted, "So is that your biggest, deepest, darkest secret, then? That even though you're a good Italian boy, you like pineapple on your pizza?"

It's not. It's not at all. I'm afraid of what my biggest, deepest, darkest secret is. And I think it might be you.

But Ren felt unmoored, still, from the bout of jealousy earlier, and from Seth's heartfelt confession. He hadn't said he loved Ren but he'd come damn close.

Knowing Seth, he felt it too, he just hadn't said it out loud because he'd been afraid of scaring Ren away.

After all, he'd freaked when confronted with one of Seth's hookups.

Ren couldn't blame him for not saying the words.

Even though there was a part of him that really wanted to hear them.

"Yes," Ren finally said. "Now you know the worst of me."

"Nah, I think I know the best too," Seth said.

Ren left Seth sleeping in his bed, and got ready for work, beating Gabe there by twenty minutes.

Twenty minutes during which he cut up an entire bag of onions, chopped garlic, his knife flashing in the early morning sunshine, and started in on the day's meatballs.

"You're here early . . . and you're . . ." Gabe's forehead creased as he took in what Ren had accomplished already. "You're busy. Is everything okay?"

"Why wouldn't it be okay?" Ren said.

But it wasn't okay.

After he and Seth had fucked—okay, even Ren had to admit that it wasn't just straight fucking anymore, there were way too many feelings involved, but every time he thought the words, *making love*, his brain freaked out—he'd lain awake, and tried not to freak out some more.

He'd failed.

Seth had fallen asleep, and he'd stayed up most of the night, only sleeping in fits and starts, with weird, terrible dreams.

Which all ended the same way: with him losing Seth.

Logically, Ren knew he wasn't going to lose Seth to a shark attack or in a terrible LA earthquake, being swallowed either by a set of jaws or a gaping maw in the earth, but he'd woken both breathless and terrified.

The last time he'd woken, before his alarm, he'd known he needed to talk to someone.

The obvious person was his cousin.

He also happened to be the most annoying, and also the most smug.

And he was going to get even smugger after this conversation, but Ren was desperate enough that he'd decided that didn't matter.

"Did something happen with you and Seth?" Gabe asked carefully as he tied his apron on.

"No," Ren said resolutely. Something hadn't just happened. Something had been happening this whole damn time.

"Then what's this all about," Gabe wondered as he got the big pot out, ready to start the red sauce for the day. "You're dedicated, yeah, but I've never seen you here this early, or this preoccupied."

"I'm . . ." Ren took a deep breath, feeling his throat close up. *Don't panic, don't panic.* "I'm thinking that maybe Seth and I should start dating."

His confession was met with a wall of silence.

Gabe just stared at him. Was he confused? Shocked? Afraid that his cousin had been abducted by a race of shape-shifting aliens?

"Are you saying . . ." Gabe finally said, the words coming out slow and enunciated, like he didn't want there to be any mistake. "Are you saying that you don't think you're already dating?"

"Well, we've been on *dates*, sure," Ren said. "But . . . we've never talked about it. Not exactly. Not precisely." He had told Seth after they'd run into Carl that the trivia night had been a date. But they hadn't been *dating*, like the verb. Those had been strictly nouns.

Gabe set down his wooden spoon. "Let me be absolutely clear about this because sometimes you are so far up your own ass that you don't even see what you're doing even though you are very obviously doing it."

"Fine," Ren grumbled. "What is it?"

"You're already dating Seth. You've been on dates. You're sleeping over at his place, he's sleeping over at ours. You see him all the time. *You. Are. Dating.*"

"Okay," Ren said. "That makes sense."

Gabe shot him a look like maybe he *had* been abducted by those shape-shifting aliens. "Yes, it does," he agreed.

"Well, how about this. Maybe I should suggest to Seth that we make this a little more official."

"Like he's your boyfriend?" Gabe raised an eyebrow.

"Yes, exactly like that. Like he's my boyfriend," Ren said. He'd even said the word without stumbling over it. He was proud of this fact. Very proud.

Until Gabe threw his head back and laughed so hard it was a wonder he didn't have an aneurysm.

"Oh," he said between gasps for air, "this is too good. I knew I was in for something, but wow, this is better than I ever imagined it could be."

"What," Ren said coldly, crossing his arms over his chest, "my ignorance is that amusing?"

"No, because you're behind the curve on that one too. Seth's already your boyfriend."

"What?"

"You are his boyfriend. And he's yours."

"But," Ren objected, "we've never talked about it. Not once! How can you acquire a boyfriend without a single conversation?"

"It's actually not very difficult," Gabe said with an exaggerated patience. "You hang out with him all the time, right?"

Ren nodded.

"And you're sleeping together."

"Regularly," Ren said.

"And you aren't sleeping with anyone else?"

"Nope."

"Finally, you already admitted you were going on dates with him. I . . ." Gabe winced. "I think you passed right by that conversation and didn't have it, but . . . the end result is the same."

"I'm a boyfriend," Ren said. Not like he'd always imagined he'd say it, with despair and possibly rending his garments and gnashing his teeth, but with *wonder*. Like it was the greatest fucking thing to ever happen to him. "I'm *Seth's* boyfriend."

"If you were someone else's boyfriend, I'd be pretty surprised," Gabe said, clearly still amused by this entire conversation.

"Well, if I'm already dating him, and he's my boyfriend, there's . . . there's nothing else. It's not like I'm in love with him."

Ren froze.

Gabriel froze.

"You're . . . you're not?" Gabe wondered into the silence.

Ren stared at him. "You think I am?"

Gabriel rested a hip against the stove. "What do you think you are?"

Ren thought of all the things he'd tried not to think about, all the feelings that he'd shoved into a box labeled, *Do Not Understand* and *Do Not Open*. Everything he'd avoided looking at too closely.

Yeah, the dating and the boyfriend things were both puzzle pieces that had now fallen nicely and neatly into place. But this was . . . this was way more than that.

"I think he's in love with me," Ren said, and this time he tested out the word. *Love*. He'd always believed that it would feel like the end, like a dead fucking end, but instead, when he said it, it felt like a horizon opening up, a future expanding, a new life beginning.

Not better or worse than before, but different.

But also, totally fucking better because Seth was in it and Ren wasn't going to lose him.

He ripped off his apron. Like actually totally ripped it.

And here Ren had been surprised that he hadn't torn any garments in his sudden, painful realization.

"I have to go," he said, grabbing his keys.

"I figured as much." Gabe was still laughing under his breath. "Be back for the lunch rush, okay?"

"No promises," Ren said, and took the stairs out of the truck faster than he ever had before, and when he hit flat ground, he broke out into a run. No promises, because he'd never actually loved someone before, and now he did, and every single bet he'd ever made was fucking off, because *this was for real*.

By the time he made it to the loft building, he felt slightly ridiculous.

Ridiculous, sweaty, and also out of breath.

But also determined.

Except when he unlocked the front door and did a thorough search of the interior, Seth wasn't there anymore.

He'd left, too.

Ren felt so dumb. Why hadn't he said anything last night? The moment had been right. Sure, a sidewalk in a semi-decent Los Angeles neighborhood wasn't the epitome of romance, but that was okay, because it was *them.* It was Ren and Seth and they were *epic* and *destined* and *written in the fucking stars.*

No extra romance was needed, because they had plenty of it to go around, just between the two of them.

He stood in the middle of the living room, still panting from his desperate run, and tried to think. Where had Seth said he was going to be today?

The most obvious answer was that he'd be at the office.

Of course he could also be at the gym, or at his house, or at a client's. All of those were possibilities.

The closest one was the office. He'd try there first.

Ren bypassed the elevator, and took the stairs at a fast, jogging pace. At this rate, he wouldn't need to work out for the next week, but that was okay. He could arrive a mess, because Seth loved him, and he loved Seth right back. His heart *sang* with the knowledge of it.

And it wasn't because he was hot or charming or gave the best blowjob in Los Angeles. It was because they fit together, like they were made for each other. Because Ren cared about what happened to him, because Ren made him laugh, because Ren made him feel less alone in the world.

And most importantly, because Ren was never going to let him go.

By the time he reached the office that housed Seth and Lennox's business, his breath was rough and ragged, but instead of pausing to get it back under control, he pushed the front door open anyway.

The main office was divided into two sections: a room with several desks, with Lennox's and Seth's laptops on them, and a few spare desks, when they had employees come in, and another room, which was a conference room where they met clients.

The office was empty.

Ren moved on recklessly, pushing open the conference room door.

Only to stop in his tracks.

There was Seth, a button-down shirt on with a *tie*, and a pair of tight navy slacks that fit him so well that Ren wanted to peel him out of them with his *teeth*.

Next to him were two of the most attractive people that Ren had ever seen. And he looked at *Seth* regularly. Slept next to him too.

They looked familiar, and Ren realized, a moment too late, what Seth had told him he'd be doing this morning: finalizing and signing his contract with Diego and Benji from Star Shadow.

And all three of them—the two hugely popular pop stars and his *boyfriend*, his fucking *boyfriend*—were staring at him.

"Lorenzo," Seth said in that drawl of his, just edged with the Southern accent he'd grown up with, "did we have something planned that I didn't remember?"

He knew that they didn't, so no doubt he was trying to save face.

But Ren was beyond saving face.

Which . . . that said it all, didn't it?

Ren shook his head. "I need to talk to you."

"I'm . . . I'm a little busy," Seth said, clearly trying to be diplomatic.

Could he wait? Ren supposed he could. But he'd come all the way here to say it, and he wasn't going to leave with it unsaid.

"Could you just take five minutes? I promise to make it quick."

The one that Ren was pretty sure was Benji—he'd had that *horrible* solo album when Star Shadow had been on a break—smiled at Seth. "Seems pretty important," he said, his expression knowing and amused.

Seth shot him a look that said, *I don't know what you're doing, but I'm willing to go along with it because it's you.*

Though Ren had known, unequivocally, that Seth loved him back, the knowledge sang through him a second time, twice as loud as the first.

"It's important," Ren reassured him. "Very important. Life-altering. Life-changing."

"You'd better talk to the guy," Diego said in that soft-spoken way of his.

"I'll . . ." Seth hesitated. "I'll be right back."

He followed Ren out the door, and shut it behind him.

"What's going on?" he demanded to know. "Are you okay? Is everything at the food truck lot okay?"

"Everything is fine. At least it seemed to be," Ren said. "I came here because . . . well, you know that movie, *When Harry Met Sally*?"

Seth stared at him, incredulous. "You came here to make a date to watch one of your romantic comedies?"

"No," Ren said. "But one of the characters says something that I never understood but I suddenly do now. He says that when you realize you want to spend the rest of your life with someone, you want the rest of your life to start *right now*."

"And . . . this is how you feel?" That Seth looked surprised was an understatement. But Ren pressed forward anyway. He'd come here, hadn't he? He'd run all the way here. There'd been times he'd refused to go on dates with guys because he was having a bad hair day.

But his hair was sweaty and mussed and a mess, and he discovered that he did not give a single shit. And he knew that Seth wouldn't either, because he loved him.

He loved him.

"I've been very stupid," Ren said gravely, reaching for Seth's hands, gripping them tightly. "Incredibly stupid . . . monumentally stupid . . . blindly stupid . . ."

The corner of Seth's mouth quirked up. "Blind, huh?"

"Unbelievably," Ren said seriously. "I didn't know we were dating. I mean, I *knew*, but I wouldn't think about it. And I did the same thing when it was clear we were doing more than dating, that I was your boyfriend. I'm your boyfriend, right?"

Maybe Gabe had been wrong. Ren didn't think so, but he held his breath anyway, and watched as a slow, brilliant smile broke over Seth's features, like the first rays of sunshine.

"Yes," Seth said. "I would consider you my boyfriend."

"Then there's nothing left to be confused about," Ren said. "I love you, you love me, and *that's* what I came here and had to say, because once I realized, I couldn't leave it unsaid. Not any longer."

Seth pulled him in, his hands cradling Ren's face. He *didn't* give a shit that he was a mess. Ren's heart soared. "I do love you," he said. "And I knew you loved me, too, but it sure feels good to hear it." He hesitated. "You're not going to freak out and run, right?"

"I did freak out," Ren said honestly, because there was no room left not to see in his heart what Seth meant to him. It was shining like a beacon, burning more brightly now than it had before. It was inescapable, and Ren realized, with a rush, that he didn't *want* to escape it. He wanted to embrace it. "But when I ran, I ran straight to you."

Seth kissed him then. It was messy and it was awkward and it was more than a little damp, but Ren had discovered that none of that mattered.

Love was what really mattered.

EPILOGUE

"CAN YOU BELIEVE THAT it's been a whole year?" Tony asked as they all sat at two long sets of tables that had been shoved together. The Fickle Cup and the Funky Cup had joined together to cater the event, where the lot was closed, and instead of serving food to others, for once the food was being served to them.

"Yes," both tables answered him in complete unison.

Ren grinned.

It had been a long year, but a great one, anyway.

"Hey, if anyone gets to complain about how much work we did," Tony said, still grinning like every day of grinding had been worth it, and it *had* been, "it should be me."

There was a whole chorus of disagreement. Gabe was shaking his head, Tate and Ash were laughing and pointing at something Tate's sister, Rachel, had said. Ross was grinning at Shaw. Alexis was gesturing wildly to Jackson. And Ren? Well, he was pressed right up next to Seth, and it turned out that was his favorite place in the world to be.

The last three weeks had been the best ones that Ren could remember.

Because now with no lies, no confusion, and nothing holding them back, Ren was beginning to realize just how great being in a relationship was.

Well, the key was probably that he was in the *right* relationship. He couldn't imagine ever having done this with anybody else, but with Seth? It felt real and it felt natural and Ren never wanted it to end.

"Actually," Lucas said, standing up next to Tony. "I think it should be me."

"Oh?" Tony said, shooting his boyfriend a smile. "Why is that?"

"Because anything you deal with, well, it rolls down to me," Lucas said.

There was plenty of response to that, along with lots of laughter and also some pointed comments about how they'd all learned not to visit the storage shed after a particularly trying day.

They'd all gotten an eyeful of Lucas comforting Tony—or Tony comforting himself by comforting Lucas—more than once.

"I guess that's true," Tony said, scratching his chin. "What do you propose to do about it?"

Lucas gave him a long, speculative look, and to everyone's shock—Ren was shocked, and he could see the exact same expression on just about everyone's faces around them—went down on one knee. "I propose," he said, the edge of his voice a little shaky and nervous, "that I want things to roll down to me for the rest of our lives. I don't care that those things might suck, or they might make our lives harder. We created this place, and it's been amazing. The hardest, and best, year of my life. I want to share this with you, every year forward, not just unofficially, but officially. The most officially." Lucas pulled a ring, shining and silver, from his pocket and held it up.

Tony stared at his boyfriend. And then at the ring. And then back at his boyfriend.

They'd been together for years at this point, and Ren knew how solid they were. Solid enough, but also unconventional enough that nobody he knew had actually expected this.

But it made sense, now that Ren thought about it.

Lucas would want things to be official.

He would want to make it real, and tie it in a bow with red tape. His past made everything make more sense.

"You want to get married," Tony stated. He looked surprised too. Maybe the most surprised.

"I want to marry *you*," Lucas said with vehement certainty.

"And I . . . I want to marry you too," Tony said, and they were kissing, and the table was clapping and catcalling, and it was a great fucking moment.

But Ren had experienced so many of those lately, it was hard to get worked up about this one.

"That was beautiful," Gabe said with a misty-eyed sigh. "Absolutely fucking beautiful."

"You'd definitely be the person to think so," Ren teased. "The King of Feelings loves a good proposal. Who knew?

Everyone."

Sean laughed. "Should I expect half a dozen proposals? Rooms full of roses? Heartfelt speeches?"

"Hey," Ren said, elbowing Sean, "you knew what you were signing up for."

"I know," Sean said, shooting a gooey, sentimental look at Gabe. "And I'd still do it all over again."

"Aw, we're adorable, too," Gabe said, meeting Sean's goo with some goo of his own. Ren gave them approximately two months after Tony and Lucas tied the knot before they did it themselves. "But, here's the thing. You can't call me the King of Feelings anymore."

"Oh?" Ren raised an eyebrow.

"That implies that I'm the only one who enjoys all this emotion," Gabe observed. "And"—he paused pointedly, staring right at where Ren was pressed up next to Seth—"we know that's not true now."

"How about," Seth said, his hand reaching over to squeeze Ren's knee, "we call you the *Prince* of Feelings?"

Ren considered this.

Feelings, he'd learned, not only weren't the enemy, they could be very enjoyable.

With the right person.

He turned and looked Seth right in the eye. "Only," he said firmly, "if it's a joint title."

"You good with him pulling you into this?" Gabe asked.

But Seth just nodded. Seriously and solemnly. "Absolutely," he said. "Lorenzo can pull me into anything he wants."

Ren grinned, because he'd known it was true, but it was glorious to hear Seth say it.

And much later that night, when they'd found the one dark corner—the one that Lennox was always threatening to light up on the lot, though he never did, because he and Ash enjoyed using it too much—after they'd finished kissing because they hadn't been able to keep their mouths, or their hands, off each other one second longer, Ren realized something else.

"Someday," he said, murmuring into Seth's lips, "someday I'm going to do that to you, too."

Seth smiled. "Three weeks of being a boyfriend and you're already ready to propose?"

"Not yet," Ren said. "I didn't say *now*, I said someday. Because I want that. I want *you*."

"And you'll have me," Seth said, leaning in and pressing a kiss to his cheek. "Today, tomorrow, and every day after."

BETH'S BOOKS

FOOD TRUCK WARRIORS

Drive Me Crazy - Lucas is just looking for some summer fun while Tony wants it all. But when their undeniable chemistry heats up the food truck kitchen, all bets are off.

Kiss & Tell - a New Year's Eve novella set in the Food Truck Warriors universe. Jackson lives to work, but what happens when he runs into Greek food truck owner, Alexis? When midnight strikes, sparks fly, and two lives change forever.

Hit the Brakes - Tate has had a crush on famous football player Chase since high school. But what happens when Chase suggests they fake a relationship to give Tate's food truck a much-needed boost?

On a Roll - Sean and Gabriel accidentally named their food truck the exact same thing. Can they stop arguing about it long enough to fall in love?

Full Speed Ahead - Lennox isn't the only one keeping secrets. A stalker has discovered one about Ash, and when Lennox intervenes, the electric chemistry between him and Ash erupts into something very much like love.

Wheels Down - Shaw isn't Ross' friend—Ross isn't sure he has friends, anyway—until he discovers that Shaw is actually so much more than just his friend. He's his lover, and his partner, and his salvation.

Ride or Die - Ren & Seth's story and the final Food Truck Warriors novel. Can Seth woo and win Ren's bad boy heart once and for all?

KITCHEN GODS - Available on audio

Complete Box Set - including all four novels, and additional bonus content.

Bite Me - Miles' and Evan's story. They were sure they were enemies . . . until they were sure they weren't.

Catch Me - Wyatt and Ryan's story. Their relationship is completely fake . . . until it isn't.

Worship Me - a short story about Matt and Alex from Catch Me.

Savor Me - Xander and Damon's story. They're partners in a new restaurant . . . until they're so much more.

Indulge Me - Kian and Bastian's story. Working together is a necessity, but their mutual love? It's every bit an unnecessary indulgence.

LOS ANGELES RIPTIDE

The Rivalry - Rival. Enemy. Teammate. Friend. Lover. Two very different quarterbacks end up playing for the same team, fighting for the same starting spot - and end up fighting for each other, too. *Available on audio.*

Rough Contact - Their romance is forbidden. Their love is a secret. Neal and Jamie are the Romeo and Juliet of football - with all the feels, and much less tragedy.

The Red Zone - With Alec's help, Spencer can change everything about his life he's come to hate. An extraordinary future—and an undeniably extraordinary man—are waiting for him.

STAR SHADOW

Complete Box Set - including all four novels, and an exclusive short story.

Terrible Things - a little grittier, a little darker, a little more terrible. A rock star romance. Available on audio.

Impossible Things - Benji & Diego's story, and the sequel to Terrible Things. Available on audio.

Hazardous Things - Felix's had a crush on Max forever. But he's straight. Ish. Right?

Extraordinary Things - The final book of the Star Shadow series. Revisits Leo & Caleb's love story.

STANDALONES

Merry Elf-ing Christmas - a North Pole elf who doesn't belong, and an engineer who doesn't realize what he's missing in his life is Christmas magic. Coming November 18.

The Rainbow Clause - Shy NFL quarterback meets immovable object AKA the journalist assigned to write his coming out profile. Sparks are definitely gonna fly. Available on audio.

All Screwed Up - David is Griffin's annoying contractor. So why does Griffin want David to nail him? An enemies to lovers romantic comedy co-authored with Brittany Cournoyer.

Snow Job - Micah & Jake have always been enemies. They used to be stepbrothers. But they could be so much more.

Taste on my Tongue - Kitchen Wars is the hottest new reality show on TV, but pop star Landon can't even turn an oven on. Will baker Quentin be able to give him a culinary education so they can win?

Wrapped with Love - Losing Jordan is the biggest regret of Reed's life. Will Secret Santa and a little holiday magic be able to repair what was broken?

Fairytale of LaGuardia - Once upon a holiday season, a hockey player and a baseball player walked into a bar . . .and the rest is history. A Christmas story co-authored with A.E. Wasp.

Musical Notes - Two teachers with nothing in common, except a high school musical that's only three weeks away from Opening Night.

ENCHANTED FOLKLORE

Yours, Forever After - a lost Prince, a lonely bookworm and a surprisingly chatty unicorn go on the quest of a lifetime to save their kingdoms from an evil sorceress. Now available in the Complete Edition, featuring an epilogue novella.

Yours, Everlasting - Evrard . . .Rhys . . .Evander . . . Evander has gone by many names in his thousands of years alive. He's also lived many lives. But while he may have left his past as the Guardian of Secrets behind, it refuses to stay buried.

ABOUT BETH

A lifelong Pacific Northwester, **Beth Bolden** has just recently moved to North Carolina with her supportive husband. Beth still believes in Keeping Portland Weird, and intends to be just as weird in Raleigh.

Beth has been writing practically since she learned the alphabet. Unfortunately, her first foray into novel writing, titled *Big Bear with Sparkly Earrings*, wasn't a bestseller, but hope springs eternal. She's published twenty-eight novels and seven novellas.

Join Beth's Boldest, her Reader's Group
Subscribe to Beth's Newsletter
Follow Beth on BookBub
Facebook / Instagram / Twitter
www.bethbolden.com

ACKNOWLEDGMENTS

A HUGE thank you to everyone who supported this series and me as an author from *Drive Me Crazy*. It's because of you that I didn't want to stop writing with *Full Speed Ahead*, and I ended up writing *two* more books LOL.

Also I don't think I could write *any* books without Jacki James. Her honesty and support means the world to me. Thank you, Jacki!

Another huge shoutout to Angela, Emily, Louise, and Megan for being fantastic beta readers and always making me dig deeper.

Thanks again to Cate Ashwood for continuing this series for me, and for designing my favorite cover of the entire series.

Last but never least, thank you to my understanding husband, who doesn't even comment when we eat dinner after eight.

Made in United States
North Haven, CT
25 January 2022